DRUM UP *the* DAWN

Book one of
Galaxy Girl

by Kate Christie

SECOND GROWTH

Copyright © 2020 by Kate Christie

Second Growth Books
Seattle, WA

All rights reserved. No part of this book may be reproduced or transmitted in any form or by any means, electronic or mechanical, including photocopying, without permission in writing from the author.

This is a work of fiction. Names, characters, organizations, events, and incidents are either the products of the author's imagination or used in a fictitious manner. Any resemblance to actual organizations, persons (living or dead), events, or incidents is purely coincidental.

Printed in the United States of America on acid-free paper
First published 2020

Cover Design: Kate Christie

ISBN-13: 979-8-6953874-3-8

ACKNOWLEDGMENTS

I owe thanks to my early readers, Kris and Charley, whose willingness to read unedited drafts was so appreciated. Another thanks goes to Margaret Burris, who is always ready and willing to copyedit—even at the last moment. Thank you, team! Any errors in the following pages are solely mine.

CHAPTER ONE

If not for the nightmare, Kenzie Shepherd would have been nowhere near her favorite coffee shop the moment the tweaker decided to hold it up. Instead, she would have been at work on the fifth floor of Emerald City Media listening to Aaron Mulvaney, her department head, drone on about budget cuts and click-through rates, falling subscription numbers and how they were lucky to even be employed in an industry struggling to stay afloat in the new media reality. But sometime during the previous night, she'd awakened in her dark studio, pulse pounding in her ears, eyes seeking out the flames still flickering against her eyelids.

It had taken long minutes to calm her mind, to convince herself that she was safe, that it had just been a dream. The same dream, in fact, that had haunted her for years, recurring at odd times without warning. For an indeterminate space of time, she'd struggled to get back to sleep, only to succumb at last to a slumber so deep she'd missed her alarm. She'd only awakened when the text alert she'd set for her sister went off: "Danger, Will Robinson. Danger."

The text hadn't been an actual emergency (unless a funny dog video was an emergency). After rushing around her condo, Kenzie had tugged on her raincoat and run for the bus, automatically checking her speed so that she wouldn't attract attention. Normally, she liked to walk the mile and a half to work even on rainy spring mornings like this one, but today she didn't have the luxury. Caffeine, on the other hand, was not a luxury. It was a necessity. She'd barely hesitated before joining the short line at Cloudtastic Coffee. She was already ridiculously late; what difference could another five minutes make?

At first, she wasn't sure the kid in the Nike balaclava leaning over the front counter was actually trying to rob the coffee shop. Then she caught the eye of the barista at the cash register—Courtney, a pierced twenty-something Kenzie had gotten to know in the three years she'd worked in Belltown. The look on Courtney's face wasn't wild or fearful but rather resigned, as if she could fully believe that this was, in fact, happening.

Kenzie didn't stop to consider consequences. She didn't hear her sister's voice in her head, warning her to stay hidden. She didn't think about xenophobes or terrorist splinter groups. She simply acted. Time seemed to slow, individual seconds drawing themselves out as if she had pressed a giant pause button hovering above the planet. The people around her froze, and even sound and light waves decelerated. In the space between moments that only she seemed able to navigate, she relieved the would-be thief of his mask and gun in one swift swoop. Before a single second could slip past, she was out of the coffee shop and down the street, ducking into a narrow alley a block and a half away. There, behind a rusting green dumpster, she removed the bullets from the handgun and used her inhuman strength to bend the barrel into a pretzel. Satisfied it was inoperable, she stuffed the gun in the bottom of her messenger bag, tossed the balaclava in the trash bin, and rejoined the foot traffic on the busy city sidewalk, ducking her head so that the brim on her raincoat's hood blocked her face from view.

Almost immediately a police car careened past on the wet street, siren wailing. That was fast. But then police cars weren't exactly few and far between in downtown Seattle. Nor were video cameras, she realized, freezing momentarily. A pedestrian ducked past her, muttering under his breath, and she unfroze. The coffee shop had at least one security camera, which meant her actions had likely been captured on film. Even if they hadn't, Courtney knew her name and where she worked. She had looked Kenzie in the eye just before she'd "blurred," as Kenzie's sister called it. Courtney would tell the police what she'd seen, wouldn't she? *Who* she'd seen? They might not believe her, and the video might be too grainy in the dimly lit interior on a dark Seattle morning to show much. But the report could find its way to the eyes and ears of a Sentinel agent.

The historic brick building that housed the Emerald City Media company loomed just ahead, and Kenzie's pulse pounded erratically for the second time that morning as she followed a man in a business suit inside. What had she just done? A decade of hiding from Panopticon, possibly blown in an instant.

The elevator to the ECM floor was faster than taking the stairs at a normal pace. Kenzie distracted herself from her dislike of small spaces by rehearsing the inevitable argument with her sister: She'd *had* to act; she couldn't just stand there and let Courtney get threatened by a meth head with a gun. Besides, it was over. No way to go back and change the past now. If she'd had that particular superpower, a botched hold-up of a coffee shop wasn't the scene she would choose to revisit.

Aaron gave her a frown when she slid into an empty chair in the conference room, but he didn't comment. He was from the Midwest and relied heavily on non-verbal communication, Kenzie had noticed in her two years of reporting to him.

Her best friend, Matt Greene, leaned forward from two seats down to mouth at her, "Dude, you're late!"

"Dude, I know," she responded in similar fashion.

Her phone buzzed, and she checked it surreptitiously. Antonio Santos, her "other best friend," as he had christened himself, had sent her a gif of a basketball player missing a basket. She watched it twice, but she had no idea what meaning she was supposed to derive from the image. Still, she glanced down the conference table to where Antonio was sitting surrounded by his "writer buds"—mostly sports journalists like him—and gave him the amused smile she hoped he was waiting for. Then she turned her gaze toward the PowerPoint projection at the front of the room that contained website user data related to the number of characters in email newsletter subject lines, headlines, and story snips.

Sure enough, she'd arrived in time for yet another depressing meeting on the declining popularity of traditional news media.

Her sister's comment when she'd declared her major at the University of Washington half a decade earlier came back to her now, as it often did: *Are you sure you want to join a sinking ship?* But she hadn't listened, and now here she was wondering daily if her job would exist in a week, month, year. At least she was multi-talented, with skills in writing, photography, and video production. The U-Dub journalism department encouraged their graduates to be versatile—wisely, in Kenzie's opinion.

While Aaron droned on, she held her phone under the edge of the notebook she was never without, scrolling through Twitter for any Seattle news and crime hashtags that might reference the coffee shop assault. But there was nothing—yet.

"Kenzie," Aaron said, his voice edged with something she couldn't quite read, "I'd like to talk to you. Everyone else, get back to work. Thanks, team."

Antonio gave her a surreptitious thumbs-up on his way out, while Matt brushed past and murmured teasingly, "Oooh, someone's in trouble."

"Zip it," she muttered, elbowing him perhaps a tad too hard, judging from his sharp intake of breath. *Whoops.*

The edge in her boss's voice, she soon learned, was eagerness, something she didn't often associate with him. Irritation and general all-around curmudgeonry, yes. Fangirl levels of agitation? Not so much.

"Are you still working on the trade show write-up?" he asked, hand smoothing back one of the few patches of buzzed hair that still remained on his mostly bald head.

"Yes. I should have it in time for the afternoon deadline," she said, though it would take a Herculean effort to complete the piece. She was fully capable of such effort, if a tad unwilling, so it wasn't a genuine falsehood, was it?

"Scrap it for now. I have another assignment for you," he said, and waved her along with him as he left the conference room. "You're familiar with Ava Westbrook?"

Kenzie blinked as she accompanied him through the newsroom to his office with its rectangular window that looked out over Belltown, Elliott Bay gray and gloomy in the distance. Of course she knew who Ava Westbrook was. As the daughter of General Alexander Westbrook, founder of Panopticon—the US government's alien identification and regulation bureau—Ava was definitely on Kenzie's radar. As an innovative engineer who had recently moved to Seattle to take over as chief operations officer at her family's company, Hyperion Tech, she was doubly of interest.

"Not, like, personally," she said.

"I didn't mean personally." Aaron's voice was impatient as he slid into his chair and typed in the password to his sleek desktop computer. "She's basically been a recluse since her brother's trial, but today that changes. Todd Warren is going to interview her at her office this afternoon, and I want you along to take photographs. It's just the kind of exclusive we need to lift our numbers."

Kenzie's eyes narrowed slightly. Todd Warren was a veteran war reporter who didn't normally cover the tech industry. That was Kenzie's beat, along with Matt and a handful of other staff. Then again, the arrest and imprisonment of Ava Westbrook's older brother, Nicholas, the previous year wasn't traditional tech news, either, and yet, here they were.

"Of course," she said neutrally, already planning her phone call to her sister.

"I trust you can get up to speed on the Westbrooks on your own?" Aaron asked, his eyes fixed on one of his two massive screens.

"Absolutely."

"Good. Then get to it."

She got to it, ignoring Matt's questioning look as she made a beeline through the newsroom, headed for the women's restroom with her phone in the pocket of her khakis. There were two women already there, and she had to smile politely through a conversation about morning beverages before, at last, she was alone. This room was the only one on her floor that she could guarantee was free of surveillance equipment. She leaned against the door to the hall, punched a shortcut key on her phone, and waited for her sister to pick up.

"Kenzie? Are you okay?" Sloane sounded concerned.

But then, she often sounded concerned. It was understandable, given the current cultural climate around alien-human relations. While a decent number of people knew that Kenzie had been adopted by the Shepherd-Hendersons when she was twelve, only a handful were aware that she hadn't been born on Earth.

"I'm fine," she assured her sister, and then paused. Should she tell her about the coffee shop? But no, as long as social media stayed quiet, she should be fine. Ava Westbrook, on the other hand, was a more pressing concern.

"You can't go there," Sloane declared before Kenzie had even finished describing her assignment. "That'd be like walking into the lion's den willingly."

Through her phone's speaker, Kenzie could hear the click of shoes against concrete and pictured her big sister pacing the central floor of Seattle's Panopticon office, the blue, red, and black circular seal painted over much of its surface. At the top of the circle were the words, "PANOPTICON: AN EYE ON HUMANITY" while the bottom of the circle read, "United States of America." At the center was an image of a tower with a spotlight that reminded Kenzie of a lighthouse. Matt said it looked more like "some creepy-ass Sauron tower shit" out of *Lord of the Rings*. To be honest, he had a point.

"There's no evidence linking Ava Westbrook to Sentinel," Kenzie argued, keeping an ear out for approaching footsteps. "Unless you have information I don't know about?"

This was a sore point between them. Her sister often withheld information on the basis of the oath of confidentiality she had sworn the day she joined Panopticon. Which was fair, but still.

"Oh, little sister, there is so much you don't know about," Sloane predictably replied. "But no, there's nothing to connect Ava Westbrook to Sentinel. Other than the fact HER FATHER FUNDED IT AND HER BROTHER RAN IT."

If she'd been human, Kenzie would have winced at her sister's elevated tone. As it was, she merely rolled her eyes. "Obviously. That's why I called you."

"So we're agreed, then? You're not going on this little interview?"

Kenzie took a calming breath, reminding herself that her sister meant well with her bullying tactics. "Except I am."

"But—"

"Sloane. I do not tell you how to do your job, do I?"

"That's because I am a trained government agent, while you are…"

"Invulnerable? Is that the word you're looking for?"

Sloane sputtered, and Kenzie momentarily felt bad for lording her alien advantages (as their parents had delicately referred to the powers exhibited by natives of Zattalia, her home planet) over her sister. But sometimes such gloating was necessary.

"Fine," her sister said grouchily. "But I want to have eyes and ears on that office, got it?"

"Maybe. If it's convenient. Otherwise, I'll text you when I'm done."

"Kenzie Min Zat Shepherd—" her sister started.

"Gotta go," Kenzie interrupted cheerily. "Love you, sis. Bye-ee!"

As an unregistered alien, it was useful having a sister high up in the local Panopticon office, but knowing when to cut and run, as the idiom went, was also a good thing.

Back at her desk, Kenzie pulled up Nexis and typed in "Nicholas Westbrook." As the results poured in—*oh my god*, she thought, eyes wide as she stared at the sheer number of relevant headlines—she noticed Matt waving at her from above the top of her monitor. Their desks were separated only by a low cubicle wall, a situation that sometimes reduced her work efficiency. But they had spent countless hours studying together in the Gothic reading room at U-Dub's library—eerily reminiscent, they'd agreed, of the Great Hall at Hogwarts—and they'd both managed to graduate with honors. When it mattered, they worked well together.

"What's up, bub?" she asked, barely glancing up from her screen. She clicked on a link to a news story near the top of the results: "Marine Captain Nicholas Westbrook indicted on charges of alien intimidation, harassment, kidnapping, and murder." Sounded about right.

"So what did Vaney say?" Matt asked, invoking their private nickname for the boss.

"Warren and I are interviewing Ava Westbrook this afternoon."

Matt actually—and unsurprisingly to everyone who worked near him—squealed. He could be as excitable as Kenzie, which was probably what had drawn them together their first year of college. "You are not!"

"No, really, I am."

"Are you going to ask her about Sentinel?"

Kenzie glanced around quickly, but no one nearby appeared to be listening. "Of course not. And lower your voice."

"Sorry." At least he had the grace to look abashed. He'd known about her other worldly identity for almost as long as they'd been friends, and he wasn't always the best at being inconspicuous, a fact that drove her sister crazy. "But seriously, what a sweet assignment. I mean, I know she's related to alien-hating warmongers, but Ava Westbrook is hot *and* nerdy."

Definitely not Kenzie's favorite type of woman.

Except she was—warmongering family members aside, of course. Kenzie had never shared the tiny fact of her bisexuality with Matt, though. Actually, she'd never shared it with anyone, not even her sister. She'd always figured it would come up if and when there was a reason—like a girlfriend or at least an impending date. So far, neither situation had arisen.

She cleared her throat pointedly. "I have to do a bunch of research, okay?"

"Oh, okay. I see you. Have fun with your 'research,'" he said.

She ignored his air quotes to focus on her screen again. Matt was right about one thing—the Westbrooks were literal warmongers. The General, the architect behind Panopticon, had created the US government agency to keep an eye not on humanity, as its motto claimed, but squarely on non-humans. Rumor had it the original name was supposed to be Bureau of Alien Affairs, but the acronym didn't work so an alternative had been chosen. General Westbrook had died a number of years earlier in a grisly murder-suicide carried out by a distraught alien who'd claimed Panopticon killed his family, an allegation that had never been adequately confirmed or denied, in Kenzie's opinion.

After the General's death, his son Nicholas had secretly used his position as head of Sentinel—Panopticon's military arm—to track down registered and unregistered aliens alike, subjecting them to a variety of experiments in the supposed name of keeping humans safe from off-worlders. After an alien with friends in the federal government managed to escape Sentinel's clutches, Nicholas Westbrook had been arrested and his unit disbanded. Numerous operatives had escaped, however, and rumor had it that Sentinel had recreated itself as an underground terrorist group with an avowedly anti-alien agenda.

This was why Kenzie's adopted parents had contended registration was risky and encouraged her to pass as human instead. There were too many xenophobic humans in positions of power, they'd argued even before Sentinel's actions came to light, with the tools and desire to harm those like Kenzie whose powers made them seem like potential threats. But was Ava Westbrook like her father and brother? And what about her mother, Dr. Amelia Thornton? A physicist by training who up until recently had run the family's multi-billion-dollar business, Hyperion Tech, makers of assorted drone and robotics technologies, Dr. Thornton had resigned a few months earlier to pursue "personal matters." Her opinion on aliens was mostly undocumented, though some of Hyperion's products had a distinctly pro-human, anti-off-worlder bent.

Similarly, Ava Westbrook's sentiment toward aliens was unknown. In Kenzie's opinion, Ava had something going for her that her mother lacked: She had testified against her brother at his trial, providing cell phone and email records that had helped the federal government make their case against their wayward soldier. But just because Ava appeared to believe in law and order didn't mean she thought off-world refugees belonged on Earth.

Kenzie's stomach growled. Time for her mid-morning snack. Any further questions about the Westbrook family's political beliefs would have to wait.

#

Ava Westbrook's landline buzzed a moment before her assistant's voice echoed through the spacious office. "The reporters from Emerald City Media are here. Should I send them in?"

She hesitated before pressing the conference button. "Not yet. I'll let you know when I'm ready."

"Yes, Miss Westbrook," Chloe said, a hint of a smirk

in her voice.

Ava ignored the semi-impertinent tone and added another item to her endless to-do list: *Interview for a new assistant.* She had inherited Chloe from her mother along with her current title, Chief Operations Officer. Frankly, neither had been especially wanted. Ava had been perfectly happy as head of Research and Development in Hyperion's New York office, but then her brother had gone off the rails and her mother had jumped ship. To keep the company in the family, Hyperion needed at least two members of the Thornton clan in leadership positions, and she had decided that the position being offered was an opportunity she couldn't pass up. While Victoria, her mother's cousin, had agreed to become CEO and president of the board, Ava had taken on the role that would allow her to oversee the company's culture.

As COO, she was convinced she could guide Hyperion away from its roots in weapons systems and robotics and into more progressive industries like artificial intelligence and clean energy. She was confident that with time, she could help the organization recognize the business sense in changing courses. Recent growth in wind power, solar photovoltaics, and fuel cell technologies presented a huge financial opportunity. Hyperion could be on the forefront of the inevitable move away from petroleum products—which were finite—toward renewable resources that weren't only better for the environment but offered significantly less long-term risk.

Ava spun in her seat, taking a breath to settle her anxiety over the impending interview. While her mother's former assistant might not be ideal, she had to admit that the office digs were spectacular. A wall of windows opened onto a balcony that looked out over Seattle's vibrant downtown and Elliott Bay, with the Olympic Mountains visible to the west on a clear day and Mt. Rainier's impressive mass dwarfing the Cascade Range to the south. Still, she missed her comfortable, windowless lab back in New York. Seattle felt like a small town compared to the crazy energy of Manhattan. Missed, too, the sense of quiet competence of working in R&D. She had never quite been able to shake her name, but her projects had spoken for themselves. No one whispered charges of nepotism when her nano technology brought in billions. Since coming to Seattle, though, the whispers had grown to a near chorus. It didn't help that despite her MBA, she felt out of her depth at the helm of a company mired in controversy, thanks to her brother's depraved crimes against Earth's alien community.

She stared out at the gray clouds hanging over the city and bay on a cool spring day. This interview was just another obligation she didn't want to deal with. But Victoria wasn't giving her a choice, and worrying wouldn't prevent the meeting from taking place. Better to simply get it over with as quickly as possible.

Swiveling her chair back to face the interior of her office, she pressed the intercom button. "Chloe, please send my visitors in."

"Yes, Miss Westbrook."

Chloe's insistence on invoking her last name at every turn felt purposeful, particularly given that Ava had asked her not to. Maybe she should place finding a new assistant at the top of that endless list.

The double doors at one end of the wide room opened, and as the first of two figures entered, Ava rose and stepped forward to meet the pair. She was rehearsing her greeting—strong but polite—in her mind when she focused on the woman in the lead, and all at once she forgot about first impressions with the local press. This reporter was beautiful, with blonde hair pulled away from her face in a neat chignon, blue eyes that were inquisitive behind chunky black frames, and broad shoulders that seemed out of place on a writer. Not that Ava minded them. In fact, muscles paired with ephemeral beauty was one of her favorite combinations.

Inwardly, Ava groaned. Great. Now she was a nervous *gay* mess for her first interview with the media as Hyperion's COO.

She took another deep breath and fastened a smile to her face, turning her attention to the man hulking behind the female reporter. Her stomach dropped again but far less pleasantly as Todd Warren stared back at her. Ava knew this man. He had penned several inflammatory articles about Sentinel in general and her brother in particular at the time of the trial. Nothing he had written had been inaccurate, of course; it was just that Ava would have appreciated a tad less besmirching of the Westbrook name given that her brother was mentally ill and her father wasn't around to defend himself.

"Mr. Warren," she said silkily, waving the pair toward her desk. "What a surprise. I didn't realize you were based at Emerald City Media."

"Not all writers work out of New York," he replied, holding out one of the chairs for his colleague.

And, *ew*. Chivalry equated a bit too closely with misogyny in Ava's mind. Apparently, Warren's fellow reporter agreed—she gave him a narrow-eyed look before pulling out the other chair for herself and settling into it. Then she sprang back to her feet, nearly knocking the chair over.

"Sorry, I'm Kenzie Shepherd," she announced in a rush, and thrust her hand toward Ava almost forcefully.

Ava couldn't help smiling at the other woman's awkwardness. It was always good to realize you weren't the only nervous one in the room. "Miss Shepherd," she said, and delicately took the extended hand in her own. Which was a mistake, she realized belatedly, as her mind decided to catalog the unusual warmth and softness of the skin against hers, of the strength in the long, elegant fingers gripping her own, of the fascinating blue color of the other woman's eyes as they widened slightly…

Right. That was more than enough chaotic gay energy for a meeting with the press.

Ava released Kenzie's hand and turned away. Instead of returning to her executive chair, she detoured to an armoire along a nearby wall. "Can I get you anything to drink?" she asked as she poured herself a glass of water from a Brita pitcher.

"No, thank you," Warren said. "Actually, I wanted to ask—"

"And you, Miss Shepherd?" Ava interrupted. "Would you care for a beverage? I have water, soda, or even something a bit more interesting, if you're so inclined." *Oh my god, Ava, shut up shut up shut up,* she told herself. Flirting with a pretty reporter was not a good idea even without Todd Warren present to witness the exchange.

Kenzie ducked her head, and Ava stared as the other woman's neck turned a delicate shade of rose. "No, thank you."

Crap. She was straight, wasn't she, and Ava had made her uncomfortable. Just another embarrassing social exchange in the life of a nerdy lesbian technophile. There was a reason Ava preferred laboratories to executive suites, product demonstrations to feature article interviews.

She took a long gulp of water and returned to her desk. "So," she said breezily, pretending the last minute hadn't actually happened. "What can I help the two of you with?"

The interview format was pretty much what she had anticipated: questions about her ascension at Hyperion, about where her mother had gotten to, about the difficulties for the family-owned company around her brother's xenophobic assaults on alien refugees. Warren, like most members of the press Ava had met, was clearly a progressive when it came to alien relations, and she tried not to bristle too overtly at the way he lumped Hyperion and the Westbrook family in with Nick's bizarre acts. Her brother had never been officially diagnosed with personality disorder, but it didn't take much imagination to see a correlation between their father's death and Nick's paranoid delusions. And yes, she had helped put him away, but that was because it had been the right thing to do. It didn't mean she didn't love her brother less, even if she would never forgive him for the terrible things he had done.

She could feel Kenzie's curious gaze on her as Warren made yet another snide suggestion about Hyperion's technological focus on the alien community, and it was probably that awareness that made her suddenly push back from her desk, shaking her head. "No, you know what? I'm not doing this. I know what it looks like from the outside, and I know what you think you see. But Hyperion isn't anti-alien, and neither am I, Mr. Warren."

"Really?" he asked, his tone dubious.

"Really," she said firmly. "My interests lie in helping all the communities of Earth, no matter where they may have originated. We all share this planet now, and frankly, there are far graver issues that need our focus. Climate change is the single most complex threat facing every living being on Earth, and I am more interested both personally and professionally in finding a solution to the melting of the permafrost and the increasing acidification of our oceans than I am in debating who belongs and who doesn't. Frankly, we don't have the luxury to focus on the wrong priorities, which is why I'm determined to make Hyperion Tech a leading proponent in the fight to slow climate change—for the sake of the planet *and* for the sake of my family's reputation."

And, oh, *crap*, Victoria was going to be so pissed, Ava realized as her irritation ebbed as quickly as it had risen. These were definitely not the talking points she was supposed to be rolling out to the press. Careful neutrality was the safe route, not proudly proclaiming her personal views on the human-alien question. But too bad. Her mother and Victoria had promoted her knowing exactly where she stood on these issues. No way was she going to stay in the proverbial closet.

Victoria was currently at an off-site meeting, however, while Kenzie Shepherd was sitting directly across from Ava, a slow smile blooming as she appeared to digest her statement. Well, that was something, anyway. She'd managed to impress the straight girl.

"Huh," Warren said, still sounding like he thought she was about to raise her hand in Sentinel's once-secret pro-human salute. "I haven't heard you say those things before. Why is that?"

And off they went again, covering the same old territory. Ava fell back on the neat sound bites her PR chief had drilled into her, and the interview wrapped up a short time later. Except they weren't done yet, Ava realized. Kenzie had pulled a digital camera from her messenger bag and was holding it up.

"Could I get a couple of photos of you?" she asked almost shyly.

"Of course," Ava said, nodding graciously even though she longed to refuse. In R&D, the glossies had featured her team or their results, not her. "Where do you want me?"

This time, the blush was less rose and more red. Kenzie bit her lip and looked away, eyes alighting on the sofa. "What about there?"

Ava rose and walked to the couch. At least she had worn a skirt. Her curves might seem less noticeable in a jacket and pencil skirt. She settled on the cool leather couch, a mid-century modern in cream that, frankly, was the least comfortable piece of furniture she had ever encountered. Her mother had said it kept her visitors from relaxing too much. Yet another item on Ava's to-do list: *Buy a new office couch.*

Kenzie fussed with the settings on the camera before approaching and kneeling before her. Ava wasn't sure if she should smile or not. Before she could decide, Kenzie lifted the camera and asked, "So what's your favorite food?"

The question threw her slightly. "My favorite food?"

"You know, the things you put into your body to keep it going?"

Ava smiled at the friendly look in Kenzie's eyes, and—*there.* The camera's shutter audibly clicked a few times. "I see what you're doing, Miss Shepherd."

"It's Kenzie." She winked cheekily and volunteered, "Mine is sushi. Have you been to Shiro's in Belltown yet?"

Though Ava recognized Kenzie's strategy to relax her, that awareness didn't appear to lessen the tactic's effectiveness. "I haven't," she admitted. "I only moved to Seattle a short time ago."

"Oh, that's right. Well, you should definitely check it out. I go there like three times a week—it's on my way home from work, which is frankly a bit dangerous for my bank account."

"Shiro's, in Belltown," Ava repeated, filing away the name for future reference. In her opinion, you could never have too many sushi recommendations.

"It's totally the best," Kenzie said, occasionally snapping photos as she changed positions and spots around the couch. "Although, I mean, obviously there are tons of others since Seattle is the closest American city to Japan. Or, at least, the closest in the lower forty-eight."

She was adorable and even a touch masculine in her khakis and collared shirt, lean muscles evident as her sleeves shifted across her arms. Ava was tantalized enough to say, her voice teasing, "So is this a PSA or an invitation?"

Kenzie's head shot up and she stared at Ava, a clear question in her eyes. The shutter clicked as their gazes held, and then Kenzie glanced down at the camera and cleared her throat. "Um, I probably have what I need. Want to take a look and let me know your thoughts?"

Ava couldn't remember ever being given a choice about which photo ran with a story about her family's company. She nodded, inhaling subtly (she hoped) as Kenzie dropped onto the couch beside her, their arms and legs almost touching. Kenzie held up the camera so that Ava could see assorted stills of herself, and she paged through them, impressed by the quality. The final shot captured her smirking at Kenzie, one eyebrow slightly raised, and she realized she looked—a little bit devious, really. More like her mother and brother and less like the remote, all-business persona she'd worked hard to develop since coming to work at Hyperion.

"So, what do you think?" Kenzie asked.

"I think you're very good at your job," Ava said, and glanced up. This close, she could see the flecks of dark gray among the blue of Kenzie's irises and realized that was why her eyes seemed darker than they actually were. She could see the freckles dotting Kenzie's face, too, so light they almost weren't there.

"You should take a few more," Warren said, his voice too loud in the quiet room. "Just to be sure."

Kenzie blinked a few times and rose, ducking her head, while irritation rose sharp and fast in Ava again. She got quite enough mansplaining at Hyperion, thank you very much. She stood, too, clasping her hands together in front of her as she turned an icy glare on the senior reporter. "Unfortunately, that's all the time I have for you, Mr. Warren. If you have additional questions, I'm sure my assistant would be happy to help."

Predictably, Warren hemmed and hawed, but Ava was resolute as she ushered the pair to the door. Just before they reached it, she couldn't resist the urge to touch Kenzie, brushing her palm against the other woman's forearm.

"It was nice meeting you, Kenzie. I hope this isn't the last time we talk?" she asked, because apparently being rebuffed by pretty blonde reporters was a kink she hadn't previously known she possessed.

Kenzie paused. "I hope it isn't, either, Miss Westbrook."

"Please, call me Ava."

"Ava," Kenzie repeated, nodding. Then, with a last small smile, she followed Warren out of the office.

Ava resisted the urge to watch her walk away and instead let the double doors fall closed. Then she returned to her desk, dropped into her chair, and propped her head in both hands. Had she really just done that? Had she actually flirted with a member of the press? Where were her ethics? Or, forget ethics—where was her common sense? Ava was usually so practical, but Kenzie Shepherd had flashed her nervous smile and Ava's composure had vanished. All she had been able to think was what a shame that Todd Warren had come along for the interview.

She picked up her phone and texted, "I am such a goob."

Her best friend's reply came quickly: "DUH!" A moment later, another message appeared. "Wait, what's the context?"

"I flirted with a straight reporter during an interview and then told her I hoped we would meet again." She added a forehead smacking emoji. Normally she didn't have much of an emoji game, but desperate times and so forth.

"Aw, look at u trying to get ur game on!" Beatrice typed back, and included a clapping emoji.

"I hate you," Ava typed. Then she added, "I miss you. Hugs to the boys."

"Miss u too, babe. ILY!"

A cascade of hearts, rainbow flags, and kisses followed, and Ava smiled fondly before setting down her phone and turning back to her massive computer screen. Her to-do list wasn't going to complete itself, which was just as well. Staying busy was the only way to distract her from the conviction she'd made a complete idiot of herself in front of the attractive reporter. If she was lucky, this really would be the last time they talked.

A pang of what felt almost like regret surfaced, but Ava shoved it down deep, burying it with practiced ease beneath her mountain of current responsibilities. Westbrooks did not dwell on past mistakes, her father had often declared. They marched forward, carrying the rest of the company with them.

Of her own volition, Ava's fingers typed "Kenzie Shepherd" into a search field, and down the rabbit hole she happily went even though her father—not to mention Hyperion Tech's shareholders—would definitely not approve.

CHAPTER TWO

It all started with Courtney's Instagram post.

Well, Kenzie could admit that "it" actually began with her own decision to intercede in a robbery despite every reason not to. But the police didn't contact her in the days that followed the incident at Cloudtastic, and social media stayed quiet, with no mention that she could find of a superpowered individual playing Robin Hood in downtown Seattle. The lack of local authorities breaking down her door combined with an absence of online speculation to give her a false sense of security, and she ended up spending more time on Dropbox staring dreamily at the photos she'd taken of Ava Westbrook than worrying about potentially outing herself.

That is, until Thursday morning, when she noticed "#SuperSeattleite" trending locally. Gnawing her lower lip, she clicked on the hashtag and discovered the original post that had started it. User @CourtneyLicious had included a shot of herself in her green Cloudtastic T-shirt and apron smiling into the camera with a caption that read, "So guys, I wish I knew the identity of the masked avenger—or hooded avenger, I guess I should say—who helped out during an attempted robbery last week, because I would totally give them a coffee on the house. But, alas, I don't. Whoever they are, I just hope they know I appreciate them. P.S. This is NOT an invitation to Seattleites at large to come assail me for free coffee, so don't even bother, my dudes."

She hadn't included #SuperSeattleite, but it was a slow news day and some bored hacker type had gotten hold of a grainy video feed that clearly showed Kenzie's back as she blurred into action.

Fudge, Kenzie thought, scrolling nervously through the list of retweets and replies. Sloane was going to—

Her text alert went off—*Danger, Will Robinson*—and she flinched as she read her sister's furious text: "WTF DID YOU DO!!!!"

She turned off her notifications and set down her phone, but that didn't stop the avalanche of anxiety currently ravaging her nervous system as she closed Twitter and returned to her story in progress. She'd been staring blindly at the tech industry's latest earnings report (and not at Ava Westbrook's photos, especially not that last shot where she was gazing absolutely predatorily at Kenzie; although Kenzie's inability to read human expressions and intentions was legendary, so there was that) for at least five minutes when Matt suddenly swiveled his chair about and scooted it around to her side, waving his phone in the air.

"Why didn't you tell me about this?" he demanded, his whisper more like a poorly hidden shout of excitement, in Kenzie's opinion.

Fully aware what he was referencing, she pretended to squint down at the screen. "What? I don't—what?"

He leveled an impatient look at her. "Dude, that's totally you."

"Who?"

"There," he said, pausing the video to point at her

back.

"No, it isn't."

"Yes, it is! They're your height and build, plus I recognize your raincoat."

"It's from REI. It could literally belong to anyone in Seattle."

"It literally belongs to you. Besides, check the time stamp—that's the day you were late to the meeting. It's totally you."

"It's someone who looks like me," she insisted, glancing around to see if anyone was looking their way. They were not, and as far as she knew, she was the only person in the newsroom with enhanced hearing abilities. Not to mention, super vision, flight, super strength, and the ability to move faster than the human eye could follow, to list a few of the powers the Shepherds had insisted she keep hidden since coming to Earth a dozen years earlier.

Matt waved a hand. "I don't know why you're denying this to me, of all people. I'm the one who's been telling you for years to do this exact thing."

Kenzie closed her eyes. "Please, not the superhero lecture again. For the last time, you cannot be my Alfred or Q or whatever, okay? It's not my duty to save humankind from itself, Matt."

"I hear you," he said unexpectedly. "But what about saving alienkind from humanity? After everything Sentinel has done in the last few years, I get that coming out isn't exactly safe. But Sentinel has made life super scary for a ton of other people, too, and not every off-worlder has your abilities, you know."

She expelled a breath because, *dang it*, he had a point. This was actually the exact argument she'd been staging with Sloane semi-regularly—and wildly unsuccessfully—ever since Nicholas Westbrook's crimes had come to light.

"Besides, I've got so many ideas for a costume!" Matt

added, grinning. "And a name! How about APB?"

"Um, like the police?"

"Yeah, but in this case it would stand for Alien Protection Bureau."

Kenzie rolled her eyes. He had read way too many comic books for her to ever take him seriously. "And on that note, get back to work before we both suffer the wrath of Vaney."

He hesitated before scooting away. "Fine. But this conversation isn't over."

She was perfectly aware of that fact.

Still, her sister had a job to do as did she, so at least that confrontation should hold off for a while. As she worked on the boring article about a certain local tech behemoth's continued rise up every list of measurable success, yada yada yada, she occasionally flicked back to Twitter to check the #SuperSeattleite tag. As the day went on, the tenor of the comments changed, morphing from a combination of excitement and the inevitable alien-bashing from thirty-year-old male virgins to a growing cacophony of questions.

In a tweet with more than a thousand likes, one user decried, "If #SuperSeattleite straight up has Wonder Woman's powers, why isn't she using them to help the rest of us? #slacker #selfish #seriously?"

The responses ranged from "How do you know the super alien is female?" (which inspired its own, separate argument over the hero's shoulders: "way too broad for a chick" versus "clearly tapering into a feminine form") to "Way to sound entitled, Becky," and "I'm not sure we want to encourage someone who passes for human AND has that kind of power to feel comfortable in their own skin." But the replies that got the most retweets and likes were the ones that agreed with the original post. Kenzie checked Instagram briefly, but the response was similar across platforms. Seattle, a well-known liberal haven for off-worlders, was apparently thirsty for a hero.

"Thirsty" reminded her of the interview with Ava Westbrook, and she sighed and put her head down on her desk for an oh-so-brief moment. Sometimes being a non-native Earth inhabitant was ridiculously difficult. Not because of the plethora of Earth languages to learn; the Alliance ship's AI had made sure she was fluent in the planet's top ten languages before she landed. But even an AI as advanced as the one on that ship struggled with culturally conditioned aspects of interaction like body language, idioms, or sarcasm. More than ninety percent of human communication was non-verbal, and as a result, Kenzie felt uncertain about her ability to accurately parse what was being communicated at least fifty percent of the time. Possibly more.

Had Ava been angling for an invitation to sushi, or had she simply enjoyed making Kenzie blush? Had she genuinely hoped they would meet again, or was that just something people from the East Coast said? Did Ava have any idea how impossible it would be for them to become friends, let alone have flirty sushi dates? But of course she didn't because Kenzie's alien identity was a secret.

Except, possibly, on Instagram and Twitter.

Mulvaney picked that moment to stroll through the bullpen. "I don't pay you to nap, Shepherd," he commented, and continued on toward his private office.

Right, Kenzie thought, lifting her head. Back to work. At least this article would give her more time before Sloane attempted to lock her in her condo and throw away the key. Or, worse, lock her in a Panopticon cell, which could conceivably hold her but only because Sloane knew her weaknesses. Along with their parents and D'aman, Kenzie's former Alliance caseworker, Sloane was one of the only people in the world who knew that she hailed from Zattalia, a planet whose citizens had been forced to become space nomads after they'd used up all of their natural resources—sort of like Earth was in the process of doing right now. For centuries, none of the more advanced planets in the Alliance had allowed large groups of Zattalians to settle in their territory, not only because her ancestors had destroyed their own planet through greed but also because of the genetically modified abilities that meant they were perceived as a threat to most other life forms.

If Kenzie was being honest, Zattalians *may* have helped create that animosity by, you know, keeping people from other planets as slaves for a few millennia. But they'd liberated the slaves like a thousand generations earlier, so really, to Kenzie's mind, the peoples of the universe were kind of holding a grudge. On Earth, that would be like disliking medieval Christians for hunting down and killing tens of thousands of women for being "witches" during the sixteenth and seventeenth centuries. Or hating Germans because a couple of generations earlier, the Nazis had tried to annihilate the Jewish people in a broader quest to take over the planet and rule it under an iron fist.

Come to think of it, Kenzie wasn't a huge fan of Christians or Germans for those very reasons. Maybe the universe's grudge against the people of Zattalia was more understandable than she'd previously allowed.

Either way, only a very few humans knew how to weaken her and the rest of her brethren, assuming there were any other Zattalians left. The asteroid strike that had taken out their fleet—the largest Zattalian fleet in the known universe, her parents had once told her—had apparently left next to no survivors, according to intelligence her adopted family had been given. In fact, Kenzie might be the last daughter of Zattalia, for all she knew.

No pressure, really.

Work could only shield her from her sister's wrath for so long. By six that evening, she knew she had to leave the building or Sloane would storm her current position and yell at her in front of her colleagues who worked the evening shift. She definitely didn't want that, so as she jogged down the five flights of stairs, she pulled out her phone and finally responded to her sister's half dozen increasingly succinct messages: "Sorry, just reading these now. Headed home. Want to have Chinese at my place? My treat." She added a few smiley, cheerful emojis for good measure and hit send.

Her phone vibrated almost immediately with a message: "I'm already here."

Crap.

A photo soon followed of Kenzie's kitchen table, white cardboard containers from their mutual favorite Chinese restaurant arranged neatly at one end, and she brightened. Maybe the upcoming lecture wouldn't be so bad, after all, accompanied as it would be by dumplings, egg rolls, spicy fish filet, and noodles. Her mouth was already watering.

As she exited the building, she glimpsed the silver tower a dozen blocks to the south that bore the Hyperion Tech logo, and spared a thought for Ava Westbrook. Was she still at work on the top floor, the dying light from the sunset piercing her wall of glass windows? If she'd wanted, Kenzie could have trained her augmented vision on the windows in question and checked up on Hyperion's newly minted executive. If she'd really wanted, she could have flown up to Ava's balcony and peered in at her from closer quarters. But not only had she promised Sloane and their mother, Jane, that she wouldn't use her flight powers in the city, she also doubted that a Westbrook would view such a visit in a positive light, no matter what progressive views they professed to possess. The fact was Ava came from a family that not only stereotyped the aliens who had taken refuge on Earth but actively encouraged others to fear them. Whatever Ava's personal beliefs, the Westbrooks had used their extraordinary power and resources to harm, even *kill* innocent aliens. A daughter of such a family—no matter how attractive and personable—could never be a close friend, let alone anything more.

Kenzie forced herself to turn away and run to the nearby stop where her bus had just pulled up. But not too fast, of course. No need to have any #SuperSeattleite sightings tonight. Sloane's blood pressure was probably high enough.

The bus ride home to her condo on Queen Anne only took ten minutes. At the top of the hill, Kenzie disembarked at the Five Spot and headed for the Galer Street Stairs. She'd had the song "Seasons of Love" from *Rent* stuck in her head all week, so she sang it quietly to herself as she walked the short distance to the former Queen Anne High School, an impressive concrete edifice squeezed between cell phone towers overlooking the Space Needle and the rest of the Seattle skyline. *Rent* was one of her favorite Broadway shows, although, honestly, there were few Broadway shows she didn't adore.

A fountain greeted her as she approached her building, water burbling gently, and she gazed around in appreciation at the historic building's Neoclassical exterior, amazed as ever that she got to call such an interesting place home. Immediately after college, she'd lived in a shared apartment with two girls she'd known from school. But then aliens started disappearing, especially those who had been successfully passing as human, and Kenzie's parents, both professors at Western Washington University, had decided it was no longer safe for her to live with humans. They'd issued an ultimatum: move back in with them in

Bellingham, 90 miles north of Seattle, or let them help her find someplace secure. She'd ended up here in a fourth-floor studio with fifteen-foot ceilings and floor-to-ceiling windows that looked out over a quiet alley. Just down the hall, a rooftop deck offered residents comfy furniture, heat lamps, and killer views of the Space Needle. As a bonus, Sloane lived only a few blocks away.

Or, at least, usually her proximity was a bonus. Tonight, Kenzie was kind of regretting the spare key she'd given her over-protective big sister.

The interior of her building was elegant and understated, dark wood floors covered with tasteful runners and the lobby walls lined with black and white photos from the previous century. Kenzie typically used the stairs, but tonight she took the slow, wood-paneled elevator to her floor, putting off the inevitable for as long as she could. At last she stood before her door, eyes closed, mentally preparing for Sloane's ire. It would be fine, she reassured herself. If she'd survived her sister's fury that time she'd flown to Vancouver for her favorite dim sum—notably, without an airplane—she would get through this, too.

She pushed open the door and called out a cheerful, "Lucy, I'm home," hoping the *Gilmore Girls* reference would relax her sister's temper. But as she kicked off her shoes and walked down the narrow hallway into the studio's great room, she realized that even the Gilmores couldn't help her now.

Sloane was seated at the butcher block kitchen island at the edge of the kitchen space, a half-empty bottle of wine in front of her. The dining table behind her looked like it had in the photo she'd texted, and Kenzie's shoulders dropped when she realized Sloane had polished off several glasses of wine on an empty stomach. That couldn't be good.

"Hi," she tried.

"Hi," Sloane said, her voice flat, her brown eyes flatter. Her short hair was standing up in places as if she'd been running her hands through it in frustration.

Definitely not good.

Flustered, Kenzie spun around and headed back down the hallway, taking her time as she pulled off her jacket and set it and her shoes in the front closet. She still hadn't come up with a convincing lie. After all the falsehoods she had dreamt up during her time on Earth, shouldn't she be better at pulling the wool over her sister's eyes?

Back in the kitchen, she hesitated before moving forward to hug her sister. But a single look stopped her in her tracks.

"Seriously, Kenzie? We are not hugging. I cannot believe you right now."

The best course of action, Kenzie knew from experience, was to get food into her sister's body to soak up the alcohol. As if to assist this venture, her own stomach growled. Loudly.

Sloane expelled a breath. "Fine. We can eat. But then we're talking about what happened, okay?"

"Yes, of course!" Kenzie grinned at her dour older sister and only just stopped herself from blurring to the table. She couldn't help it, though. A reprieve *and* the best noodles in town?

Sure enough, once Sloane had some food in her belly, her mood shifted. Not by a lot, but the look she cast Kenzie across the dining table a few minutes later was more worried than angry.

"I understand the impulse to act, Kenz, I really do," she said. "I mean, it would be hypocritical for me to tell you not to intervene in a crime, given that's basically what I do on a daily basis. But Cloudtastic is your regular coffee shop. You're unbelievably lucky the barista didn't recognize you."

Kenzie paused. Was this the moment to tell her sister she was fairly certain that Courtney did, in fact, know her and was apparently just guarding her identity for unknown reasons? Yeah, nope. No need to ruin a perfectly good meal.

"I know," she said instead, gaze trained on the last container of pot stickers. "Do you want...?"

Sloane shook her head, an indulgent smile clearly trying to slip unnoticed onto her mouth. It failed. "What am I going to do with you? At least tell me you disposed of the gun responsibly."

Crap. "Um, about that..."

"Where is the gun, Kenzie?" her sister whisper-shouted, mindful of the neighbors.

The walls were decently insulated, which had been one of the selling points for their parents. But in general, Kenzie thought as she went to retrieve the pretzel-shaped handgun from the reusable grocery bag she'd shoved it into three days earlier, keeping their voices down was a really good rule.

It took a while, but a pint of ice cream and two episodes of the new *Gilmore Girls* finally softened Sloane to the point where she seemed more like Kenzie's caring older sister than the tough, black leather-clad government agent she had become somewhere along the way.

"I just worry about you, Kenz, you know that," Sloane practically whined, her head on Kenzie's shoulder as they snuggled together under a cozy blanket on the couch that took up most of one windowless wall.

"I know. I worry about you too, Slo-mo," she said, ruffling her sister's hair in a way Sloane pretended to dislike but secretly, Kenzie was sure, enjoyed.

Sloane twitched away, eyebrows scrunched together. "It's hardly the same thing. I don't have a target on my back."

    Kenzie gave her a skeptical look. "I mean, are you sure about that?"

    "No, of course Sentinel would take any one of us out if they could. But that's different. It's nothing personal. It's a war, and they're on one side and I happen to be on the other. With you, though, it's completely personal. They hate you for who you are."

    Kenzie hunched her shoulders and stared at the flat-screen television hanging on the opposite wall, her first purchase after she moved in. Matt had helped her choose a home theater system, and while the high-definition video and surround sound was currently wasted on Lorelai and Rory Gilmore, it made watching Harry Potter and *Lord of the Rings* a thousand times more fun.

    "I'm sorry," Sloane said when Kenzie remained silent. "I know you already know that. I'm just worried, okay?"

    Kenzie glanced back at her sister, eyeing her carefully. "Is there something going on with Sentinel I should know about?"

    Sloane didn't look at her as she shrugged, focusing her energy on unearthing a large chunk of cookie dough from the surrounding ice cream. "Not really."

    Kenzie listened for what her sister wasn't saying, honing her augmented hearing on her sister's heart rate while, at the same time, focusing her super sight on Sloane's forehead, where telltale droplets of perspiration were trying to form.

    She coughed and said, "Bullshit," but as usual she didn't quite get the timing right.

    Her sister snickered. "The whole point is for the cough to mask the sound of the curse," she said, just as she'd done every other time Kenzie had tried that particular human vocal move.

    "Whatever. The point is, I can tell you're lying. Alien

advantages, remember?"

Sloane looked back at the television, her smirk slipping. "I remember." She was quiet for a minute, but Kenzie waited her out. Finally, she admitted, "There's been an increase in chatter."

Kenzie bit her lip. Another truly not good thing. "About what?"

"It has something to do with Nicholas Westbrook. That's all I know."

Nicholas Westbrook? Of course it had to do with him. Kenzie's heart sank. She'd been considering telling Sloane about her afternoon at Hyperion Tech, mostly so she could try to find a way to ask her super-gay sister if she thought Ava Westbrook had been flirting with her. Now, however, that seemed like a topic better left untouched—for so many reasons. Someday she would come out as bi to her sister. Just, not today, apparently.

"Are they going to try to break him out or something?" she asked.

"I really don't know."

"Would you tell me if you did?"

"Probably not."

"Right." Danged government NDAs.

"Just, do me a favor and try to keep a low profile for the next little bit?" Sloane asked. "I know Comic Book Boy is always trying to get you to don a cape and pick an ubernerdy superhero name, but if you could hold off on doing that anytime soon, I would appreciate it."

Kenzie expelled a breath. "I mean, it wouldn't be *that* nerdy…"

"Kenz," her sister said, voice low. "Mom and Dad would appreciate it, too."

"That's a low blow and you know it," she protested.

Sloane fluttered her eyelashes innocently. "Is it

working?"

Kenzie looked back at the screen, where Rory and Lorelai were still bickering affectionately. "Fine," she grumbled. "I'll tell Matt #SuperSeattleite is not happening."

For now, she thought but didn't add. She could keep secrets, too.

"Thank you," Sloane said, snuggling closer again.

Kenzie could actually hear Sloane's heart rate settle, could sense the rush of blood through her sister's body ease into a more normal pace. Silently, she cursed her alienness for the thousandth time since arriving on Earth. It would have been so much easier not to know.

#

Ava set her computer to sleep mode, turned off the lamp on the desk, and pulled her purse from the drawer. Another long day poring over paperwork instead of tinkering in her lab, and tomorrow would be more of the same, even if it was a Saturday. Maybe someday she would get caught up, but she couldn't imagine it.

Her assistant had left hours earlier at her insistence. Chloe's reluctance to leave the office gave additional credence to a theory Ava had been working on—that her mother's former employee might actually still be in her employ and was diligently tracking and reporting Ava's activities. The question was why? Her mother had jumped ship voluntarily, though mysteriously, in Ava's opinion. Amelia insisted she was simply ready for a change, but at the same time, she refused to share details of whatever new venture had caught her eye. Of course, it wouldn't be the first time her mother had spied on her, so maybe there was no great mystery. Either way, it was definitely time to find a new assistant.

Hyperion's executive floor—the top floor in the building—was dark and quiet, except for the sound of a voice in the office down the hall. Ava tried to move soundlessly toward the elevator. She wasn't in the mood to see Victoria. She especially wasn't in the mood to talk to her after the CEO had made it clear she didn't approve of the "pro-alien propaganda" Ava had "spewed" to the ECM reporters the previous week. Victoria's response might not have been surprising, but it was disappointing. Another bigot in the family—hooray.

That thought led to another: Kenzie Shepherd. In truth, she had thought of the journalist regularly since the day they'd met. She knew Kenzie worked at the opposite end of downtown, but she couldn't help keeping an eye out for a flash of blonde hair as she grabbed coffee in the Starbucks down the street or ate lunch at the Pink Door, her new favorite restaurant in Seattle. Alas, she had not yet managed to run into one of the only people she knew in a city of three and a half million.

In the elevator, her finger hovered over the button that housed The Westbrook, a luxury hotel owned by her family's holding company. She hadn't bothered to find an apartment yet because the hotel suite her mother had booked for her was gorgeous. Besides, it wasn't like she was there that much.

The elevator doors closed, and Ava pushed the ground floor button. At the same time, she sent a text to Hyperion's executive car service. She was in the mood for sushi.

When the flash of blonde hair at the restaurant counter actually materialized into a familiar face and surprised blue eyes, Ava was momentarily speechless. It wasn't like she'd truly expected to see Kenzie. After all, it was a Friday, and most people had probably eaten dinner by this time of night. But here she was, the very person Ava had been thinking about all week.

"Oh my gosh, Ava!" Kenzie said, approaching with a broad smile. "I can't believe you're here!"

"Well, someone did say their sushi was the best," she said, smiling back as if she weren't embarrassed to have been caught stalking Kenzie's favorite restaurant. Was it really stalking if it had taken her a week and a half to get around to it, though? It was more the poring over Kenzie's public social media feeds that fit the description. Not to mention reading every article she'd ever written and finding every photo she'd had published, even for *The Daily*, the University of Washington's student newspaper. Those activities definitely seemed questionable, in hindsight.

"I wondered if you might come here," Kenzie said, and then paused, eyes widening slightly as if she had given something away.

Interesting. Was it possible the stalking wasn't entirely one-sided? Could Kenzie Shepherd be somewhere on the queer spectrum too? Ava's smile turned flirty as she touched Kenzie's arm. "And I wondered if I might run into you here."

Kenzie stared at her, expression unreadable, for a long moment. Then she said, "What did you think of the article?"

Ava drew her hand back. "I found it unexpectedly lacking in negativity," she admitted. Instead of trashing her and Hyperion, the article—which had featured both Kenzie's and Warren's bylines—had been noticeably more positive than the company's recent press. Hers, too, for that matter.

Kenzie smiled. "I might have had something to do with that."

Ava nodded appreciatively. "Thank you for not lumping me in with the rest of my family."

"I believe in judging people based on their words and actions, not on the words and actions of others."

Was she for real? But Ava couldn't find any hint of sarcasm or irony in her bearing. On the contrary, Kenzie seemed completely earnest.

Ava was saved from replying by the cashier calling Kenzie's name. She watched the transaction curiously, noting how Kenzie conversed longer than she would have expected with the older woman at the counter. Right. A regular, obviously.

Food in hand, Kenzie returned to Ava, smiling sheepishly as she waved two large reusable bags in apparent farewell. "I should probably let you order, shouldn't I."

"I suppose so." Ava eyed the bags. "That isn't all for you, is it?"

"Oh! Um, no?"

Ava raised an eyebrow.

"I mean, most of it, yeah, but I'm having drinks with friends at my place, so…"

"I see," Ava said, struck by a sudden pang. If she were still in Manhattan, she would have been doing much the same. Instead, here she was in a new city in the Pacific Northwest, a part of the country that prized waterproof jackets and hiking boots over silk blouses and Louboutins. For the hundredth time, she questioned her continued loyalty to a family who didn't appear to have the same compunction when it came to her.

"What about you?" Kenzie asked. "Big plans tonight?"

"No, I just left work. I haven't made any plans past sushi."

Kenzie bit her lip, which was adorable and distracting just like everything else about her. Maybe that was why Ava nearly missed her next words, spoken in a rush: "Any interest in coming over?"

"Coming over?" she echoed, trying to process the

meaning of the question."

"Yeah. I live on Queen Anne." Kenzie waved vaguely in a northward direction. "It's nice out, so we're having drinks on the patio."

"The patio?" Ava repeated because apparently her brain was feeling especially sluggish during this portion of their conversation. Most of her brain power seemed caught up in the realization that Kenzie appeared to be asking her over. For drinks. Tonight.

"My building has a rooftop patio that looks out over the city. There's a view of the Space Needle. Oh, and heat lamps! There are totally heat lamps if you're someone who, you know, gets cold."

Adorable and nerdy was a potent combination, in Ava's opinion. And yet, even though she would love to spend more time with Kenzie Shepherd, even though she was lonely and didn't know anyone in Seattle other than her mother's cousin and a boarding school classmate she'd never particularly liked, she paused. Kenzie's friends were likely to know who she was. More worrisome, they would almost assuredly know who her brother was—and what he'd done.

"It's okay if you don't want to," Kenzie said, her shoulders falling slightly. "I only thought since you're new in town—"

"No, I'd love to," Ava interrupted. "It's just, the Westbrook name doesn't make it all that easy to be social, I've found. Especially lately."

Kenzie frowned, a slight V forming between her eyebrows. "I didn't think of that. I promise, though, my friends are totally open-minded."

Ava didn't doubt that. But did their open minds extend to a conservative, militaristic family that was embarrassingly vocal about loving guns and hating anyone who hadn't been born on Earth? Still, Ava didn't encounter many people who made her want to risk the complications that came with trying to have friends. Delusional siblings aside, being one of the wealthiest women under 40 in the world made it difficult to find people she could trust.

Decision made, she nodded and said, "I'd like that. Thank you for the invitation."

"Really?" Kenzie appeared almost shocked by her response. But then her wide smile returned, blue eyes warming with seemingly genuine happiness. "Awesome! That's so great. I can text you the address, and when your order is ready you could come over?"

"Sounds good," Ava said, and gave Kenzie her private cell phone number, the one only a handful of people on the planet possessed.

A moment later, Kenzie practically skipped out of the restaurant, waving enthusiastically at Ava who waved back with a tad more decorum. An invitation to hang out *and* a smooth request for her number—maybe Kenzie Shepherd really wasn't so straight, after all.

While the restaurant prepared her seaweed salad, dragon roll, and order of salmon nigiri, Ava had the company driver take her home to change. With the downtown buildings flashing past beyond her window, she texted Bea, a silly grin on her face: "I have a friends date with the journalist!"

"Hold on!" came the reply. "U, making friends? How?!"

She filled her best friend in on her evening so far, and Bea agreed that either her sushi timing had been ridiculously fortuitous or, just possibly, Kenzie had been spending more time than usual at her favorite restaurant in hopes of running into Ava.

"I have a good feeling about this," Bea wrote.

Ava's phone buzzed again immediately, and a photo

came through of Bea and her husband, James, grinning cheesy selfie smiles and brandishing earnest thumbs-ups. Bea's, Ava knew, was ironic, while James's probably wasn't. She sent back a laughing emoji just as the car pulled up in front of her building. "Gotta jet," she typed. "I have a social gathering to attend. Give Rowan a kiss from me."

"Let sleeping babies lie! Also, ur sex starved body begs u 2 restrain ur inner nerd tonite."

Whatever. It hadn't been that long. Besides, with her luck, it seemed likely that Kenzie was just a friendly, absurdly clueless straight woman. Either way, it wasn't like Ava would be getting action anytime soon.

"GTG," Ava texted back. "ILY!" She didn't usually resort to text shorthand, but her driver was looking at her expectantly and, more importantly, Kenzie Shepherd was waiting for her.

Now she just had to figure out what to wear.

Ava readjusted her sweater and looked up at the rear entrance of the former Queen Anne High School, waiting for Kenzie to answer her text. She felt overdressed. Not that that was anything new; she seemed to spend much of her time in Seattle feeling overdressed.

"Ava! Hey!"

The voice was coming from above, and Ava looked up, squinting against the lights on the outside of the building. Kenzie was hanging over the edge of the roof, her eager waves looking like they might tip her over the edge at any moment. Was she that drunk already? It had only been 45 minutes since they'd run into each other downtown.

"Hi," Ava called, barely holding back a strangled *be careful* as she waved.

"I'll be right down!"

"Okay," Ava said faintly, but Kenzie was already

disappearing behind the railing.

In what seemed like no time at all, Kenzie was holding the door open for her and gesturing her inside the foyer.

"I'm so glad you made it!" she said as she led Ava to a stairwell. "We'll just stop by my place and grab you something to drink, okay?"

"Okay," Ava repeated, allowing herself to be swept along on the tide of Kenzie's enthusiasm.

The condo ended up being a rather small studio, which was—fine. She was building equity and it was better than having roommates, Kenzie told her, though sometimes she did feel lonely without anyone to talk to. Personally, Ava had never had roommates, nor could she remember ever having been inside a studio before. She looked around curiously as Kenzie led her down a narrow hall into the great room. The high ceilings and tall windows gave the space a sense of airiness she could appreciate, and the sleeping loft above the kitchen made it feel more like a one-bedroom. Instead of a ladder, a black iron spiral staircase stretched up to the loft. Somehow, the whimsical staircase seemed to match Kenzie perfectly.

The decor did, too. The great room was decorated in warm colors, with a gray and dark red wool rug occupying most of the floor and a cream-colored sectional that left plenty of space for a wide square coffee table covered in magazines and books. A quarter of the wall opposite the sectional was taken up by a large bookshelf, and a cursory glance at the loft space revealed at least two more bookshelves, all occupied with more books than knickknacks.

"I'm old-fashioned," Kenzie said, following her gaze. "I prefer the feel and smell of paper to e-books. I guess that makes me a bad Millennial, right?"

"I wouldn't know," Ava said. "I've been told I'm the worst Millennial ever."

"Who told you that?" Kenzie asked as she pulled a glass out from one of the cupboards and placed it on the butcher block island at the edge of the kitchen.

"Beatrice, my best friend." Her head tilted sideways, reminding Ava of a Labrador retriever Bea's family had owned when they were young. "Where does she live?"

"LA."

"Ooh, California. I know as a Washingtonian I'm supposed to hate it, but I sort of like California."

Ava wasn't sure what to say to that. She was well-versed in the biases of the East Coast—New Jersey was unarguably the armpit of New York—but West Coast prejudices eluded her. She only nodded and glanced at the drink selection.

"So, what can I get you?" Kenzie asked. "We've got beer, wine, rum, vodka, whiskey. Oh, and apple juice, too, if you don't drink."

Ava examined the whiskey bottle. Kenzie appeared to be a typical Millennial when it came to alcohol, anyway—quantity over quality. "I'll have a glass of pinot noir," she said. It was hard to ruin pinot noir.

Kenzie looked at the array somewhat helplessly until Ava pointed at a bottle of red wine. "Right! That's Mika's favorite. She's my sister's girlfriend."

"Your sister's *girlfriend?*" Ava repeated, hoping she sounded suitably casual. She was really hoping that Kenzie meant the gay kind of girlfriend, not the soccer mom type.

"Yep. Sloane, my sister, just came out recently. You're cool with that, right?" she asked as she poured way too much wine into the glass, her gaze fixed on the task before her.

"Very," Ava said, wondering if this was the moment to reveal her own Sapphic tendencies.

Before she could decide, the door to the corridor opened suddenly and a short-haired brunette in a leather jacket strode in, her walk brash and confident. "Hey, Kenz, sorry I'm late—" Her voice cut off as her gaze alighted on Ava. "Wait. What is *she* doing here?"

So much for open minds.

As she had learned to do since her brother's arrest, Ava stood straighter and stared down her would-be antagonist even though her conflict-averse inner self longed to make an immediate retreat. At the kitchen island, Kenzie morphed suddenly from friendly pup to growling wolf, her body visibly taut as she faced the newcomer.

"Are you serious, Sloane?" she demanded. "She's here because I invited her."

"You invited her? I thought you said your relationship was professional," the woman who was evidently Kenzie's sister shot back, her wary gaze never leaving Ava.

Relationship? That meant they must have talked about her, and Kenzie had apparently assured her sister they weren't friends. Great. Just perfect. This was why Ava was happier drinking alone and reading herself to sleep. Unlike Kenzie, she adored the comfort and ease of e-books, and had at least a dozen in progress on her Kindle at any given time. In fact, maybe she would be better off at home tonight with one of those than witnessing the Shepherd sisters stand-off.

"Who I choose to be friends with is none of your business," Kenzie said, her voice harsher than Ava would have imagined possible.

"Are you kidding? It's completely my business."

"No, it's not."

And yeah, that was more than enough of that.

"It's okay, Kenzie," Ava said, adjusting her purse over her shoulder. "I'm actually fairly tired. Maybe I should just head home."

Kenzie glanced at her, stricken. "No, Ava, you don't have to go. Just wait here for a sec, okay? Don't go anywhere. Please."

Before Ava could respond, Kenzie was speed-walking her sister down the hall and out into the exterior corridor. Ava could hear their voices, low and furious, but she couldn't make out what they were saying. She sighed, fully able to believe where her night had taken her. Since Nick had gone off the deep end, this was what her life had become. At least there was alcohol. She gulped down the wine Kenzie had poured and touched her tongue to her lips. Not bad for two buck chuck, really.

A moment later, Kenzie returned with her sister at her side. Sloane Shepherd wasn't exactly apologetic, but her hostility at least had lessened. Somewhat. Kenzie elbowed her in the ribs, and Ava saw her wince.

"I'm sorry we got off on the wrong foot," Sloane said, her voice even. "I'm an agent at the bureau, so it was a little jarring seeing you here in my sister's home."

Ava stared, only barely keeping her jaw from dropping. Kenzie's sister worked for Panopticon? No wonder she was so opposed to Kenzie being friends with a Westbrook. So many questions swirled through Ava's mind, but they all vanished as Kenzie stepped forward and clasped her hand. The other woman's palm was warm, almost hot, her grasp loose but firm, and Ava felt a shiver cascade down her spine.

"Please don't go. I promise my other friends aren't as scary as my sister." Sloane huffed behind her, and Kenzie shot her a look. "Oh, come on, you know they're not."

She *was* a bit scary, though Ava would rather have been tortured by her brother's goons than admit as much. "Okay," she relented. "But only because I'm absolutely starving."

"Thank you," Kenzie said, her seriousness giving way

to a relieved smile.

As they left the condo, Kenzie made a show of carrying Ava's takeout bag for her while Ava brought her glass of wine and the rest of the bottle, at Kenzie's insistence. Sloane followed them along the corridor, and Ava felt the Panopticon agent's stare burning holes in her back the entire way to the rooftop patio.

As they stepped outside, however, she forgot to worry about Sloane Shepherd. The skyline of downtown Seattle lay before them, edged by the darkness of Puget Sound at one end and the darkness of the Cascade Mountains at the other. It was an entirely different view of Seattle than she was accustomed to, and just for a moment she felt another pang of homesickness for her apartment in Manhattan and its familiar views of Central Park. Then Kenzie's hand brushed the small of her back, urging her forward, and the longing for any place other than where she was now vanished.

She stepped forward, aware of the curious faces turned toward them from a collection of patio chairs and couches arranged about one of the promised heat lamps. Bea always said you just had to act like you belonged, which was easy enough when you were a beautiful former pop star married to a former NBA star. But Ava could channel some of her best friend's boldness. After all, she'd gone to MIT, and she was a kickass engineer with an apartment on Central Park West, a beach house in Malibu, and a leadership position in one of the most powerful tech firms in the world. These friends of Kenzie's couldn't be anywhere near as vicious as the calculating old white men on Hyperion's board of directors she was forced to confront at least once a month. And if they were, well, she had always enjoyed a challenge.

"Hey, guys, this is Ava," Kenzie said, hand still barely touching her back. "Ava, this is everyone."

"Hi, Ava!" a chorus of voices rang out.

She smiled, feeling her nerves beginning to float away on the tide of friendliness and two buck chuck. Maybe everything would be okay, after all. At least, for tonight.

CHAPTER THREE

This was going well, Kenzie thought, relaxing against the faux rattan couch she and Ava were sharing with Matt, the Seattle skyline sparkling in the distance under cloudy but rain-free skies. It was definitely going better than she could have anticipated earlier when she ran into Ava at Shiro Sushi, where Kenzie had been hanging out a totally normal amount of time all week—assuming that every night after work could be considered normal. Good thing she wasn't human or all that mercury might take a toll.

She still couldn't quite believe she'd invited Ava to come back to her place. She'd meant it when she decided after their first meeting that she shouldn't pursue a friendship with Ava, but then days upon days had passed since the interview, and her resolution to stay cold and unfriendly had ebbed. When she'd seen Ava standing in the entryway to Shiro Sushi, the only thing she could think was FINALLY. That, and she wasn't ready to say goodbye again. The next thing she'd known, she was blurting out that harebrained invitation. Even more startling, Ava had agreed to come.

It was probably best that she hadn't planned that line

in advance, or she definitely would have botched it. Not that it was a *line*. Kenzie wasn't hitting on her, unless of course Ava wanted to be hit on, and even then Kenzie was a bit sketchy on the dating habits of women-loving women. She'd known she found women attractive for a while, but due to her non-human status, she'd previously avoided getting too close to humans of any gender—except Chris Larsen her last two years of college. A Mormon who didn't believe in sex before marriage, Chris had never pressured her to do more than make out occasionally. He had been sweet and funny, and also an optimal cover for an alien in hiding. Dating a fellow alien would have been easier, she presumed, but she didn't know that many. And as far as she knew, there wasn't a Tinder for off-worlders. Although, really, there should be. She could only imagine the categories: Humanoid seeking humanoid, non-psionics only. Or, Bryllian seeking Bryllian, pacifists need not apply…

Anyway, Ava was different. From almost the moment they met, she'd stirred something new in Kenzie, something surprising—and, if she was being honest, a bit disturbing—in its intensity. That intensity had been on display earlier when Sloane showed up and acted like a total jerk toward Ava.

"I'm not joking, Sloane," Kenzie had hissed in the corridor outside her loft, "shape up or ship out."

Her sister had scoffed at the ridiculous idiom for a moment before blinking at Kenzie. "Wait, you're serious?"

"As a heart attack."

"You would choose Nicholas Westbrook's sister over me?" Sloane had asked, her eyes narrowing.

"Her name is Ava, and just because her brother is dangerous doesn't mean she is," Kenzie had said, arms folded stubbornly across her chest. Then she'd relented slightly. "Look, you're making a big deal out of nothing. I ran into her randomly tonight and she seemed like she could use a friend. She's got to be lonely, Sloane. Can't you be nice for one night?"

Sloane had sighed and nudged Kenzie's cheerful welcome mat with the toe of her boot. "I thought you were going to say 'for once in your life.'"

"That too," Kenzie had said, smiling a little.

"But don't you think it's a little coincidental?" Sloane had asked, gazing back at her with troubled eyes. "You outed yourself in that coffee shop last week, and now suddenly Ava Westbrook is in your kitchen? You're the only Zattalian within a hundred light-years, Kenzie."

She hadn't admitted that the same thought had occurred to her. Instead, she'd shrugged and said, "I'm the one who introduced myself to her, not the other way around. Anyway, you're the one who says to keep your friends close and your enemies closer."

"That was Hanna from *Pretty Little Liars*, you dork. So which is Ava, then: friend or enemy?"

Kenzie had rolled her eyes and reached for the door. "Be nice, or I'm telling Mika."

"*Pfft*. Like I care," Sloane had said as she followed her back inside, but Kenzie knew a bluff when she saw one. At least, from her sister. Maybe not so much from other people.

Thankfully, Sloane had reined in her suspicious nature, and while Sloane's girlfriend Mika and their other friends had been visibly surprised to meet Ava, they were also being friendly and welcoming, just as Kenzie had promised. Now that Ava had finished her sushi, Matt had engaged her in a discussion of her years in R&D at Hyperion and her onetime supremacy in a national robotics league. Which, hello, Kenzie was totally going to Google that later.

"Wait, what are you talking about?" Sloane asked now,

honing in on their conversation.

"Ava was captain of a robotics design team in college that won consecutive national championships," Matt explained, his voice higher pitched than usual.

"And you know this because…?" Antonio asked, his smirk alerting everyone gathered to the fact that he was about to make fun of Matt—as usual.

Sometimes Kenzie wondered why they put up with Antonio's jock boy humor, but he'd interned at ECM the same summer Kenzie had, and they'd been friends ever since. In the beginning, she might have had a tiny crush on him, with his confident smile and his pretty curls and the way he made her feel appreciated and *seen*. She'd even revealed her unregistered status to him because she hadn't wanted any secrets between them. But then the college girlfriend he'd conveniently forgotten to mention visited from Portland, and Kenzie's crush had evaporated. Still, he was a good guy, occasional lapses in judgment aside, and Kenzie knew she could trust him. That was more important than any crush.

"I know this because robotics design is awesome," Matt said. "And, you know, I might have competed myself back in the day."

Kenzie watched as Ava immediately steered the conversation toward Matt's robotics design experience at U-Dub, which temporarily drew the spotlight away from her. While Matt described his team's entry the year they made the quarterfinals, Kenzie leaned closer to Ava.

"I noticed you left that particular feat off your official company bio," she said softly, inhaling the combination of caramel vanilla with a hint of warm, woodsy cedar from Ava's perfume, fainter now in the evening than it had been the afternoon Kenzie interviewed her.

Ava pursed her wine-reddened lips and said, voice similarly low, "Somehow I thought it might be unwise to brag about building an indestructible, murderous robot."

She had a point, Kenzie acknowledged—world-dominating Westbrooks and all of that.

"In my defense," Ava added, her breath whispering tantalizingly across Kenzie's cheek, "I had no way of knowing at the time that my brother would develop robotic technology designed to kill actual people."

By people, she meant aliens—another sign she didn't share her family's stance on off-worlders. Ava's tone was self-deprecating, but Kenzie thought she could see genuine pain reflected in her eyes, which even in the relative darkness of the rooftop patio were a shade of green that made Kenzie want to stare. Sloane would notice any extra attention she showed Ava, though, and the last thing Kenzie needed was her sister publicly calling out her nascent interest in the other woman *in front of Ava*.

"Ah," she said lamely, and reached for her own glass of wine. Human alcohol had little effect on her physiology, but it tasted good and, as a bonus, kept her hands occupied.

"So, do you and your friends come up here often?" Ava asked in the same soft, intimate tone meant only for her.

Kenzie pushed up her glasses and nodded. "Most weekends. Although in the winter or if it's raining, we go to The Queen's Ale House instead. It's just a few blocks up Queen Anne Ave."

"The Queen's Ale House? That sounds like something straight out of the West End."

"Of London?" Kenzie asked, and then said, "Of course you meant London. Like, West End Boys, and Piccadilly Circus, and the theater district..." With difficulty, she stopped herself from additional rambling.

"Maybe you can take me there sometime," Ava said, nearly whispering in Kenzie's ear.

"London?" Kenzie all but squeaked. "Oh, you meant the pub, didn't you?"

"I did," Ava said, her eyes amused but more in a fond way than in a sarcastic mean girls way.

Kenzie saw Sloane's gaze narrow in on them and hastily put a respectable amount of space between herself and Ava. "Absolutely," she said, nodding. "Definitely. Anytime."

Ava laughed under her breath, but Kenzie heard her plainly. Danged alien advantages.

She tuned back into the general conversation only to discover that Matt was still extolling Ava's accomplishments, his eyes shining. It was possible Kenzie wasn't the only one with an ill-fated crush on Hyperion's chief operations officer.

"You should have seen their entry the first year they won," her best friend all but gushed. "It totally revolutionized robot combat."

"Robot *combat*?" Sloane's eyebrows descended to a most unfortunate degree.

"He's exaggerating," Ava started to say, but Matt was already off and running about MechaDeath, the robot Ava's team had developed featuring a miter saw, grinding wheel, armored exoskeleton, and high-efficiency internal combustion engine.

Holding her phone to one side, Kenzie (subtly, she hoped) Googled Ava's name and "MechaDeath." Sure enough, there was an article about the Robot Combat League Championships a dozen years earlier, and even a picture of a young Ava and her teammates standing beside their winning design. A paragraph below the photo explained that after the competition, the team had sold the internal combustion engine schematics to a GE subsidiary. That was how Ava had made her first million, completely independently of the Westbrook name.

Her *first* million? Kenzie had somehow managed to forget that the woman seated next to her on her rooftop deck drinking cheap red wine and laughing with her friends belonged to one of the wealthiest families in the world. What was harder to forget was that most of that money came from the coffers of her mother's company, known for its patents on lasers, drones, and surveillance equipment of the variety Sentinel had used to monitor Earth's alien population. Was currently using? According to Sloane, even Panopticon didn't know if the terrorist group was still operating. With its leadership in prison and several high-profile members killed in arrest attempts, Sentinel was at the very least in disarray. But that didn't mean the splinter group had disbanded.

Just then, Ava glanced over at her and shrugged helplessly, a small smile adorning her beautiful lips. Kenzie smiled back. Yes, the night was going well. Now, if she could only keep Sloane's suspicions about Ava's family from bringing her down.

The following morning, Kenzie's phone notified her of a new text from Ava Westbrook: a note of thanks that included a photo of a mug of steaming coffee, the view of Elliott Bay in the distance similar to the view from Hyperion's executive wing.

After she finished squealing silently—*AVA TEXTED ME OH MY GOD*—Kenzie typed back, "You're very welcome. I was happy you joined us. But... are you at work?"

"No," Ava replied. "I don't have an apartment yet, so I'm living for now in a hotel suite in Hyperion Tower."

Several things occurred to Kenzie as she lay in bed, staring at her phone. Number one, Ava, like her, was a full-sentence-with-correct-grammar texter. Definite heart eyes about that. Number two, Ava lived in a no doubt luxurious suite in the same skyscraper where she worked as a high-profile executive. Why, exactly, was she texting Kenzie, a junior reporter who had only recently moved into her own place? She must really be lonely, just as Kenzie had told her sister. That, or she was the erstwhile mastermind of some nefarious long con to capture Kenzie—the only Zattalian in the near universe—and deliver her to Sentinel's newest secret base.

Freaking Sloane and her overblown suspicions. Or were they? After all, Kenzie could still be clueless when it came to humans and their intentions.

"Beautiful view," Kenzie wrote back, opting for impersonal.

"Not bad at all," Ava agreed, similarly neutral.

And then, nothing. Just silence. Was she waiting for Kenzie to respond to her initial overture? That was how human friendships worked, so probably she was—assuming she wanted to be friends. But Kenzie couldn't stop comparing Ava's life to her own and noticing how preposterous that assumption seemed. Was Ava like Jenna Grant from high school who had seemed to like Kenzie when she was new to Bellingham but had soon stopped texting and calling once a group of popular girls adopted her into their clique? Probably. That, or evil. Possibly both.

After a bit, she unglued her eyes from her phone screen and floated down to the kitchen, where she made quick work of half a box of Cheerios while she waited for her own coffee to percolate. Maybe she would go for a jog around Greenlake before her weekly brunch date with her sister and Mika. The abundance of dogs on the popular city trail always cheered her up. Not that she needed cheering up—except that, all at once, she totally did.

Kenzie avoided Cloudtastic for weeks before daring to darken its doorstep again. In that time, the Super Seattleite hashtag on Twitter had died away, and Sloane had stopped chastising her for playing at hero. Now she was more annoyed with Kenzie for befriending Ava Westbrook. Not like she had any real reason to worry—since their brief, awkward text exchange two days earlier, Kenzie hadn't heard from Ava, nor had she reached out herself. The friendship ball was solidly in Kenzie's court, and she couldn't decide whose gut she should trust: her own or Sloane's.

As a non-native resident of Earth, she had long allowed Sloane's opinions—and those of their parents—to inform her decisions. That was why she had never played sports or become a police officer or firefighter or otherwise done anything that might risk revealing her identity. She knew they had her best interests in mind, and so she let them, the people who had taken her in after she lost everything, guide her. For a long time, that had worked. But now she was out in the world on her own, and everything seemed different. If Sloane and their parents had their way, she would simply walk past a burning building and ignore the people and animals suffering and even dying inside. But that wasn't right, was it? Saving her own skin—and her family's, too, since Sentinel targeted both aliens *and* the humans who helped them—couldn't be more important than rescuing people who couldn't save themselves, could it?

If she had listened to Sloane, she wouldn't have gone back to Cloudtastic at all, ever. But on Monday morning, with her tragically short text thread with Ava hanging over her, Kenzie was feeling jittery and jazzed, more than ready to take on the world—or at least, her bossy older sister. Instead of visiting the Starbucks near her building as Sloane had counseled, she braved the line at Cloudtastic. She didn't, however, wear her rain coat this time. Instead, she wore a fleece vest, donned her glasses (which she hadn't been wearing the day of the hold-up, thanks to the rain), and wove her hair into a complex bun comprised of double French braids, hoping that these measures would help disguise her #SuperSeattleite alter ego.

She was halfway to the counter when she made eye contact with Courtney. The other woman's eyes widened, and she appeared to bite back a smile before turning back to her current customer. *Crap.* She knew, didn't she? Kenzie vacillated, wondering if she should cut her losses and leave. But then, what if Courtney took that as some sort of rejection and promptly revealed her identity to the world? *Aargh.* Sloane had once again been right about Earth matters. Kenzie should have listened.

In the end, she couldn't decide on the right course of action, so she did the easiest thing—she kept moving forward in line until soon she was standing in front of Courtney, smiling tentatively and hoping everything would turn out for the best.

"Miss Shepherd, it's nice to see you," Courtney said, nodding.

"You, too. How have you been?"

"Oh, you know. A little bit of drama but fortunately, I had a guardian angel looking out for me." She gazed significantly at Kenzie.

"Right!" Kenzie pushed up her glasses even though they weren't remotely slipping. "I heard about that. I'm glad you weren't hurt."

"So was my mother," Courtney said. "Your usual?"

"Um, yeah," Kenzie said, the barista's words warming her. Courtney had a mother who Kenzie had made happy. *Wow.* She was seriously going to tear up. On impulse she added, "Oh, and can I get another drink?"

Courtney gazed at her in surprise. "Of course. What will it be?"

Kenzie fumbled her phone until she found the picture

she wanted. "Sorry, is that enough to go on?"

Courtney squinted at the screen. Then she nodded decisively. "Café au lait. Italian roast, I'm guessing. Coming right up."

"Great, thank you." She waited for Courtney to ring her up, but the barista looked past her as if ready for the next customer. "Don't I have to pay...?"

"Not today," Courtney said, and smiled, her brown eyes warm. "It's on the house, Kenzie. Next," she added in a louder voice, her gaze sliding to the customer behind Kenzie. "What can I get you, sir?"

Kenzie moved away, mumbling her thanks. Probably best not to call attention to her free order. If #SuperSeattleite trended again with a clear picture of her face, there would be no saving her from Sloane's wrath.

A few minutes later, she caught a bus south toward the central business district, wondering at her sanity as she did so. There were so many reasons this was a potentially dumb move to make, but she was terrible in text and didn't want to start the work week off on the wrong foot.

The receptionist in the downstairs lobby gave her a polite nod. "Miss Shepherd, isn't it? Here for a follow-up?"

She nodded, smiling. "Yes, thanks." Kenzie was used to being recognized by strangers—ECM included head shots with their reporters' bylines because they supposedly appeared more approachable that way. It definitely meant she was approached more, and not always by happy readers.

When the receptionist lifted his phone and punched in an extension, Kenzie listened in more closely than usual. She didn't typically use her powers to invade other people's privacy—she had a system of checks and balances she followed fairly strictly—but her nerves got the better of her this time.

"I have Miss Shepherd here for a follow-up."

"Miss Shepherd?" The voice at the other end sounded confused. "I don't have her on the schedule. Please hold for a moment." There was quite a long pause during which the receptionist continued to smile blandly at Kenzie, and then the voice came back. "It's fine. Send her up."

Whew. So maybe not a terrible idea after all. Of course, there was still plenty of opportunity for Kenzie to say or do the wrong thing. She was fairly accomplished at that.

Just like last time she'd visited, a plainclothes security officer escorted her to an elevator set off from the others and used a special pass to access the 44th floor. Visitor pass dangling from the hem of her vest, she watched the digital numbers change as the elevator rose quickly and quietly. She wasn't a fan of small spaces and could have run up the stairs faster, but not without giving herself away. Grainy videos could only save her so many times.

It occurred to her that she was voluntarily triggering her own claustrophobia, and yeah, she would definitely not be telling Sloane about this.

The elevator dinged, and Kenzie took a deep breath. She could do this. She would have to do this—her name had already been announced.

"Kenzie?"

The voice startled her, and she quickly stepped out of the elevator to find Ava waiting in the alcove outside her office, her assistant avidly watching the exchange.

"Hi!" Kenzie said brightly, then lowered her voice to a normal-ish tone. "I mean, how are you?"

"I'm good," Ava said, her smile bemused. "But this is a surprise. What are you doing here?"

She pushed up her glasses and invented an excuse: "My editor wanted a follow-up, so I thought I would bring you coffee as a bribe for a few minutes of your time." While she might not often use her powers to eavesdrop, she lied more than was entirely healthy, she was pretty sure.

Ava's smile dimmed a bit. "Coffee is always an acceptable bribe. I think I can spare you five minutes." She glanced at her assistant, who nodded. "All right, then. Come on in."

Kenzie followed her into the wide, sunlit office. It was lighter than she remembered from last time she was here. She squinted at the wall of windows. Did Ava's windows have an automatic tinting function? Then again, why wouldn't they? This was Hyperion, one of the most advanced tech companies in the world.

"So, do I get to drink the coffee, or are you just here for the view?" Ava asked as she rounded her desk and perched on the edge of her chair, her voice as husky and compelling as Kenzie remembered.

"Oh, right!" She stepped forward and set the to-go cup on the pristine white desk. "Sorry, I wasn't sure what your order was, so I had the barista choose."

Ava picked up the cup and removed the lid, breathing in the scent. "Italian roast?" she asked. When Kenzie nodded, Ava took a sip. "It's good. Better than that corporate swill around the corner. Where's it from?"

That was the moment Kenzie realized her error. If she said Cloudtastic and Ava had heard about the #SuperSeattleite intervention... Before she could decide how to answer, Ava checked the logo on the side of the cup: "CC" printed in a sans-serif font across a fluffy white cloud, blue sky in the background and an outline of the Space Needle in the foreground.

"Wait," Ava said, "I've seen this logo before. Isn't it from the shop where all that business—"

The phone on the desk buzzed loudly, and Kenzie almost leapt through the ceiling. What had she been thinking, drawing Ava Westbrook's attention to a possible connection between herself and #SuperSeattleite? Ava was a literal genius, with multiple degrees in technology from

MIT and an MBA from Harvard. If anyone could follow a trail of diminishing clues, it was her.

"Yes?" Ava said into the intercom, her tone clipped.

"You wanted me to remind you about Victoria's meeting request," the assistant said, sounding far too officious for Kenzie's liking.

"Thank you." Ava glanced up at Kenzie, her expression apologetic. "While this is a lovely surprise, I'm afraid I don't have much time. What kind of follow-up was your editor looking for?"

"Um." Kenzie stared into Ava's green eyes, much more noticeable today with her fair skin glowing in the morning light and her dark hair pulled back in a low, tight chignon. On Friday night, Kenzie had almost swooned when Ava appeared at her building with her hair spilling in waves over her shoulders, dressed in a fuzzy black sweater and dark skinny jeans instead of her usual business garb. Her lipstick was more evident this morning, too, sharply defining the edges of her full lips in a way that made Kenzie long to smudge it with her thumb.

"Yes?" Ava pressed, the ghost of a smile on those lovely lips.

"I'm supposed to ask about your perfume," Kenzie improvised.

"My perfume." Ava sounded as if she were one hundred percent certain Kenzie was full of crap.

"It's for ECM's fashion blog," she said quickly. "A bunch of our readers wrote in asking about your style. You know, like your clothes and make-up?"

Ava's head tilted. "I thought you wrote for the tech division."

Kenzie was pretty sure the subject of her beat assignment hadn't come up during the interview or over drinks. Ava could only know Kenzie covered the tech industry if she'd been stalking Kenzie back. Reverse stalking? Whatever.

Quickly, Ava added, "Of course, I'm happy to give your readers a glimpse into my fashion routine. I'm only afraid they might be a bit underwhelmed."

"I doubt that." Kenzie pulled her notebook and pen from her messenger bag as she sat down in the chair across from Ava. The wildly uncomfortable chair, she soon remembered, arching her spine away from the rigid plastic back. She had forgotten about this particular instrument of torture.

Ava laughed at her semi-outraged expression. "Sorry, the furniture in here is a holdover from my mother's time. Now, what questions did your readers have?"

"Let me check." Kenzie bent her head over her phone as if she had a list of questions stored in the cloud. In fact, she was Googling "celebrity fashion style" and jotting down snippets of the search results. Thank god, as usual, for Google.

It only took a few minutes of chatting to cover cosmetics, suits, perfume—Kenzie was unreasonably thrilled to learn Ava's favorite was a unisex scent—footwear, and work-out gear. Which left casual wear, according to Kenzie's hastily fabricated notes.

"That sweater you wore on Friday was so soft," she commented, finishing a note on Ava's preferred sneakers to work out in.

"It's cashmere," Ava said, and fiddled with the cuff of her plum-colored suit jacket. "Speaking of Friday, I was wondering if I offended you in some way."

Kenzie looked up quickly. "What? No. Why?"

Ava moved her computer mouse in a circle, eyes on her monitor. "No reason. It's just, you didn't seem very—chatty, I suppose, when I texted you the next day. I wondered if it was because of something I'd done."

"Of course not," Kenzie said forcefully. "If anything, I

was worried my sister might have offended you."

Ava waved a hand. "She was fine. I've seen so much worse since my brother… Well, you know."

"You have?" Kenzie frowned. "But that's not fair."

"Oh." Ava looked at her across the desk. "Well, no, maybe not. But fairness has little to do with anything, in my experience."

It was a generous way of calling out her characteristic naivete, Kenzie knew, and she ducked her head, pretending to write another note so she wouldn't have to meet Ava's gaze.

"No lingering terror of MechaDeath, then?" Ava asked.

Kenzie couldn't resist a small smile at that. "Nope."

"Good. I'm glad to hear it."

Kenzie looked up again, her smile widening as she saw Ava's. She could do this, couldn't she? She could be friends with Ava Westbrook, no matter what Sloane—and their parents, probably—thought.

A knock sounded at the door, and Ava's smile slipped. She sighed under her breath and called out, "Yes, Chloe?"

The assistant poked her head through. "It's time."

"I'll be out in a moment." She waited until the doors closed to glance at Kenzie, one elegant eyebrow lifted in resignation. "Work calls. Do you have enough for your story?"

Kenzie was tempted to say she would need another meeting to wrap up, but her journalist's ethics were already on thin enough ice as it was. Reluctantly, she nodded. "Yes. Oh—except, can I take a quick photo?"

"But you don't have your camera."

"I have an iPhone," Kenzie said, holding it up, "and if it doesn't turn out, we have unused shots from last week. Would that be okay?"

Ava paused for a moment, running her hand over her hair. "Yes, it's fine. If you think so."

Kenzie, who was fairly sure it would be impossible to take a bad shot of Ava, had her pose in a few different spots in the office, the morning light soft and inviting. Ava's smile was nervous at first, but by the time they finished, it had taken on the same relaxed, intimate quality as the previous time. As she gathered her things, Kenzie tried not to dwell overly much on why that might be.

Unlike the first interview, Ava walked her to the elevator and used a keycard to activate the down button. Then she stepped back, arms folded across the slight curve of her belly. "So. Thanks again for the coffee."

"Was it the right order?" Kenzie asked, clamping down on the urge to come up with a reason to see her again. The friendship ball was back in Ava's court now, assuming Kenzie understood the sports metaphor correctly.

"It was. Your barista is good." She squinted at Kenzie and seemed about to say something else when the elevator dinged. "Anyway."

"Anyway," Kenzie echoed. The doors opened and she stepped on, bracing herself for the small space.

"See you around?" Ava asked, her shoulders slightly hunched.

"I hope so," Kenzie said, and then the doors slid closed and she fell back against the rear wall, breathing in through her nose and out through her mouth like she'd learned to do soon after coming to live on Earth.

Who was she kidding? She could never be friends with Ava Westbrook, and not because she worried the other woman might be a terrorist. She couldn't be friends with Ava Westbrook because she wanted to kiss her more than she'd ever wanted to kiss anyone in her life. But while Ava might consider herself pro-alien in theory, did she really want to kiss one?

As Kenzie left Ava's building and headed back to Belltown, she had a feeling she'd rather not know the answer to that question.

It was her own fault for thinking about burning buildings, Kenzie thought a couple of nights later as she tightened her raincoat hood and prepared to vault to the third floor of an apartment complex where her augmented vision told her that a woman, child, and cat were hiding from the smoke and flames roaring through the increasingly unstable structure. A floor above was an older person, judging from their frail structure. She would have to come back for them, she decided even as time slowed and she fit herself between glowing sparks and crumbling timbers. Her skin was invulnerable—mostly—but she could smell her raincoat melting in the intense heat and willed her body to move even faster.

In seconds, she'd lifted the mattress off the mother and child, secured them in her arms, and leapt back to the ground, depositing them in front of an aid vehicle. The cat was between her and the older person, so she blurred to it first and the white-haired woman second. Back on the ground, she found a second aid team and deposited the woman with them. The cat seemed fine, so she handed it to a stunned police officer and turned away, her raincoat hood barely holding together. Then she sprinted off into the darkness. Once she was a safe distance away, she found a dark alley and lifted off into the sky, where she hovered in the branches of a tree. She paused there and checked the scene one more time to make sure she hadn't left anyone behind. There was no sign of motion, so that was good. The interior of every living body was chaotic; if anyone had been left alive, she would be able to sense a beating heart, the air whistling through constricted airways, the blood flowing through intact veins at speeds almost faster than she could move.

Breathing out a sigh of relief, she flew the rest of the way home, careful not to risk colliding with any aircraft. Low-hanging clouds simultaneously reflected the city's light and obscured her movements, providing her a welcome cover. Otherwise she would have had to walk home, melted raincoat or not.

She touched down in the school playground across the street from her building, choosing a corner where vegetation grew up the chain link fence and obscured the area from view. In another minute, she was entering her building and running up the stairs, making sure each stairwell and corridor was empty before traversing them. The last thing she needed was a neighbor spotting her entering her studio with ashes and soot in her hair.

At home at last, she took a shower, scrubbing the fire's remnants from her body. Black and white puddles dripped from her hair and skin, and she stood under the warm water for a long time, trying to forget the terrified look on the mother and child's faces, the way the elderly woman had flinched away from her, the feel of the cat's claws as it tried to wrest itself from her grasp. They had all seemed more afraid of her than of the fire. That wasn't how it was supposed to be, was it? In the movies, in Matt's comic books, in the stories of heroes with superpowers, the people who were rescued all seemed so grateful to their rescuers. Kenzie would never hurt a person or animal, and yet they had all stared at her with horror, eyes voicing the unspoken question, *"What are you?"*

But they were alive, she reminded herself as she toweled off. They were alive and that was what mattered, however ambivalent they felt about their rescuer.

She was pulling on comfy PJs with little green aliens—a joke gift from Matt two Christmases earlier—when her front door opened.

"Kenzie?" a familiar voice called out.

She peered over the edge of the loft. "I'm here, Sloane."

"Are you okay?" Her sister stopped in the middle of the great room, staring up at her anxiously. "I saw the news. It was you, wasn't it?"

She could have lied, but Sloane usually saw right through her. After all, she was the one who had taught Kenzie to lie.

"Yes," she admitted, coming down the spiral staircase more slowly than usual. "But it wasn't my fault. I mean, it was in a way because I was the one who made the decision to go in there, but—"

She stopped talking as her sister threw her arms around her. "Shut up, you idiot," Sloane said. "You did good, okay?"

"I—did?"

"Yes. You saved a woman and her daughter! You're a goddamn hero."

Kenzie released a long breath and buried her face in her sister's shoulder. "I don't think I could take it right now if you were mad at me," she admitted.

Sloane pulled away and checked Kenzie's face, frowning. "Hey, I'm sorry. I didn't mean to be harsh before. You know I just worry about you."

Kenzie shook her head and swiped at the tears leaking from her eyes. "It's not you. It's just—they looked at me like I was a monster. Like I was worse than the *fire*."

"Kenzie," Sloane said, and her voice broke slightly. "I'm sure they were just scared."

The thing about teaching someone the basic tenets of lying was that then they could tell when you were lying, too. Kenzie gazed at her sister, wanting to believe her. But she couldn't, not entirely. Still, she swallowed down her tears and forced a smile. "Ice cream?"

"Ice cream," Sloane agreed. "Let me just text Mika and let her know I'm staying at your place tonight."

"You don't have to—" Kenzie started.

But Sloane cut her off. "I want to, little sis. Okay?" she asked, her voice still doing that trembly thing that always broke Kenzie's heart.

"Okay," she said, and turned away to retrieve one of the many pints of ice cream from the freezer.

Honestly, she was glad to have Sloane beside her that night, her familiar snoring steady and comforting as Kenzie stared up at the loft's low ceiling and waited for dawn.

#

Ava scrolled through her Twitter feed, reading local trends idly as she waited for her lunch order at the company café. #SuperSeattleite was trending again today, thanks to an amazing photo that had captured the would-be hero emerging from the flames carrying a mother and child she'd rescued from an apartment fire the night before. Her face was mostly obscured, but astute social media users had deduced she shared the same build as the coffee shop hero and—particularly damning—was wearing the same raincoat.

There was something familiar about her, Ava thought, squinting at her screen. Could she be a Hyperion employee? Company policy required all non-humans to be registered with the proper authorities—a policy Ava didn't personally favor—and as far as she knew, there were no aliens at the local office who fit the profile of this individual: able to move faster than the human eye could track; invulnerable to smoke and fire; and able to leap buildings and/or fly. Actually, there weren't many aliens who could do all those things. Most had no special abilities, and those who did usually had one or two at most. This

Super Seattleite person represented the type of alien her brother had feared most: one who couldn't be contained by police or other authorities; one who would, as her brother had said at his trial, be king.

King. As if gender had anything to do with it. Not all species were sexually dimorphous, as her brother knew better than most. The military had apparently made him more sexist than she remembered from childhood. But then, he had been so much older, already a teenager when she'd been adopted. She wasn't convinced she'd ever really known him at all.

She glanced out the window at the view of the nearby Columbia Tower, where she was a member of the exclusive club on the 75th floor—another unwanted family gift. What was the name of the alien her brother had obsessed over, the one who looked human but possessed untold powers? Oh, right: natives of the ruined planet Zattalia, located 35 light-years from Earth. Rumor had it they could fly faster than the speed of sound, were invulnerable, and had nearly limitless powers of strength, sight, and hearing. Rumor also had it there weren't many in the Milky Way, since Earth's home galaxy was considered a bit of a backwater by the rest of the universe.

But reality hadn't stopped Nick from being terrified that one or more would arrive and attempt to take over the planet. Zattalians were known for their long history of enslaving less technically gifted populations, and even though Earth as a non-space voyaging planet fell under the general protection of the Alliance—a peaceful coalition of spacefaring civilizations that had existed for a full Earth millennium—Nick had watched *Star Wars* enough times to be convinced that it wouldn't take much for the balance of good in the universe to shift; for the Alliance to become, basically, the Sith Empire.

He wasn't alone in his fears, either. Ironically, his

actions and those of his followers had placed Earth at risk. Part of being eligible for protection under the Alliance's charter—and for eventual full-scale acceptance as a member planet, though Earth was nowhere near that stage yet—was to welcome alien refugees that the Alliance placed on Earth. By attacking those refugees, Sentinel had jeopardized Earth's position in the Alliance, potentially leaving the planet vulnerable to attacks from the very alien invaders Nick feared most.

But people suffering from borderline personality disorder were difficult to reason with since they didn't know that their delusions weren't real. Moreover, fear was a powerful motivator, and Nick was a smart, charismatic guy who knew how to lead. With him at the helm, Sentinel had set up a secret base and begun kidnapping aliens to experiment on. Nick claimed his intention had been to find the weakness of every alien refugee species so that humans could never be vulnerable to attack, but somewhere along the way, he began to focus on developing the technology to transfer alien powers to humans. Creating super soldiers would protect the planet, he'd argued, even though all that would really do, in Ava's opinion, was create an army of potential human despots instead of alien ones.

Men. Honestly, if they could only stop seeing the world—and the universe, for that matter—as a hierarchical system, maybe Earth wouldn't be where it currently was.

"Miss Westbrook," the cafeteria aide called, smiling nervously at her.

"Thanks, Grace," she said, smiling back as she took the to-go order. She added cutlery and napkins to her lunch bag and then checked her phone. Her car was waiting.

The drive uptown took only a few minutes. Seattle traffic was nothing compared to Manhattan, partly because Seattle was so much smaller but also because Seattle was

West Coast laid-back. Ava had to admit that the relaxed nature of the city was appealing, as was not being recognized and spit on everywhere she went. Maybe her mother had been right to move to the West Coast office after her father died. Ava hadn't thought so at the time, but now Seattle felt almost like a fresh start. Assuming the press would allow her to have one.

The building her driver stopped in front of reminded her of the East Village, with its neat brick exterior and the ornate stonework at the edge of the roof. Ava took a deep breath and slipped out of the car.

"If I'm not back in five minutes, I'll see you in an hour," she told Ramón, the driver.

"Yes, Miss Westbrook," he said, nodding at her.

Ava had asked him weeks ago to call her by her first name, but he'd informed her that he was old-fashioned, and she'd let it go. Now she simply nodded back, stepped across the sidewalk, and looked at the building's communications console. It didn't take long to find the correct buzzer.

Almost immediately a disembodied voice sounded: "May I help you?"

She smiled into the security camera and said, "I'm Ava Westbrook. I'm here to—"

The sound of the door unlocking cut her off. On rare occasions, it could be good to be a Westbrook.

The lobby was quintessential Seattle—exposed brick, polished hardwood floors with inlaid stone tiles, framed photographs of snowy mountains and fields of wildflowers, and giant rustic timbers that looked like they had been cut almost whole from formerly towering redwoods. Ava took the elevator to the fifth floor and emerged to find a reception desk located outside what looked like a pair of locked doors, with two receptionists seated a few feet apart. They certainly took their security seriously here—but then, they probably had to. Her brother's followers and their ilk had targeted media outlets, claiming that the mainstream press was covering up acts of alien violence.

"Miss Westbrook," one of the twenty-something receptionists said, nodding at her. "Do you have an appointment?"

"No, actually, I have lunch," she said, holding up the bag from Hyperion's cafeteria. As she did so, it occurred to her that this was perhaps not the least conspicuous approach she could have taken.

"I see," the young woman said, frowning slightly. The man beside her, who looked all of twelve years old, snuck a glance at Ava. "And who are you here for?"

"Kenzie Shepherd," she said confidently. She had learned at a young age that if you acted like your request was reasonable, others would believe it was, too.

The receptionist typed in an extension on her phone, and Ava could hear it ring and ring until the automated sound of voicemail picked up. When Ava had texted Kenzie that morning, as had become their daily habit over the past week, she had mentioned she would be at ECM all day working on a story. Had she been called away? Or, worse, had she lied?

"She's not answering," the woman said. "Would you like me to try someone else?"

At that moment, one of the doors to the main office opened. Matt Greene, Kenzie's friend, poked his head out. "Ava? What are you doing here?"

"Looking for Kenzie," she said, waving the bag again. "I come bearing french fries and turkey sandwiches."

"Ooh, for me?" he asked, grinning as he stepped out into the reception area.

"Not unless she likes to share."

He coughed. "No, she definitely does not. Follow me.

She's up on the roof."

What was it about this woman and her affinity for high places? Ava preferred her heights to be bounded by steel and glass, personally, but for Kenzie, she was willing to brave a six-story drop.

"Is this how you repay all the reporters who interview you?" Matt asked, smiling over his shoulder as he led her to a stairwell.

"Not generally," she said, following him up the stairs. "But I work so much that it isn't all that easy to meet new people, so…" She trailed off, hoping she didn't sound too forward. But Kenzie was the one who had brought her coffee, and before that, she'd invited Ava over for drinks. Ava didn't think she was reading the signals incorrectly.

"I know what you mean," Matt said as he turned at the top of a landing and headed up a much narrower set of stairs. "I read once that sixty percent of Millennials surveyed said that work friendships are important to their happiness."

"Did you and Kenzie meet here at ECM?" she asked, her voice studiously casual.

"No, we went to school together. She interned here our senior year and then hooked me up with a job after we graduated."

Did their relationship involve a different type of hooking up, too? But their personal history was none of her business, Ava reminded herself.

Just as Matt reached the door at the top of the steps, it burst open, sunlight streaking into the dim stairwell. Startled, Ava blinked. When her vision cleared, there was Kenzie, smiling, her hair a halo of blonde in the sunshine.

"Well, hi, guys," she said, not sounding the least bit surprised to see Ava at her place of work.

Had Matt texted her in advance? But no, Ava would have noticed.

"Hey," Matt said, "look who dropped by to see you?" His tone sounded teasing but, at the same time, it contained a note of warning.

Ava could have sworn he'd liked her the other night, but she supposed it was understandable if he'd changed his mind. Being friends with a Westbrook was a bit like hanging a target on your back.

"I know," Kenzie said, and then as Matt's stare intensified, she added, "I mean, I thought I heard your voices just now."

Ava glanced between Kenzie and her friend, wondering what she was missing.

"What a wonderful surprise, Ava!" Kenzie said, still smiling brightly. "Do you have business at ECM?"

"No," Ava said, "unless you consider lunch business." She held up the bag, trying to assume the confidence of a superhero pose minus the actual pose.

"Lunch?" Kenzie repeated.

Ava pressed forward with assumed blitheness, even though her little surprise seemed like it might be on the verge of crashing and burning. "You mentioned you were stuck at work, so I thought I would bring lunch to you. You know, to repay you for coffee the other day."

"Coffee the other day?" Matt echoed, smirking at Kenzie in a way that told Ava this was the first he was hearing of Kenzie's most recent visit to Hyperion.

"Bye, Matt," Kenzie said pointedly, and pushed him toward the stairs.

He lurched back as if he weighed nothing, eyes shooting semi-amused daggers at Kenzie, and Ava knew she was definitely missing something.

"It's really great to see you. What did you bring me?" Kenzie asked as she led Ava toward a table with a wide umbrella in one corner of the rooftop patio. In the opposite corner, a group of people in business casual outfits were enjoying their lunches and the May sunshine—and very clearly watching Ava and Kenzie. "I mean, us. What did you bring us?"

"Kale salad," she started, and then, as Kenzie's face screwed up into unadulterated horror, she hurried to add, "french fries, and turkey sandwiches."

"Oh," Kenzie said, her face clearing. "Well, those sound good, anyway."

"You're not a fan of kale?" Ava enquired, filing away the result of that particular lesbian litmus test. It wasn't that *all* queer women loved kale and kombucha, necessarily, but enough women-loving women did for Ava to consider those particular stereotypes statistically significant.

"Kale, lettuce, spinach, vegetables, take your pick," Kenzie said, waving her arms a bit maniacally.

And, wow. She really didn't like vegetables.

Kenzie pulled out an empty chair for Ava with a flourish, thereby confusing her gaydar once again, and they settled in to eat lunch looking out over the bay and the skyscrapers of Seattle's central business district gleaming in the distance.

"Dang, these fries are really good," Kenzie commented after her first taste of the crinkle cut potatoes she'd slathered in ketchup.

Salad bad, french fries and sushi good, Ava noted, readjusting her perception of her lunch companion. Somehow, those two tastes didn't seem to track. Sushi, after all, contained seaweed, which was a sea vegetable. Maybe Kenzie made an allowance because it came from the ocean…?

Ava caught herself. She was subjecting Kenzie to romantic partner levels of analysis when there was no concrete indication she was anything other than straight.

She did have a lesbian sister, and the gay gene did run in families. Plus there was her sculpted physique. Ava's eyes lingered on Kenzie's hands, noting her long, elegant fingers topped with short, unpainted nails. Another checkmark on the list of common lesbian attributes.

"So. What do you like to do when you're not working or hanging out on rooftops?" she asked.

"I like to do all the normal things," Kenzie said, her eyes on her sandwich.

What an odd response. "Okay, but specifically, what kinds of things?"

"Drawing, eating ice cream, reading, bingeing *Game of Thrones* with my sister." She looked up and pointed suddenly. "There's your building. See?"

"I do," Ava said, and gave her a raised eyebrow. Kenzie would rather talk about Hyperion than about hobbies outside of work? Perhaps it had been wishful thinking on Ava's part to believe Kenzie might have any real interest in being friends, after all.

"You're easy to find because your building's right next to the Columbia Tower. But what about you?" she added, the second half of her turkey sandwich in hand. She ate with a neat efficiency that Ava couldn't help admiring. "What do you do outside of work?"

"Work some more." Ava laughed at the look of consternation Kenzie sent her. "What? I like work. I used to like it even more back when I had my own lab."

"Your own lab," Kenzie said, sounding more envious than Ava would have expected. "What kinds of things did you build? Other than murderous robots, of course."

And there, a lip bite and flirtatious comment—those were the kinds of confusing signs Ava couldn't stop noticing. Was Kenzie straight or wasn't she? Would Ava ever get the courage to ask her or wouldn't she?

Alas, she did not magically obtain the necessary

courage over lunch. Instead, she chatted with Kenzie about aerodynamics and fluid mechanics, composite structures and cellular solids. Kenzie was noticeably knowledgeable about mechanical engineering because, she informed Ava, she'd minored in the field at U-Dub. Oh, and her father Dr. Benjamin Shepherd was a materials science professor at Western Washington University while her mother was Dr. Jane Henderson, the biochemist. Had Ava heard of her?

Ava pretended to be surprised by this revelation even though she already knew who Kenzie's famous mother was, just as she had already known Matt and Kenzie had gone to school together. But pretending not to be a casual stalker was still important at this stage of getting to know Kenzie. Depending on where things went, it might remain that way.

"Those are some impressive science genetics," Ava commented, trying one of the fries before they could vanish entirely. Salty and filling—definitely not her favorite. She helped herself to more kale.

"Um." Kenzie shuffled in place. "It's not genetic. At least, not in the way you mean. Sloane and I aren't related biologically."

Ava looked up at her. "You're not?"

"No." Kenzie pushed up her glasses. "Jane and Benjamin adopted me when I was twelve. My parents were killed in a—in a fire."

"I'm so sorry," Ava said, touching her arm. "Twelve is old to have to reinvent your world."

Kenzie looked down at Ava's hand on her forearm, pale against Kenzie's slightly bronzed skin. "Yeah, it really was. But at least I remember my family. Some ref—people aren't as lucky."

Ava pulled her hand back, her spine straightening against the cheap metal patio chair that probably came from Lowe's or that other home store whose name she could never quite remember. It almost sounded like Kenzie knew about her mother. But how? Ava's parents had gone to great lengths to conceal her adoption. The answer leapt out at her: Sloane. Of course Ava's parentage would be available to an agent of Panopticon; her father might have created the file himself. He had been a stickler for details and order. As a career military officer in charge of the largest alien monitoring unit in the world, he'd had to be.

"Are you okay?" Kenzie asked.

"Yes. No. Or, I suppose I was thinking about what you said."

"Oh?" Kenzie's expression was open and curious as ever, her hands relaxed on the table. There was no telltale sign of anxiety, no evasive gaze, no tension of any kind to indicate she might be hiding something.

Maybe, Ava thought, she had been wrong. Perhaps Sloane, who had looked at Ava on Friday night as if she represented a credible threat to Kenzie's safety, had not in fact used her security clearance to look into Ava's past. Even if she had, could Ava really blame her for looking out for her younger sister? Ava's security team had fielded multiple threats against her life since her brother's descent into madness. And look what had happened to their father. Realistically, Ava probably *was* a credible threat to anyone she spent much time with.

"I was thinking you're right," she admitted. "You are lucky to remember your past. I don't have much to hold onto myself in that respect."

Kenzie's eyes widened. "Wait—are you saying you're adopted, too?"

Ava nodded, even more reassured by her response. Kenzie couldn't be that good of an actor, could she? "My mother died when I was four. She was a long-time employee at Hyperion, actually, which is how I came to live with the Westbrooks."

"Four?" Kenzie shook her head and touched Ava's hand briefly. "That's so young. Do you remember her at all?"

Ava noticed she didn't ask about her father, and was grateful for the grace Kenzie offered. "A little. She looked like me quite a bit, so that's nice, in a way."

"I know what you mean. I look like my mother, too."

They were quiet for a moment, sounds filtering in from the other table and from the street far below, but it was a comfortable silence, and Ava was suddenly, tremendously glad she'd decided to drop in on Kenzie.

After a little while, Ava spoke again. "So we were both adopted into families with scientists. How did your parents balance their career demands with the responsibilities of parenting?"

Kenzie's head tilted to one side. "What do you mean?"

"Well, generally scientists have so many professional responsibilities that it can be hard to carve out family time. My mother, for example, solved that issue by sending me to boarding school when I was thirteen."

Kenzie looked sympathetic. "I remember reading that somewhere. It must have been hard to leave everyone and everything you knew."

"It was." Westbrooks didn't feel sorry for themselves, though, so she hastened to add, "But I wanted to go. It was an amazing educational opportunity, and my best friend was going, so it was a win-win. Anyway, that's how my parents dealt with competing demands. What about yours?"

Kenzie glanced out over nearby buildings toward the water that was never far away in downtown Seattle. "Sloane and I were lucky because Western is more of a teaching university than a research one, so our parents never really had to choose between us and their careers.

Sloane says the pressure to publish and win grants at U-Dub was insane when she was in grad school. But Western is small, only twelve thousand or so, and it doesn't have doctoral programs."

Somehow, Ava wasn't surprised that Kenzie and Sloane's parents had managed to find balance in their work and home lives. "What's Bellingham like? I've heard good things."

Kenzie visibly brightened, nearly forgetting about food—but not quite—as she described her hometown, a small city of 70,000 only 20 miles from the Canadian border, tucked between Puget Sound and the North Cascade Mountains. The populace was into all of the Northwest things, and so were the Shepherd-Hendersons: hiking among moss-draped evergreens, kayaking crystalline mountain lakes, participating in local multi-sport events, and playing in the snow in the easily accessible mountains.

"It sounds like an idyllic place to grow up," Ava commented.

Kenzie swallowed her last bite of sandwich and grinned at her. "You don't really think that, do you?"

"Excuse me?" Ava asked, arching an eyebrow.

"I mean, no offense, but you don't exactly look like the hiking type."

"Offense taken," Ava said, laughing. "I'll have you know that New England has quite a few mountains. Some of them are even close to three thousand feet high."

"Three thousand," Kenzie scoffed. "I hate to tell you, my friend, but those are hills."

Ava felt her smile soften at Kenzie's choice of words: *my friend*. She could only be so lucky.

Her phone chose that moment to vibrate—*ugh*, a meeting reminder. She glanced up from the screen to find Kenzie watching her, blue eyes dark in the umbrella's shadow.

"You have to go, huh?" Kenzie almost sounded like she shared Ava's regret that their lunch was coming to an end—or maybe that was just more wishful thinking.

"I do," Ava agreed. Ramón would be downstairs momentarily, but she took her time organizing the leftovers, unwilling to lose the companionship of their lunch date just yet. Kenzie was easy to talk to, and nice to look at, and she smelled good… *And* she was probably straight, given the odds on such matters. More importantly, Kenzie was a member of the Seattle press. Boundaries were good; definitely time to remember those.

"Anyway," Ava said, "thanks for letting me drop in like this. I'm glad you hadn't already eaten lunch."

Kenzie snorted softly. "Oh, I totally had."

Ava glanced up at her. "What?"

"This was my second lunch," Kenzie clarified. "And it was delicious. Except for the kale, which is all yours." She pushed the compostable box with the remaining salad toward Ava as if it were radioactive.

Her second lunch? Where in god's name did she put all of those calories? Ava had known girls and women back east who routinely cycled between bingeing and purging, but Kenzie seemed like the last person on the planet who would do that.

"I have a really fast metabolism," Kenzie said, apparently interpreting Ava's expression correctly.

Before her mind could pursue the tangent of Kenzie's metabolism, Ava rose and began to edge away from the table. "I should probably get going. My driver is waiting."

"Your driver?" Kenzie echoed, frowning a little as she rose, too.

"The company car is a Tesla, if that helps."

Kenzie's brow cleared, and she followed Ava to the stairwell. "I mean, I'm sure the environment is happier. I'll walk you down. I've never seen one up close."

Ava descended the seemingly endless stairs carefully, concentrating on each step. It didn't mean anything that Kenzie was walking her to her car. She was just excited to see a Tesla, that was all.

Ramón was waiting at the curb of the shady street, and stepped out to open the door for Ava as she and Kenzie approached.

"Wow," Kenzie said, and whistled. "That's a sweet ride."

The next thing Ava knew, Kenzie was introducing herself to Ramón and chatting him up about the electric car. Ava watched, simultaneously amused and entranced by the way Kenzie was able to charm her usually reticent driver. This was more words than she'd heard Ramón utter in the two months he'd been her driver.

Her phone vibrated again, another reminder for the project management meeting she would be leading in less than a half hour. As if she had somehow sensed the notification, Kenzie wrapped up her car talk with Ramón and returned to Ava's side.

"Thanks again for lunch," she said, her smile suddenly smaller and quieter. But if anything, it was more intense as she stood just beyond Ava's reach, watching her.

Should they hug? Ava had never been much of a hugger, but with Kenzie, her usual seemed all out of whack. "You're welcome," she said, and contented herself with a small smile in return. Except she wasn't contented. She wanted more—more time, more talking, more of Kenzie's earnest gazes.

Work didn't get done by itself, however, as both of her parents had been fond of saying, so Ava turned and slipped into the Tesla's back seat.

Ramón was hovering nearby, but Kenzie stepped forward and pressed the car door shut. "See you soon?"

she asked through the half-open window.

Ava nodded and felt her smile widen. "I hope so."

As Ramón guided the car away from the curb, Ava looked back and watched Kenzie's figure grow smaller. Then the car turned a corner, and Kenzie was lost from view entirely.

"Nice lunch, miss?" Ramón asked, his eyes friendlier than usual in the rearview mirror.

"Yes," she told him, thinking back over the 45 minutes she and Kenzie had spent together on the roof of ECM, talking and laughing like normal people. Since her father's murder and her brother's arrest, Ava hadn't often felt that way—*normal*. "It was a very nice lunch."

Seattle wasn't so bad, she thought, watching out her window as the Belltown walk-ups gave way to the taller, shinier buildings of the central business district. In fact, it was definitely growing on her.

CHAPTER FOUR

"I know I said you did good, but that was before I realized you let someone take your picture," Sloane announced, voice tinged with obvious disapproval as she let herself into Kenzie's condo.

Kenzie paused the game of *Overwatch* she and Matt were playing. "Sorry," she mouthed at him. He only shrugged in return and sat back against the couch, clearly unperturbed by the prospect of witnessing what promised to be the latest in a long line of Shepherd sisters skirmishes.

"You know I gave you that key for emergency purposes, right?" Kenzie said as Sloane reached the great room.

"I—" She stopped as she noticed Matt. "Oh. Hi, Greenie."

Matt snickered under his breath at the nickname. Kenzie smacked him, reducing the force at the last second to prevent any broken bones. She didn't actually think her sister would magically surmise that Kenzie and Matt had gone to Value Village after work to shop for the Super Seattleite costume that was even now sitting in her closet, but it was Sloane. She worked in mysterious ways. And, also, she was an expert at—and huge proponent of the widespread use of—surveillance.

"You were saying?" Kenzie asked, trying to reel her sister back on topic.

Sloane glanced from Kenzie to Matt and back again. "You know exactly what I was saying."

Matt piped up helpfully, "You mean that awesome photo of her emerging all heroic from the fire with that mom and kid in her arms?"

Sloane's look turned dangerous. "He knows?" she demanded.

"I didn't tell him," Kenzie defended herself. "He figured it out, okay?"

"I'm just that good," he said, breathing on his nails and polishing them against his shirt.

And yes, Kenzie could see what a giant dork he was, but she loved him anyway.

Sloane pointed at him. "If you tell anyone else, Greene…"

She left the threat unspoken, which was significantly more terrifying, in Kenzie's opinion. "Of course he's not going to tell anyone. Right, Mattie?"

He locked his lips and threw away the key. "Scout's honor."

That meant something, since he was an Eagle Scout. In his defense, he claimed there hadn't been much else to do growing up on Whidbey Island. It was either join the scouts or ride in the back of open pickup trucks while your buddies tried to throw you out at top speeds. Matt had always been prone to motion sickness, so the decision had been a no-brainer.

Shaking her head, Sloane headed for the refrigerator and helped herself to one of the microbrews Matt kept there.

"That's twice in a matter of weeks—that I know of. Tell me, Kenz: Are you planning to keep doing the hero thing?" she asked, dropping down on the couch beside Kenzie and subjecting her to one of her famous stares.

"I don't know." Kenzie held her gaze, but she couldn't keep herself from blinking rapidly. Seriously, why did she bother trying to lie to her not-so-secret agent sister? Kenzie had always been the type of person whose emotions were readily apparent to pretty much anyone with functioning vision, let alone someone with extensive training in the art and science of interrogation.

But were her emotions evident to Ava Westbrook? Had Ava realized Kenzie had a crush on her and that was why her phone had remained quiet since their impromptu lunch date? Or maybe Ava was simply busy because, after all, she was a top executive at a huge corporation. God, Kenzie was such an idiot.

"Oh my god, you're such an idiot!" Sloane pointed her bottle at Kenzie. "If you keep playing at this crap, Panopticon is totally going to catch you at it, and then any number of agency moles will be only too happy to feed your exact coordinates to Sentinel."

To be honest, that hadn't occurred to her. Kenzie stood up and headed for the kitchen to replenish her glass of wine. "What am I supposed to do, then, just let people die when I could save them?"

"Why not? People die every day, Kenzie. You're not responsible for saving humanity from itself, remember?"

"That fire was started by a faulty electrical wire, which is hardly humanity's fault. Besides, you and Mom and Dad are the ones who always said that, not me."

"Right. Like anything we said ever stopped you."

Kenzie nearly broke her wine glass. "You—I don't—what?"

Sloane rolled her eyes so hard that Kenzie was a little surprised they didn't get stuck. "Come on, Kenz, don't act like you haven't secretly been helping people all along. It's just, now camera phones are everywhere and there's a god damn hashtag."

Kenzie blinked at her sister. Did Sloane really know about the lost children reunited with their parents by an unknown stranger, the mugging victims whose would-be attackers suddenly vanished in a blur, the hikers miraculously discovered in the middle of the Cascades by an anonymous tip, the accident victim who didn't remember being pulled from his burning car? Apparently, Kenzie wasn't as sneaky as she'd always thought.

"I never told Mom and Dad about your rescue stunts because I didn't want to worry them, and I knew it made you feel better to help people," Sloane said, her voice softening. "In your shoes, I'm sure I would have done the same thing. But this is different, Kenzie. There are multiple witnesses, not to mention photos and social media coverage, and honestly, I'm worried."

"You don't have to worry," Kenzie said, coming back to sit between her sister and best friend. She leaned into Sloane's side. "I'm invulnerable, remember?"

"Not completely."

Matt leaned forward to peer around Kenzie at her sister. "Wait, what?"

Sloane glared at him. "I don't know if you realize this, genius, but if her identity is compromised by Sentinel or any of the other crazies out there—and that includes the off-worlder crazies, because they definitely exist—you're at risk, too."

His eyebrows rose. "Oh, shit, you're right. Everyone knows the best friend is expendable. Clearly, I did not think this through."

"Clearly," Sloane said snarkily. "Freaking amateurs. I

knew you two were up to something. Just tell me what you're planning so I can try to keep you from getting yourselves killed."

Kenzie and Matt exchanged a look.

"She does have a point," he admitted. "But I'm still your Q, right?" He held up his hand.

Kenzie completed the high-five, ignoring her sister's exasperated huff. "You know it."

"Show her, then," he said, grinning. "I can't wait to see her face."

Kenzie couldn't, either. She blurred to the closet and into the bathroom with the bag, where she quickly changed into the items she and Matt had picked up. Then she sped back to the living room and skidded to a stop on the rug in the middle.

"Ta-da," she said, spinning in a slow circle.

"It's even better than I remembered," Matt said reverently, leaping up from the couch to take a closer look.

"You. Cannot. Be. Serious."

Kenzie smiled at her sister, even though her mouth wasn't visible through the mask that covered her head. Her nose was covered, too. Only her eyes shone through two wide, slanted holes. "As a heart attack. Isn't it perfect?"

"For the last time, heart attacks are not funny! And no, a black bodysuit and an alien mask are not perfect, Kenzie. Where did you even find them?"

"Value Village. And don't worry," Kenzie added as her sister's nostrils flared in warning, "Matt paid in cash while I waited outside. I even made him wear a hat and sunglasses, so they can't be traced back to me."

"Glasses only hide people's identities in comic books." Sloane turned to Matt, her eyes narrowed accusingly. "The green bug-eyed mask was your idea, wasn't it?"

He pressed a hand to his chest. "Who, me?"

Kenzie decided not to tell her sister that Matt's idea had been to shop online for adult-sized monster suits. After she'd vetoed anything with five-inch nails or bloody fangs, he'd suggested she get the one that looked like the android assassin from *Terminator 2*.

Sure. Because people in need of rescue weren't already traumatized enough.

"Actually," she said, placing her hands on her hips and standing up straighter, "it was my idea. If they're going to call us little green men, I figured I might as well look the part."

"Okay," Sloane said, nodding. "So let me ask you this: What happens next time you fly into a fire and your bodysuit burns off?"

Kenzie's hero pose faltered because, well, she hadn't thought of that, either.

"On the bright side," Matt quipped, "you wouldn't have to worry about ever being called a little green *man* again, am I right?" He held up his hand, but Kenzie pointedly ignored it this time.

"Oh my god," Sloane said yet again, pinching the top of her nose like she did right before she got a migraine. "If you're going to do this, then you absolutely have to let me help. I can source a costume—"

"I think they're technically called *suits*," Matt put in.

Sloane didn't even spare him a glance as she continued: "—that won't be traceable. And as an added bonus, it won't disintegrate the next time you decide to play hero."

Kenzie considered her options. On the one hand, she could quit helping people and let #SuperSeattleite fade away naturally. On the other, she could partner unofficially with her government agent sister, thereby gaining a ton of technical assistance. While Matt was really good at *Overwatch* and *Titan Fall*, his international intelligence game wasn't all that impressive.

"Won't helping me get you in trouble?" she asked, pulling off the mask and worrying it between her hands.

Sloane shrugged, smiling up at her sadly. "I've already broken pretty much every rule by not revealing I'm related to an off-worlder, so, you know, this would sort of be par for the course. Besides, ever since Coop disappeared, I'm not quite as gung ho as I maybe used to be."

Michael Cooper, the chief science officer for Panopticon's Seattle office, had been Sloane's mentor her first few years at the bureau. He was the one who had recruited her away from her graduate program at U-Dub with promises of making the world a better place for humans and aliens alike. He was also the first to sound the alarm about Sentinel. But soon after he'd blown the whistle, he'd vanished. Sloane had spent months chasing leads, but in the end the officer who had been promoted into Coop's position had called off the search.

Not knowing was the worst part, Sloane had confided. Kenzie knew just what she meant. When the asteroid storm had begun to overwhelm the Zattalian fleet's energy shields, her parents had put her into an escape pod on course to one of the Alliance's central systems. But her pod's hyperdrive had sustained damage, so the on-board AI had rerouted her to a refugee station not far from Earth where she had spent a few months waiting for a permanent placement.

Meanwhile, her future parents, Jane and Benjamin, had registered with the Alliance to assist refugees. Soon after the Shepherd-Hendersons had been accepted into Earth's asylum program, Kenzie had been notified there was a Terran family interested in adopting her. As a member of a wayfaring people, she'd spent more time in space than on any planet, but secretly, she'd always dreamed of finding a home world. She'd gone to meet the Shepherd-

Hendersons, and it didn't take long to recognize how lucky she would be to join their family. Later, she'd applied to the Alliance for information on her family of origin, but she hadn't gotten very far. The refugee program was known for insane levels of bureaucracy—keeping track of hundreds of inhabited planets and trillions of citizens across the far reaches of space was a complex task even for advanced species—and she'd been told that the lack of available data indicated she was probably the sole survivor of her fleet.

She'd seen her family's ship take a direct hit and explode in a hail of metal and fire shortly after her pod launched, so it wasn't like she held out much hope for their survival. But it was the *probably* that still sometimes kept her up at night.

"Kenzie?" Sloane asked, her tone hesitant.

She always seemed to know when Kenzie was thinking about her lost family. It was Sloane's human advantage, Kenzie often joked. She nodded belatedly, moving around the coffee table to snuggle back in against her sister's side. "I'd love your help. Thanks, Slo-mo."

Sloane ruffled her hair, now falling out of its messy bun thanks to the alien mask. "You got it, Speedy."

"What about me?" Matt asked, pouting in the way that always reminded Kenzie of a cranky alpaca. Although, were there any non-cranky alpacas? In her limited experience, the answer was no.

"Get in here," Kenzie said, opening her free arm. "Team work makes the dream work!"

As Matt cuddled in happily, Sloane muttered under her breath, "Lord, what have I done?"

"You know you love me," Kenzie said.

"Well, obviously."

"I love you, too."

"I love you three," Matt said.

Even Kenzie groaned at that one.

\#

Ava squinted at the photo on her phone in the early evening light streaming into her office. The building's glass walls had been designed to regulate temperature and energy use by letting in some rays of sunlight while reflecting others, but that didn't mean she didn't sometimes still have to wear sunglasses during the day.

Ah—that explained why #SuperSeattleite was now accompanied by the newly trending tag #GalaxyGirl. Seattle's new hero had undergone a makeover, and Twitter was all abuzz over the sleek, dark-colored bodysuit and matching cowl, a dim image of the Milky Way galaxy splashed across both. The requisite tool belt was slender, and the mask—Ava peered closer. Did the mask really have alien eyes? Apparently, Galaxy Girl had a sense of humor.

Girl—really? Shouldn't it be *woman*? The bodysuit made it abundantly clear that this was no child flitting about the city saving people and pets from all manner of injury. In the past 24 hours alone, according to the denizens of Twitter, she'd stopped an attempted carjacking, helped a little girl catch her runaway puppy before harm could befall either, assisted the local police with a hostage situation, and flown a car—*an entire car*—from the Ship Canal Bridge to the nearest hospital after the driver had suffered a stroke. Men probably felt better calling a female hero with such strength and power a girl, but there was more to a hero than her name.

For example, those arms, Ava thought, smiling a little as she made the blurry photo larger. If her mother could see her now, practically drooling over the physique of an off-worlder, she would probably have her committed. Good thing she couldn't see her, then. And yes, someone with this woman's abilities *was* a potential threat to humans who couldn't possibly match her in a fair fight, but when had humans ever fought fair? Besides, no one was forcing her to use her powers for good. Ava didn't believe for a second that Sentinel was entirely gone, only that they were, for now, underground. That meant coming out as an alien hero was more of a risk for this woman, whoever she was, than it was for the people of Seattle.

Her phone vibrated in her hand, and her smile widened as she saw the message: "Dinner?" Kenzie had included a selfie with the sign to Shiro Sushi just over her shoulder.

Ava hesitated before typing in, "Absolutely." She still had a couple of hours of work to get through tonight, but she could take a break and enjoy a meal with a friend. Bea would applaud her efforts to maintain a healthy work-life balance even if no one at Hyperion would.

"Coolers!" Kenzie replied. "Meet me in half an hour at 2901 Western Ave."

So bossy, Ava thought, intrigued by the notion that a bit of steel might lay beneath Kenzie's sweet surface.

"Please?!" Kenzie added.

And yes, that was more like the person Ava was getting to know.

"See you soon," she replied, already beginning to pack up.

"Yessss!! Wear something warm." She added a sweater emoji followed by an image of a landscape, with the sun setting over water. Apparently, they were dining outdoors.

Ava glanced down at her slacks and suit jacket. Good thing her hotel room was on the way.

It didn't take long to change into dark wash skinny jeans, a cream knit sweater, and a buttonless wool camel trench cinched at her waist. Soon enough she was on the elevator to the underground garage, scrolling through her message history with Kenzie. They had texted almost continuously since their lunch at ECM the previous week, mostly memes and shots of beautiful views or cute dogs spotted around town. Also food—Kenzie was serious about sustenance, though most of the meal-related selfies she'd sent included her being goofy, like taking a giant bite of an enormous cheeseburger or catching a french fry out of the air. She'd also shared descriptions of hiking trails in and around Seattle, possibly seriously but also possibly as a joke. Ava wasn't entirely sure given their weekend plans hadn't included road tripping into the woods. Instead, they'd gone for drinks with Kenzie's friends on Friday night and to brunch on Sunday morning, again with the whole crowd. Ava had been invited out to the pub on Saturday night, too, but she'd had to attend a fundraiser for Seattle Children's Hospital.

"Ooh, fancy," Kenzie had teased her via text.

"Hardly," she'd responded as she tried to decide which of her diamond earring sets to wear. Well, maybe a little fancy. For a moment, she'd considered asking Kenzie if she wanted to be her plus one, but she'd rejected the idea almost immediately. Nothing screamed "I'm gay for you" like inviting your crush to a black-tie charity gala.

Now it was Tuesday, and even though she'd seen Kenzie 48 hours earlier, it felt like so much longer. That must be why she was positively giddy at the idea of hanging out tonight—because, obviously, that was how casual work friends felt about each other.

Ramón was waiting when she exited the elevator, leaning against the Tesla parked in a reserved spot near the elevator bank. "Where are we going tonight, Miss Westbrook?" he inquired politely.

"Uptown," she said. "I think."

She slipped into the open door and waited until he had settled his sizable girth behind the wheel to provide the address from her phone. "But don't tell me what's there," she added. "I want to be surprised."

He glanced at her in the mirror as he guided the nearly silent car to the garage exit, but he didn't comment. As her driver, he knew more about her comings and goings than most people, which was why discretion was an important part of his job. Jack Treadwell, former CIA agent and current chief of security at Hyperion, personally oversaw the hiring of people like Ramón—those who had more access to the company's executives than anyone else. Treadwell would have preferred to have a security agent assigned to Ava 24/7, but so far she'd managed to convince him such coverage wasn't necessary. There were already agents at Hyperion Tower monitoring her visitors, and she did allow a single undercover operative to accompany her to public events where her presence had been advertised in advance, but otherwise she treasured her privacy.

Ava distracted herself from rush hour traffic by responding to a few work emails, but it wasn't long before Ramón was stopping the Tesla on the corner of Western Ave and Broad Street. Before Ava could even unbuckle her seatbelt, movement on the nearby sidewalk caught her attention. Kenzie was waving at her, a reusable grocery bag flapping awkwardly in her grasp. Did she have two bags? Maybe they were meeting other people. Ava tried to suppress her slight pang of dismay, but it was no use. She'd been hoping to have Kenzie all to herself this time.

Friends, she reminded herself. They weren't dating. Or were they? It was difficult to know, really.

"Ah, Miss Shepherd," Ramón said, smiling as Kenzie grinned from the sidewalk. "Enjoy yourself, Miss Westbrook."

"Thanks, Ramón," she said, blushing for no good reason as she slipped out of the car.

"You made it! Hi, Ramón," Kenzie added, ducking her head in to smile at Ava's driver.

"Hello, Kenzie."

Wait, he was calling Kenzie by her first name? Though she supposed Kenzie wasn't technically his boss, so...

"See you soon, Ramón," she said, and closed the door.

The car pulled away as Ava focused more closely on Kenzie. Her hair was pulled back in a neat chignon like the one she'd worn the day they met, a few soft strands framing her face. Her make-up was of the natural variety, her lips slightly pinker than usual. She was beautiful, and her genuine smile only made her prettier, in Ava's opinion.

Right. *Friends.*

"Where are the others?" Ava asked, and then regretted the question as Kenzie's smile faltered.

"Um, I thought it could be just us," she said, biting her lip. "Unless you'd rather—I mean, I could totally call Matt and—"

"No," Ava said quickly. "I just thought, with all that food..."

Kenzie glanced down at the bags, her brow clearing. "Oh, right. I wasn't sure what your favorites were, so I brought one of everything. Well, not *everything,* but pretty close."

Ava laughed, because of course she had. "That sounds perfect. So, what is this place, anyway?"

Kenzie perked up. "I was hoping you'd never been! It's the Olympic Sculpture Park."

Ava noticed the letters "SAM" on the side of the nearby wall. "It's a Seattle Art Museum extension site, right?"

"Exactly. This is one of my favorite places in the city to go for a picnic," Kenzie confided, leading her toward a ramp that led up along the side of a single-story building that faced Puget Sound.

As the ramp rose, the building came into clearer view. It reminded Ava of Hyperion Tower, all glass and steel and neat triangles. The view became more evident, too, and Ava nodded in appreciation at the sight of a green hillside zigzagging down toward Elliott Bay in the near distance, West Seattle and the Olympic Mountains farther afield.

"I thought we could eat here on the patio," Kenzie said, "but it turns out they're having a wedding inside the pavilion in a little while, so no one's allowed."

She sounded so disappointed that Ava reached out and looped her arm through Kenzie's, adjusting her stride so that one of the dinner bags wouldn't bump against her. "Ooh, a wedding," she said, wriggling her eyebrows at Kenzie. "We'll have to crash it later and toast the happy couple."

"What? No! We can't do that," Kenzie said, her voice higher pitched than usual, although Ava wasn't certain which made her more nervous: their proximity, or the prospect of crashing a stranger's wedding.

She laughed again and put more space between them. "Where do you suggest we eat, then? I'm famished."

"I guess we'd better find someplace fast," Kenzie said, pushing up her glasses.

They walked for a bit, passing several perfectly acceptable picnic locations, in Ava's opinion, as well as a variety of interesting art installations that they stopped to admire. There weren't many people out despite the balmy (for Seattle) weather. Apparently, picnicking in the sculpture garden wasn't a popular choice for a partly cloudy Tuesday night in May.

Midway down the hill, Kenzie brightened. "What about there?" she asked, gesturing toward a table beneath a large, slowly rotating red neon ampersand. A woman and several children were just walking away, leaving the space momentarily unoccupied.

"Perfect," Ava said, smiling.

She loved art, ancient and modern and everything in between. As they approached the table, she squinted at the gray and white parts of the installation, picking out several benches, concrete steps, and a small tree partially painted white.

"It spells out 'love & loss,'" Kenzie explained.

Ava looked closer. Beneath the neon ampersand, the white parts of the benches and steps formed the letters "l," "o," and both occurrences of "s." A white "e" had been painted on the tabletop, while the small tree featured two trunks radiating from the same base, forming a "v" that had also been painted white.

Kenzie took a seat on one of the round concrete stools and began to spread the sushi and noodle dishes out before them. She only managed to fit the contents of one bag on the small table before giving up and handing Ava a cloth napkin and a set of beautifully painted chopsticks.

"So environmentally correct," Ava commented as she surveyed the many tasty-looking rolls and dishes.

"Well, like you said, climate change *is* the most complex issue facing Earth…"

"What should I try first?" Ava asked, focusing on the food.

"Oh, man, that's a tough one," Kenzie lamented, sounding as if choosing which dish to start with was an agonizing life decision.

They nibbled on edamame while surveying the different rolls and combos. Ava loved sushi, but Kenzie's devotion to Shiro's offerings was on a whole different level.

"My favorite is the salmon nigiri," Kenzie said finally, pointing at a container within easy reach of Ava's chopsticks. "It's the kind of fish that absolutely melts in your mouth."

It was, too. Pacific sushi made even high-end New York sushi seem like the grocery store variety. Ava closed her eyes and hummed as the raw sake salmon coated her tongue with its flavors. "Delicious," she said, opening her eyes to find Kenzie watching her, eyes wide.

"Um, yeah, I know," Kenzie mumbled, nearly knocking half the containers off the table in her haste to reach a different one. She slowed her movements and glanced up at Ava with a sheepish smile. "Do you like cream cheese in your sushi roll?"

"I don't hate it," she said, her voice low and suggestive, and licked her lips, hiding a smile as Kenzie appeared to have a mild stroke on the spot. Interesting. Perhaps they were dating, after all.

It took them a full forty minutes to work their way through the smorgasbord of seafood dishes Kenzie had purchased. By "them," Ava really meant "Kenzie." Long after Ava had sat back, pleased with her choice to wear jeans with an elastic waistband, Kenzie kept going, her chopsticks seeming to move almost faster than the human eye could track at times. Ava wondered how she afforded so much food on a junior reporter's income, but then she remembered that Kenzie's parents were renowned scientists with more than one patent between them. The Henderson-Shepherd family income wouldn't be on par with the Westbrooks, but she didn't doubt they were comfortable.

Kenzie managed to keep up a running commentary on life in Seattle even as she finished off the remaining sushi, offering Ava a combined history and travelogue of Washington State's largest city. She had very specific recommendations on what to do and what not to do. For example, walk-on ferry rides for the sake of riding ferries were a definite yes while the famed Underground Tour, an exploration of the city's literally buried history, not so much. Ballard Locks for the salmon ladders during spawning season were another yes, along with the Fremont Market on any sunny Sunday. But as for Ride the Ducks, "a hard pass."

"What about the Space Needle?" Ava asked, mildly amused by the inflexibility of Kenzie's opinions.

"Honestly, the view from the Columbia Tower is way more interesting. But the top of the Space Needle does complete a full rotation in under an hour, so it's worth getting dinner there sometime."

"The Space Needle rotates?" Ava asked, suddenly more intrigued by the site she had previously considered a tourist trap.

Kenzie smiled sideways at her. "Yep. And before you ask, that isn't a PSA. It's an invitation," she added, leaning companionably into Ava's shoulder.

Companionship, however, was the last thing on Ava's mind. Kenzie's body pressing into hers made her pulse race pleasantly and warmth wend through her in a way that was a bit more than friendly. *Shite.* She was such a lesbian.

"Come on," she said suddenly, sweeping the empty containers into one of Kenzie's bags and the few still with food into the other. "I think I hear wedding music."

As it turned out, it was a gay wedding, with a pair of thirty-something men and their friends and family members dressed to the nines and dancing happily to retro music while a disco ball shot rainbow lights throughout the stunning glass and concrete building. Ava and Kenzie leaned against a concrete wall outside the pavilion, half-turned to the party and half to the sun currently tracking toward the bay in the distance.

"Who gets married on a Tuesday night?" Ava asked, but softly because the wedding party seemed genuinely happy.

"Troy and Ben, that's who," Kenzie said.

Ava shot her a look. "How do you know their names?"

"Oh. Um, I think it was on the sign on the door earlier?"

Ava was about to ask her if that was a question when a loud boom reverberated from the center of the city. Almost immediately, a cloud of black smoke could be seen rising to the south of downtown.

"Oh my god," Kenzie said, her face draining of color. She pushed away from the wall and started toward the street.

"What is it?" Ava asked, hurrying after her.

"That explosion came from near Panopticon," Kenzie said, her voice grim.

"Your sister isn't at work right now, is she?"

"No, but plenty of her fellow agents are." Kenzie stopped suddenly and turned to face Ava, pressing the grocery bags into her hands. "Can you hang onto these? I have to go."

Ava blinked. That was not at all what she'd expected. "Why?"

"I have to get down there." She gestured downtown even as she pulled out her phone and began typing away.

Ava tried to understand what she could possibly mean. Then it came to her: "Oh! You mean as a reporter?"

"Yes, of course," Kenzie said, her tone odd. "Call Ramón, okay? He'll get you someplace safe."

"Kenzie, I really don't think—"

Kenzie reached forward and hugged her. The contact was brief, but Ava lost her train of thought as she felt Kenzie's strong arms enfold her. Of course it would feel amazing to be hugged by Kenzie Shepherd.

"Just call him," Kenzie said, pulling away to tuck a strand of Ava's hair behind her ear. "Hyperion is too close to whatever's going on, and I don't want to worry about you. Please?"

"What if I don't want to worry about you?" Ava asked, hearing the waver in her own voice.

Kenzie smiled crookedly and winked at her, surprisingly confident. "You don't have to worry about me. I promise." And then she was hurrying away, phone in hand. "I'll call you later. Be safe!"

"You too," Ava replied, watching Kenzie cross the street and disappear around the edge of the building on the opposite corner. She stood there for a full minute, watching the space where Kenzie had disappeared and trying to absorb the way their night—their lives, possibly?—had just shifted. But it would take time to sink in, she knew. Catastrophe always did.

Sighing in frustration, she pulled out her own phone and dialed Ramón. Before the call could go through, the Tesla turned the corner and slowed to a halt in front of her.

"Are you okay, Miss Westbrook?" he asked, sharp eyes taking in the scene around them as he opened the back door for her.

"Yes, I'm fine," she said, and slipped inside.

He paused, hand on the door. "Where's Miss Shepherd?"

"She's a reporter," Ava said, only just keeping the irritation from her voice. "Which means she's running toward the fire."

He nodded and closed the door, speaking quietly into a mic clipped to his jacket. As the locks audibly clicked, she realized she was no longer in control of her own life.

"You're not going to take me home if I ask, are you?"

He spared her a semi-apologetic glance. "No, Miss. I have orders to take you away from the explosion, not toward it."

Ava leaned back against the leather seat. There was no use arguing. Once her security team enacted a protection protocol, she knew from experience that she was simply along for the ride. Good thing her phone was relatively charged and her data plan unlimited.

As Ramón drove north, away from the black cloud hanging ominously over downtown, Ava pulled up Twitter, trying to get a live update on whatever was happening. It wasn't long before the first video appeared on the #DowntownSeattle tag—a group of heavily armed individuals had attacked Panopticon and set off the explosion she and Kenzie had heard, leveling a portion of the building in a bid to get inside. But before they could get far, Galaxy Girl had swooped into action. Within minutes, she had rounded up the attackers, and in another quarter hour she had extinguished the flames *and* pulled half a dozen survivors from the wreckage. Not everyone had survived the assault, but Galaxy Girl's intervention had kept the bureau's casualties low.

As Ava watched the footage of the alien hero saving the day, the sense of dread that had shadowed her since the explosion slowly waned. This off-worlder, whoever she might be, was the real deal. The terrorists who had attacked Panopticon—and Ava had a fairly good guess about their identity—couldn't have expected Seattle's hero to be on the scene so quickly.

And yet… What if they had? Maybe they had attacked Panopticon to test both her power and her sense of justice. Most off-worlders had little love for the bureau. Had the attackers picked their target as a means to two ends: damaging Panopticon *and* calling out Seattle's alien hero? If so, they had certainly learned a lesson. Galaxy Girl was apparently willing to help even the government entity that, at best, would arrest her for "vigilantism" and imprison her indefinitely. At worse, Ava's father's agency would ship her off to a hidden government lab to discover the secrets lurking in her physiology. After all, Nick had gotten the idea—and the funding—to experiment on off-worlders while working for Panopticon. Though she couldn't prove it, Ava had always suspected that his plans had found support from the highest levels, including their dear, deceased father.

Now that Galaxy Girl had come to the rescue, what would Panopticon do? Would they still treat her as a hostile after she'd saved the lives of multiple agents and perhaps prevented an extended fire fight that could have led to loss of civilian lives as well? She was a widely publicized hero, thanks to social media, and she'd saved their asses. What was more, the whole world knew it. Eyewitness Twitter video didn't lie. Or, at least, not in this case.

Hours later, Ava was back home and in bed with her Kindle propped on her lap pretending to read the same page over and over again when her phone finally rang with the call she'd been waiting for.

"Hi," she breathed. "Are you okay?"

"Yeah." The lone word managed to convey a wealth of exhaustion. Kenzie cleared her throat. "Everything's fine. Sloane wasn't there but a couple of her buddies were. They made it, fortunately, but—some of the others didn't."

She sounded hoarse, strained, nothing like her usual bubbly self. And even though Ava had already asked, she repeated the question: "Yes, but are *you* okay?"

"I'm—I don't—there was a lot of blood," she said finally.

Ava sat up, her Kindle forgotten. "How were you close enough to see blood?"

"I mean, like, with a zoom lens." Voices sounded in the background, echoing oddly, and she added quickly, "I have to go. Can I call you tomorrow?"

"Yes, of course. But—"

"I'm sorry," Kenzie said. "I can't—" She released a breath that vibrated the phone speaker. When she spoke again, her voice was quieter. "I had a good time tonight. You know, before?"

Ava let her head fall forward. "I did, too. Be safe, okay?"

"Always," Kenzie said, sounding a little more like herself. "Talk to you tomorrow."

The line clicked, and Ava tossed her phone onto the comforter, a sound of irritation escaping her throat. *Jesus.* Since when was being a tech reporter so dangerous? But Kenzie wasn't just a reporter. She was also the sister of a Panopticon agent, and that meant that, like Ava, she was always going to be closer to the action than the average civilian. Closer to danger, too.

Ava rubbed her forehead. Why couldn't life ever just be normal? But then she caught herself. She still had her life and limbs and—now that the emergency was over and her security team no longer on alert—liberty. There were men and women tonight who weren't that lucky, and she would do well to remember that.

Westbrooks didn't take privilege for granted, she reminded herself, turning her Kindle back on. They appreciated it just as much as—if not more than—the next lucky bastard.

CHAPTER FIVE

Kenzie unlocked her door and pushed it open, relieved to finally be home. After tonight, she understood what the term "bone weary" meant. But it wasn't physical exhaustion making her feet drag and her shoulders slump, but rather a fatigue more existential in nature. While she'd seen car accident victims and people who had been injured in other ways, tonight was the first time she'd encountered human bodies broken and twisted in purposeful violence.

Every time she closed her eyes, she saw a rotation of terrible images—bodies bloodied and battered; flames so hot they melted metal; one corner of the west wall of the bureau crumpled as if a giant had kicked it in. Plastic explosives like the type used tonight were particularly suited to demolition, according to the Panopticon debriefing team she'd met with after the fire had been extinguished and the scene secured. There had been a brief moment when Kenzie thought the agents unhurt in the attack might try to detain her, but instead Peter MacIntosh, the man who had stepped into Coop's role as chief science officer for the Northwest bureau, had asked her politely if she would mind talking to them. As one professional to another.

By then Sloane had arrived on the scene, and Kenzie had noticed her sister's slight head shake. But what could she do? She went with MacIntosh and his team, which—fortunately—included Sloane. Her sister's non-verbal cues and occasional whispered warnings at a decibel only Kenzie's hearing could detect kept her from revealing too much during the hour-long debrief in a conference room she'd never seen on her previous visits to Sloane's place of work. She hadn't removed her cowl, and the voice modulator Sloane had given her seemed to do its job. MacIntosh, who she had met at least half a dozen times, appeared to be no closer to discovering her identity than before she'd come to Panopticon's rescue.

He'd even thanked her before an agent escorted her out. "We would have lost a lot more good people without your intervention," he'd said solemnly, nodding at her.

"I'm just glad I could help," she'd told him. And it was true. Even if Panopticon was responsible for the creation and growth of Sentinel, the single most anti-alien organization in Earth's history, Kenzie didn't want the people who worked for the bureau to die. Many of them were just like Sloane—Americans who believed in liberty and justice for all. For non-telepaths, there was no way to know by looking at someone what they felt or thought, and besides, she would only be practicing a different type of bigotry if she decided intolerance was a suitable reason to leave someone to die.

She *was* glad she'd been able to help, but she was also horrified by what she'd seen. It had taken every inch of willpower not to collapse in her sister's arms. All that blood... She'd washed it off her hands in a locker room MacIntosh had asked Sloane to escort her to before the debrief, but she wasn't sure she would ever be able to get the scent of iron out of her head. How could people be so terrible to each other? She sort of understood why humans might fear off-worlders, but how could members of the same species commit such atrocities against one another?

Probably, it was the lingering horror of what she'd witnessed that made her forget to use her augmented vision before entering her studio. If she had peered through the door and surveyed the interior, as was her usual routine, she undoubtedly would have seen the figure seated on the couch, leafing through ECM's latest weekly magazine—the issue that featured Kenzie's article on the refined fashion sense of Millennial "mover and shaker" Ava Westbrook.

"I wondered when you would get here," an unfamiliar voice said as Kenzie closed the door and kicked off her shoes.

She tensed, ready to defend herself, but the shadowy figure in the great room was faster than any human. Rising, the middle-aged Asian woman flickered like an old film, and suddenly, in her place, stood a familiar person with tiny horns, folded wings, and a wide smile: D'aman, the Alliance caseworker who had first helped Kenzie adapt to life on Earth.

"Oh my god," Kenzie said, and blurred to her old friend's side, heedlessly crashing into the taller humanoid as she hugged them. Unlike fragile humans, native Kreedilans could take a hit. "What are you doing here?"

Laughing in the deep guttural way their people had, D'aman pulled back to examine Kenzie. "It's good to see you too, youngling. Although, if you consider your recent activities, I think you'll know why I'm here."

"I haven't violated any of the refugee directives," Kenzie said, fatigue evaporating as a wave of unease swept over her.

In addition to monitoring her adaptation to life on her new planet, D'aman had also been tasked with ensuring Kenzie abided by a rather extensive list of rules and regulations that the Alliance required all non-native residents of Earth to follow. Some of the strictest rules involved the sharing of technology. For example, humans hadn't yet been approved for interstellar travel. Their willingness to use nuclear weapons on their own species, D'aman had once explained, did not inspire confidence in Alliance representatives that they could be trusted to refrain from using them on other species.

"Haven't you?" D'aman enquired, their head cocked to one side.

Kenzie turned away, dropping her messenger bag beside the coffee table and heading for the kitchen. She needed food for this conversation. Well, she needed food for most conversations, but especially tonight. She had used up most of her caloric intake from earlier fighting the terrorists.

For a moment, a memory of Ava smiling at her in the evening sunshine flashed into her mind, and she suppressed a sigh. Being able to modify the course of time would be such a killer power to possess.

"Would you like anything?" she asked as she rifled through the freezer in search of a frozen meal that would quickly satisfy her hunger pangs without reminding her of the gory carnage she'd witnessed. Pizza with red sauce was out, as was any sort of noodle or cauliflower dish. Indian food, though, should do quite nicely—chicken tikka samosas and enough naan to feed a small family. Or, you know, one hungry Zattalian.

"I ate before I arrived," D'aman said, following her to the kitchen and hopping up on one of the stools at the butcher block island.

Kenzie zapped the naan in the microwave and munched on it while the samosas heated up, dipping the flatbread in soy sauce to add even more salty goodness to its flavor. She had finished two slices of naan by the time the samosas were ready. Plate full of her favorite Indian foods, she sat down at the kitchen island and stared at one of her oldest acquaintances.

"I didn't even know you were still on Earth," she said around a mouthful of delicious chicken.

"I'm sorry if my absence has offended you. The Alliance, as you know, prefers us to maintain our distance once the initial period of adjustment has been completed successfully."

"Um," Kenzie said, frowning, "I'm pretty sure the rules say you're not allowed to read my mind, either."

"Such rules do not apply to our relationship," D'aman said. "But even if they did, I wouldn't be in violation for I didn't read your mind just now."

"Oh. Well, good," Kenzie said, her shoulders drawn up as she plowed through the food on her plate.

In addition to shapeshifting, invulnerability, and the ability to fly, Kreedilans possessed the power of telepathy. This was why they made such excellent refugee caseworkers—they could blend in anywhere and were uniquely suited to surveillance. Since their planet had been nearly destroyed a few hundred years earlier by the warlike, non-humanoid Vinckettos, there were plenty of Kreedilans looking for service off-planet. D'aman, who was three hundred years old, had left their home planet during the war, they had once confided. The rest of their family had not been so fortunate.

Kenzie's phone rang from inside her messenger bag. *Whoops.* She'd promised Sloane she would call when she got home. Probably shouldn't mention she'd remembered to call Ava before she'd even left the bureau. So far, she had kept her sister in the dark about the amount of time— both virtual and in real life—she'd been spending with Ava. Not only did she hate to imagine the magnitude of Sloane's apoplectic fit if she knew about Kenzie's feelings for Nicholas Westbrook's sister, but also, she wasn't sure yet what those feelings were. In theory, she knew how she wanted her relationship with Ava to play out, but in reality…

Whatever. That could all wait. It would have to, for now.

"It's Sloane," she told D'aman apologetically. "I have it to take it." D'aman nodded, and Kenzie slid off the stool to pace the room. "Hey, sis," she said into her phone. "I was just grabbing some food before I called you."

"Oh. Yeah, that makes sense," Sloane replied. "You did use up more energy than you usually would have to on a weekday night."

Kenzie's sensitive hearing detected the slight echo of her sister's voice that could only mean one thing. A moment later, she heard the jingle of a keychain heralding her sister's untimely arrival. She really was going to have to do something about Sloane and that key.

"I'm so sorry," she said to D'aman, purposely sending them a mental image of what was about to happen.

They flickered again, and a moment later the short, slightly stout Asian woman with a bold streak of gray running through her bob returned in their place. "My name in this form is Susan Cheng."

Kenzie nodded. "I grant you permission to speak to me without words," she said, invoking the formal phrase D'aman had taught her early on in their working relationship. Kenzie might be utter crap at lying to Sloane, but D'aman—*Susan Cheng*—was a master at deception. They—*she*—had to be.

An image of D'aman nodding and bowing slightly appeared in her mind, and Kenzie marveled for the thousandth time at the power of telepathy. Forget time travel. Mind-reading was the way to go. Or was it? Then you would have to deal with all the creepy stuff people thought about, not to mention realizing what other people actually thought about you...

Sloane's voice distracted her from her pointless mental debate. "Did you follow the protocol?" she asked as she closed the door and headed down the hallway. "Please tell me you followed the—Oh. Hello...?"

"This is Susan Cheng," Kenzie offered, eyes on the samosa she was currently slathering with soy sauce. "Susan, this is my sister, Sloane Shepherd. She lives a couple of blocks away, though she honestly spends more time here these days."

"Ha ha," Sloane said, her suspicious gaze still fixed on Kenzie's other visitor. "Nice to meet you."

"Nice to meet you, too," Susan Cheng said politely.

"How exactly do you know each other?"

"I'm Kenzie's new neighbor." She smiled as she rose to her feet and extended her hand to Sloane. "I just dropped in to say hello."

Kenzie almost snorted at that because the odds seemed high that D'aman had literally flown in from wherever they currently lived for this impromptu get-together.

After a wary moment that told Kenzie her sister would be ordering a background check ASAP, Sloane shook the smaller woman's hand. "I see. And what do you do?"

"I'm an acupuncturist."

As Kenzie stared at her old friend uncertainly, an image appeared in her mind of D'aman in their human form placing tiny needles in a faceless humanoid. That image was followed by another of a view that looked remarkably familiar.

"Which unit did you say was yours?" Kenzie asked.

"The one right below yours," Susan Cheng replied. She patted Kenzie on the shoulder, nodded to Sloane, and started off down the hall. "I'll leave you to your sister time. It was nice to meet you both. Kenzie, I would love to grab that coffee with you. My calendar is quite open at the moment."

"Right. Okay. Well, thanks for stopping by," Kenzie said to her retreating back.

"Anytime," she answered. "Really."

That sounded almost like a warning, Kenzie reflected as her new neighbor vanished into the corridor. The fact that D'aman had moved into her building clearly indicated the Kreedilan was back for more than a brief visit. Had the Alliance asked them to keep an eye on Kenzie now that she was actively using her Zattalian powers, or had D'aman initiated this renewed scrutiny on their own?

Looked like she would have to wait for that hypothetical future coffee date to find out.

"That was weird," Sloane said as soon as they were alone, frowning as she took the seat next to Kenzie. "She just randomly showed up at your door?"

Kenzie glanced down at her plate, mental wheels turning. "They—*she* was out of soy sauce," she invented, and then winced. Jesus, how racist could she get? It didn't matter that D'aman—*Susan Cheng*, she reminded herself, hoping to avoid future instances of misgendering—wasn't actually Asian.

"Soy sauce," Sloane repeated. She shook her head as if the excuse was too ridiculous to entertain. "*Anyway*, as I was saying—how did the protocol work?"

"Fine. Good, actually."

"You followed it? Really?" Sloane's eyes narrowed as she subjected Kenzie to her most agent-y look, the one Kenzie had been forced to endure way too often in recent weeks.

"Yes," Kenzie said, holding her sister's gaze. "I promise. It totally worked just like you intended, okay?"

"Well, good," Sloane said, leaning back slightly. "I just want you to be safe."

Kenzie smiled and touched her hand. "I am, thanks to you."

One of Sloane's specialties at Panopticon was contingency planning. She loved to draw up lists and schemes and anything else that required bullet points, so, naturally, she had applied this skillset to preserving Kenzie's identity. The hero suit Sloane had procured fit easily under Kenzie's regular clothes all except for the toolbelt, which was a pretty cool transformer-like contraption that she could wear as a bracelet and activate by pushing a button. But the problem of what to do with the regular clothes she shed for an unplanned emergency—and most emergencies were unplanned, Kenzie was learning—was real. One of Sloane's fears was that an agent from Panopticon or another federal or local authority might try to follow her home in order to discover her identity. As a result, the protocol Sloane had developed to preserve Kenzie's secrecy while dealing with any personal items might be a bit involved, but so far, it seemed to be working.

Tonight wasn't the first time Kenzie had invoked the protocol, which primarily involved stowing her gear for later retrieval on the roof of one of a number of buildings around town that Sloane had determined had no clear sight lines from any other buildings. Following Sloane's carefully laid plan before and after this evening's events, however, had felt more crucial than usual. Sloane had warned her in the Panopticon locker room that MacIntosh or another agent might try to place a homing device on her person during the debrief, so Kenzie had taken extra care not to allow anyone close enough to do so. Still, she'd used her super vision, as Matt called it, to make sure she was bug-free before flying away from downtown. After retrieving her bag of gear from the roof of a Sloane-approved building in Belltown, she'd made her way home via a circuitous route that involved a short flight down the twisty, shadowy back side of Capitol Hill, a brief stop in the urban wilds of Woodland Park to change back into her regular clothes, and a short bus ride and longer walk home. Kenzie had kept an eye out, but no one had appeared to be following her. She was relatively certain that her identity was still safe despite her prolonged run-in with Sloane's colleagues.

"What about you?" she asked, wiping up the last drops of soy sauce with her final samosa. "How are you doing?"

"Me?" Sloane's face instantly transformed into the mask that Kenzie always associated with her intelligence training. "I'm fine."

Kenzie gave her a look before beginning to clean up the kitchen. "It's okay if you're not, you know."

"Pssht. You know I'm trained for this kind of thing."

"Doesn't mean you can't still freak out a little," she pointed out as she washed her solitary plate.

"I don't need to freak out. It's called compartmentalizing. I'm fine, Kenz, really."

Compartmentalizing sounded an awful lot like denial to Kenzie, but then again, she wasn't exactly one to talk. Her recurring nightmare was clear evidence of that.

"Does Mika know you're here?" she asked.

"Yeah. She's actually on her way over, if that's okay?"

"Of course." Kenzie liked her sister's girlfriend, a detective with the Seattle Police Department's Alien Affairs Bureau who matched Sloane in both toughness and compassion. "Have you told her about…?" She trailed off, one finger pointed at herself.

"No, of course not."

"Well, are you going to?"

"Not until I have to. I told you, Kenzie, we can't be too careful."

"But—"

"Leave it." Sloane's voice softened. "Please?"

"Fine." She focused her hearing outside of the condo and detected the familiar rhythm of Mika's heart. She wasn't far away. "I'm going to grab a shower. Find us a movie to watch, okay?"

"Yes, ma'am," Sloane said, saluting her lazily even as she launched herself onto the comfiest part of the couch and reached for the remote.

It was just another normal night—Netflix and ice cream with two of Kenzie's favorite people in the world. But as she stood under the hot spray, wishing it could wash away the memories of the horror she'd witnessed only a matter of hours earlier, she couldn't help feeling that someone else incredibly important was missing.

#

Ava steeled herself outside Victoria's office, schooling her features into what her business school classmates had called "Game Face." Most of them had been attached to athletics in some manner, either as former athletes or current fans. Business school did seem to attract more than its fair share of sports junkies. Victoria, however, was as far from being a fan of organized sports as was humanly possible. Ava hadn't known her well growing up—she hadn't known many people from her mother's side of the family, really—but since ascending at Hyperion she had come to think of her mother's cousin as the embodiment of a snake, content to remain coiled and unobtrusive until called to attack. Her strikes were fast, accurate, and deadly, and staying out of her reach had become a daily goal for Ava. Sometimes, unfortunately, that wasn't possible.

She drew a breath, released it, and knocked.

"Come in," Hyperion's CEO called, her voice silken

and imperious at once. "Ah, Ava," she continued as Ava walked in and shut the heavy wooden door with its braided brass handle. "Thank you for coming. I'm expecting a call at any moment, or I would have come to you."

Ava doubted that very much, but she only nodded and took a seat across from Victoria. This office was just as large as Ava's but noticeably lacked a balcony. Other than that, it was almost the same, down to the built-in shelving, Danish modern furniture, and attached restroom and kitchenette. But where Ava's mother had favored the color white, Victoria was an unabashed supporter of black, dark red, and any other color that evoked vampires. Come to think of it, Ava didn't often see Victoria out in direct sunlight.

"I have a meeting coming up myself. What did you want to discuss?" Ava asked, her tone carefully neutral.

"I've heard from a few people in R&D that you have yet to greenlight the new helium-neon laser project."

"Yes, that's right," Ava said pleasantly.

Victoria paused as if this was not the answer she had been expecting. "And is there a reason for the hold-up?"

"I'm still looking at ROI numbers. It isn't clear to me who, exactly, we're targeting." As Victoria's eyes narrowed, Ava added, "From a business perspective, that is."

"Of course. But I assure you, this is not a product that requires significant market testing."

"Why is that?" Ava asked, tone still modulated despite the red flags flickering in her peripheral vision.

"For one, we already have an interested buyer. And for another, the laser market in general is a steady earner. I know optics isn't really your cup of tea—"

Ava bit the inside of her cheek to keep from snapping back. Victoria, unlike Ava and her mother, lacked formal scientific training. That was why Amelia had insisted on giving Ava the operations role—because she knew Ava understood Hyperion's technology better than Victoria ever would.

"—but our tactical lasers have always performed well."

"In that case," Ava said, "I'm sure the market research will support your position."

Victoria stared at her for a long moment before smiling thinly. "I'm sure it will as well. Thanks for coming by, Ava. It's always good to see you, dear."

"You, too," Ava replied, her smile just as false. She rose and headed for the door, where she paused, palm resting on the cold brass handle. "You said we already have a buyer?"

Victoria inclined her head in answer.

"I didn't see any mention in the project file," Ava pressed.

"I was just contacted recently."

"By whom?"

Victoria's smile vanished, and she picked up her phone. "Oh, look, here's that call now. I'll email you the information later, all right?" Without waiting for an answer, she pushed a button on her cell phone and lifted it to her ear, spinning her chair toward the wall of windows as she purred, "Bonjour, chéri. Tu vas bien?"

The brief meeting had gone about how Ava had expected, and she worried her bottom lip as she returned to her office. The attack on Panopticon a few days earlier had set her on edge, and her emotions had yet to settle. No group had come forward to take responsibility, and the mainstream media seemed to think that disgruntled aliens might somehow be involved even though there hadn't been a single alien or piece of off-world tech involved in the assault. Ava couldn't help thinking that it might be the start of Sentinel's return, even though her brother and his immediate underlings were in prison; even though the group's leadership had been dismantled. When it came to an organization that used the tenets of patriotism and pro-humanity to spread hatred and distrust, there were always "true believers" waiting in the shadows for their own chance to strike a blow for glory.

Maybe that sense of foreboding was what made her return to her hotel suite early that evening and pull up the mysterious text she'd received the day after the attack on Panopticon: "The answers can be found in Labyrinth." The message had come from an unlisted Seattle number that, when she tried calling, had been disconnected. A call to a friend in Boston had launched an investigation that, so far, hadn't turned up much. But Ava's gut told her there was something here, something that connected Hyperion to Sentinel despite her mother's longtime insistence that the family company had no connection to Panopticon or its military arm. Other than the obvious, of course.

Now, after the meeting with Victoria about Hyperion's penchant for engineering military-grade lasers, her gut was twitching again. Maybe she was simply PMSing, but it wouldn't hurt to check in again.

She was about to press the phone icon beside a name in her contacts when her text notification went off. She hesitated before clicking over to a new message from Kenzie: "The pub tonight at 8. Be there or be square!"

Ava felt a ridiculously sentimental smile take hold. "See you then!" she texted back, and added an emoji of a red square. Because, why not. She had only seen Kenzie in passing since their sushi picnic had ended so abruptly earlier in the week. A Friday night at The Queen's Ale House sounded like a perfect way to calm her uneasiness over events she couldn't control—although, obviously, she was under no illusion as to which was more important: the pub or the company being offered.

In the meantime… Switching back to her phone app, she sat back on her couch, pressed a button, and waited for an answer.

The interior of the pub located on top of Queen Anne Hill was decorated like many of the upscale pubs Ava had visited in the British Isles over the years: dark wood paneling beneath a chair rail topped by green textured wallpaper covered in posters from domestic and imported breweries. The clientele was similar, too—young urban professionals with time and money to spend.

Kenzie's friends fit that bill. For the most part, they treated her like one of the crowd. Except Antonio, Kenzie's work friend. Ava hadn't been able to get a consistent read on him yet. When he volunteered to keep her company in the group's "regular" booth while everyone else went to play pool, Ava's guard immediately went up.

At first the conversation was impersonal. Antonio mostly kept his gaze fixed on the corner of the room where Kenzie, Sloane, Mika, and Matt were currently playing pool as he queried her about her move to Seattle and offered recommendations for restaurants and downtown theaters. Meanwhile, Ava tried to remember anything Kenzie might have told her about him. The only items that came to mind were that he covered the Seattle sports scene and that Matt loved the shit out of him in that straight guy way where the nerdier one thought the sportier one was a superior human, even though the opposite was usually true. Kenzie hadn't told Ava that part. She'd noticed it herself over the past few weeks.

And then, all at once, the conversation turned. Gaze still on the pool table, Antonio said, "Remind me how you met Kenzie."

"She came to my office to interview me," Ava said, an alarm beginning to sound inside her head. After growing up in a house where everyone had secret Machiavellian plots, she recognized a lead-in when she saw one.

"Uh-huh. So, it was just random?" His voice clearly indicated his doubts on this front.

Ava tightened her grip on her glass of whiskey. "If you have something to say, Mr. Santos, I suggest you get to the point."

His eyes flew to hers before flicking back to the group playing pool. When Ava followed his gaze, she found Kenzie watching them, her look questioning. Ava gave her a casual smile and took a sip of her drink, soothed by the clink of the ice and the familiar burn in her throat.

Across the table, Antonio turned his phone face up and said, "Hold on."

As Ava watched, perplexed, he selected his music app, and soon the opening notes from the *Hamilton* soundtrack were drifting into the space between them. Out of the corner of her eye, Ava noted that Kenzie had turned back to the pool table.

"My point," Antonio said quietly, his voice nearly drowned out by the music, "is that you may not know this because you don't actually know Kenzie all that well, but she has a long history of bringing home strays and then losing interest as soon as the next one turns up."

Even though she wanted to smack the smug look off his face, Ava forced her voice to remain calm and measured, even a tad dry. "Am I to understand that I'm the stray in this scenario?"

He ignored the question, his gaze drifting back to the pool table. "Also, she's straight. In case you were wondering."

To Ava's immense irritation, a wave of anxiety washed over her, and she had to draw in a deep breath to squash an ill-advised defensive retort. Following a hunch, she drawled, "Do you know that from personal experience, or is that just wishful thinking?"

His face flushed, and she watched his fist clench on the tabletop. She had clearly found a sore point. Sometimes her early training in subterfuge and intrinsic motivation came in handy.

"I'm not—it's not—"

As he sputtered uselessly, Ava noted that Kenzie was frowning now, almost as if she could read the tension from across the room. Then Matt nudged her and, slowly, she turned back to the game.

"Spare me the false outrage," Ava said, her tone low and dangerous. "I don't know what angle you're working, but leave me out of it."

Out of the corner of her eye, Ava saw the cue ball somehow manage to skip off the table and roll across the magenta velvet rug. She was still turning to look when Kenzie was suddenly back, sliding into the booth beside her.

"Whatcha guys talking about?" she asked, her tone bright but her eyes practically boring a hole into Antonio.

And, interesting that she had picked up on their tension from a distance. Ava wouldn't have thought she was that sensitive. Not that Kenzie wasn't kind-hearted, but she didn't seem to be the best at recognizing subtext, in Ava's limited experience.

"We were just discussing the genius of Lin Manuel-Miranda," Antonio said, his smile friendly as he paused the soundtrack, his deep voice rumbling in a way Ava knew most women and gay men enjoyed—at least, women who weren't solidly at the lesbian end of the Kinsey scale.

"Is that so?" Kenzie turned to eye Ava.

"I mean, the man is a national treasure," Ava agreed, and sipped her drink. "However, I'm more a fan of Idina Menzel in *Wicked*, myself."

Her gaze remained trained on Antonio. At least he had revealed his true nature at the earliest opportunity.

"I love her in the *Frozen* movies," Kenzie said. "You know, I heard a rumor that Elsa might be gay."

Ava's eyebrow arched, and she smirked in Antonio's general direction. "I'm pretty sure I heard the same rumor."

Kenzie stopped glaring at Antonio long enough to smile sideways at her. As their gazes met and held, Ava felt her heart rate pick up again. But this time, the feeling swooping through her nervous system was warm and good, just as it always was when she was this close to Kenzie.

"Wow, Kenzie, even for you that was a spectacular bomb," Matt said as he slid in next to Antonio.

"I know, right?" Kenzie sounded almost proud of her pool table fail.

The conversation moved on then, but the mutinous look Antonio sent Ava told her that for him, at least, the game wasn't over. She wasn't surprised when, after another full round of drinks, he asked Sloane about how Kenzie used to bring home stray animals when they were younger.

"That's right," Matt said, snapping his fingers. "Didn't your mom have to put a moratorium on the rescuing?"

"It was only a temporary break," Kenzie insisted.

"What kinds of animals?" Mika asked.

Sloane ticked them off on her fingers: "Cats, dogs, baby birds, even a pair of baby possums once."

"Didn't you say it wasn't just animals?" Antonio asked. He wasn't looking at Ava, but she could feel his malevolent energy trained squarely on her. "Didn't you say it was social outcasts, too?"

Beside her, Kenzie straightened. "I wouldn't say they were—"

But her tipsy sister interrupted. "Oh my god, it was totally people too! She would befriend these kids at our school who no one else would talk to, and she would make them feel like they were the most amazing people in the world. I still don't know how you do that, Kenz."

Kenzie pushed up her glasses. "Well, I know how it feels to not fit in. Besides, I seem to recall I wasn't the only one who was nice to those kids, Sloane."

"*Pfft*. Whatever." Sloane rolled her eyes, but she was smiling.

Was that what Ava was—an outcast who no one else would talk to, one of the many whom Kenzie had made feel special? She knew Antonio had manipulated the conversation to make her think that way, but the label still resonated a little too close for comfort. Her money and familial notoriety had made it difficult for her to form new relationships for much of her adult life, and since her father's murder and her brother's descent into chaos, the situation had only grown more tenuous. There was a reason she hadn't been on a date in more than a year. She'd convinced herself she didn't need emotional intimacy, but after being around Kenzie these past weeks, she was beginning to realize she had been mistaken about quite a few things.

But what if Antonio was right? What if Kenzie saw her as little more than a pity project? Ava hadn't forgotten how Kenzie had assured her sister that their relationship was only professional sometime between the interview and the night they ran into each other at Shiro Sushi.

"Is this a PSA?" Ava had joked during that first interview. But what if it wasn't a joke at all?

She lasted as long as she could, trying to keep her anxiety in check as Mika, AKA Detective Hansen, told a story about one of her coworkers who had recently rescued what she thought was a puppy from a local shelter only to learn that it was a wolf-dog hybrid. When Mika finished, Ava decided that enough time had passed for Antonio not to know that his little scheme had drawn blood.

"Excuse me," she said as neutrally as she could manage, and slipped out of the booth.

She could feel Kenzie's eyes on her as she walked toward the women's room, her gait surprisingly steady for her state of inebriation. God, why did she always do this? As soon as someone started to get too close, she found some excuse for why the friendship must be doomed. Except, if she were being honest, she didn't want only friendship from Kenzie. After more than a handful of "friends dates," Ava still couldn't tell if Kenzie's adorable blushes and lip bites meant the attraction was mutual or if, instead, they proved she was a clueless straight girl whose friends and family members would only ever see Ava as just another Westbrook.

It was this fear that made her return to the booth a few minutes later with her professional smile very much in place, phone held aloft as if she had received an important call. "It's been fun, but unfortunately, no rest for the wicked," she announced as she reached for her purse and jacket.

There was a round of good-natured boos, and Kenzie gazed up at her with a mildly distressed look, forehead creased in the way that always made Ava long to trail her thumb across the furrowed skin, smoothing away the wrinkles.

"Do you really have to go?" Kenzie asked.

"I do. It's already morning in Asia." She paused, adjusting the strap on her purse, tempted by Kenzie's pout to stay just a little longer. But then she caught Antonio staring her down, and yes, leaving was indeed the best course of action. She'd had too much whiskey to be at the top of her game. "Thanks for the lovely evening, though. Talk to you soon?"

Kenzie nodded. "Yeah. Of course."

"See you," Ava forced herself to say, smiling at the rest

of the table.

A chorus of friendly goodbyes—none of them Antonio's, she noted—followed her out of the warmly lit pub and onto the sidewalk beyond. She walked toward the nearest intersection, phone in hand. But instead of texting her car service, she kept walking. Ramón was off duty tonight, and she didn't feel like making small talk with one of the other drivers. Instead, she dialed up her favorite moody Adele playlist on her phone, plugged one ear bud in—it wasn't safe to walk alone with both in, according to her self-defense trainer—and headed down Queen Anne Ave toward Seattle's hidden skyline.

If she thought she heard a rush of air overhead a few times on her way home that night, well, she could be forgiven the flight of fancy, couldn't she? After all, she lived in a city where an honest-to-goddess super heroine roamed the skies, brave and self-sacrificing.

Which was so much more than Ava could say for herself.

CHAPTER SIX

"Come," D'aman said, holding out their hand.

Kenzie narrowed her eyes at her former mentor/current probable Alliance watchdog. "Why?"

"Because I've missed you and I'm in the mood to go out."

"I just got home," Kenzie complained, gesturing at the jacket she hadn't even had time to remove.

It was Saturday night, and she'd gone to dinner and drinks with Sloane and their friends, as usual. She'd invited Ava along, too, but Ava had her read receipts turned off—because of course she did—so Kenzie wasn't sure if she had read the message. She definitely hadn't responded. Maybe two nights in a row was too much socializing, or maybe she simply had other plans. Or maybe, a voice inside Kenzie's head kept whispering, her silence had to do with whatever Antonio had said to her the previous night. Either way, it had taken every bit of Kenzie's willpower not to do a fly-by of Hyperion Tower on her way home from the pub. Even she could see that such hovering (literally) was not warranted. Probably.

"I am aware you just returned," D'aman said in that

slightly amused, exaggeratedly patient way they had. "Now, come. I have some place I want to take you. It involves Bandal rum..."

Ooh, alien alcohol? Now that Kenzie thought about it, she wasn't all that tired. Grabbing her keys from the hook by the door, she left her studio and followed D'aman downstairs and out onto the street. But instead of turning toward Queen Anne Avenue like she'd expected, D'aman led her to the alley behind the school across the street.

"Where exactly—" Kenzie started. But she didn't get a chance to finish as, before her eyes, D'aman morphed from a tween-sized human into a full-grown Kreedilan. Kenzie glanced around quickly, but the alleyway was dark. "What are you doing?"

"Are you wearing your suit?" they asked, ignoring her question.

"Yes, but why?"

"You'll see," D'aman said, baring their teeth in a smile. And then they launched themselves into the air, dark body and darker clothing quickly blending into the night sky.

Wasn't D'aman supposed to keep Kenzie from behaving like a Zattalian? Huffing, she changed into her suit quickly, dropped her clothes inside the pitch-black schoolyard, and shot into the sky after her fellow alien.

Kreedilans could move, and Kenzie found she had to push herself to keep up. The night air was cool up above the cloud layer, the moon bright overhead, and Kenzie laughed out loud as D'aman trolled her, allowing her to nearly catch up before shooting out of reach again. They led her away from flight traffic and out over the darker land mass east of Puget Sound, accelerating so quickly that Kenzie half expected to hear a sonic boom. Together, they streaked through the air too fast to talk, too fast to marvel at the land below or the stars above. All Kenzie could do was reach out with all of her senses to make sure they weren't about to hit a passenger jet or a flock of geese or anything else that might be moving through the sky at a fraction of their speed.

It was D'aman, though, so she already knew she was perfectly safe. Kreedilans didn't need sight or hearing to find a path through the sky. They could reach out with their minds and determine if any other sentient beings were near. A handy party trick, really. But Kenzie had been on her own with her powers for so long that she couldn't quite convince herself to relax and cede the safety of others to anyone else, not even D'aman.

Less than fifteen minutes later, Kenzie felt a gentle touch in her mind and pictured the word "Slow." Another minute of gradually reduced speeds, and they were there: Portland, Oregon, judging from the bridges crisscrossing the river that edged a vibrant downtown. Even more than Seattle, Portland was known for being especially welcoming to off-world citizens. Kenzie wasn't all that surprised when D'aman touched down in an alley and led her to an unmarked door.

"What is this place?" she asked, her voice hushed.

"It is a bar." D'aman unsnapped a pocket on their jacket and pulled out what looked like a plain black headband. "Remove your cowl, please."

She did as they requested, holding still as they placed the headband over her hair. A slight hum sounded from it, and all at once she wondered if she was making a terrible mistake. What if this wasn't D'aman at all but a different Kreedilan who was luring her into a trap and—

"What was my favorite song in eighth grade?" she demanded.

Their movements paused. "I believe it was by a band known as the Flaming Lips, but I do not remember the title."

When she was first with the Shepherd-Hendersons,

she had gone through an emo music stage. *Yoshimi Battles the Pink Robots* was one of her favorite albums back then, as strange as it was wonderful, and "All We Have is Now" used to be her favorite song. If she was being honest, it still was.

"It is I, youngling," D'aman said. "Shall I share one of our mutual memories to allay your concerns?"

"Yes, please."

D'aman closed their eyes, and soon Kenzie saw it: the first time they had gone flying together and Kenzie could barely make it off the ground. And yet, she had been so spectacularly happy at the sensation of moving freely through the air. When the lesson ended, though, the guilt at feeling light and free while the rest of her people were dead and gone had brought her to her knees. The memory was from D'aman's perspective, and it included details she could not have known, such as how her pain had reminded them of their own at surviving the loss of their family during the war with the Vinckettos.

"It is you," she said. "I'm sorry, I shouldn't have…"

"Do not apologize. I have taught you well if you are alert to the dangers of this world. This is why I am giving you the headband to wear tonight. It is of Taammen origin and will change your appearance slightly, thereby allowing you to move among the bar's patrons with impunity."

"Slightly?" Kenzie enquired.

"Your hair, eyes, and clothes. Or so I was told."

Native Taammens, Kenzie remembered, possessed a form of telekinesis that gave them the ability to cloak not only themselves but external objects, too. "But if we're going to be among aliens, why do I need to hide my identity?"

"Because even among our kind, there are those who would sell you out. Some for money, but more in order to save themselves or their loved ones."

Kenzie was still absorbing this information when D'aman turned and knocked on the door in a specific, elaborate pattern.

She had heard of these—secret pop-up alien bars, because you couldn't exactly advertise such an establishment. That would be literal suicide. Even before Sentinel made the bullying of off-worlders international news, aliens had been disappearing and turning up dead almost since the first year the Alliance had made contact. Maybe not frequently enough to trigger a universal investigation, but often enough that aliens living on Earth understood that gathering in public spaces came with risks. The only option for semi-public entertainment was to continuously move their meeting spaces and hope the haters didn't catch them.

The door opened a crack, and D'aman leaned forward, still in their Kreedilan form. A small gasp sounded, and then Kenzie heard chains and bolts sliding out of the way. The door opened, and a tiny Elasion stepped out, beaming up at D'aman.

"My friend!" the Elasion crowed in a tinny, high-pitched voice. "I thought you would never get here."

"We flew as quickly as was wise," D'aman replied, their voice sounding even deeper than usual in contrast.

Elasions were small, red-skinned humanoids with a fondness for metal trinkets. The creature facing them clanged a bit as she (Kenzie was pretty sure they were a she) exchanged a brief hug with D'aman and then turned to gaze upon her.

"Is this her?" the Elasion enquired. "Is this Galaxy Girl?"

Kenzie glanced uncertainly at D'aman.

"Don't worry," D'aman said. "Melodie agreed to have her memory expunged later as long as she could have one drink with you."

"I am so happy to meet you," Melodie said, beaming up at her. "You are doing so much for all of us by taking up the hero's mantle."

"Oh, well, thanks," Kenzie said, smiling back tentatively.

"Come in, come in," Melodie added, leaning her head out to case the alley.

"It's safe," D'aman assured her, and waved Kenzie ahead.

The interior was dark and cramped, and Kenzie frowned slightly. Then she squinted at the far wall, focusing her super vision. The real bar lay beyond this room, windowless and wide, teeming with color and motion.

"Follow me," Melodie said, cackling as she gazed up at Kenzie.

Another secret knock, and two enormous bouncers with rhino-like heads—Troolimpigos from the Prinzian system, if Kenzie remembered correctly—asked Melodie for the password.

"RRsstthurissmy," she said, almost hissing the word, and the bouncers waved her inside.

Kenzie honestly had no idea what language the password had been in. After all, it had been more than a dozen years since she'd come to Earth, and the study of off-world languages would have made her stand out in a way that her adopted parents weren't comfortable with.

She stepped forward to follow Melodie into the bar, but the bouncers shifted together, forming an intimidating wall to block her path. She probably could have knocked them over with her pinkie finger, but she wasn't in the mood for a confrontation. Not that she ever was, really.

"No humans," the two creatures said in unison.

"I'm not human," she said, the statement surprisingly

freeing. It wasn't often she could declare her non-human status in a public space. In fact, she was pretty sure she had never once done so.

"Prove it," one of the bouncers said.

She levitated off the floor, and the Troolimpigos exchanged a look before stepping aside and allowing her entry.

They hadn't made it far before another alien blocked their path. This one was tall and thin with green scales and holes where most humanoids had ears. "No humans," they grated.

"It's okay. She's with me," D'aman said, their arm around her shoulder, eyes boring into the hostile alien's eyes.

The green man faltered and stepped back, gaze suddenly blank in a way that let Kenzie know D'aman had used their Kreedilan powers to change his mind for him. She glanced up at her former mentor, her brow wrinkling.

"It appears I should have requested a non-human disguise for you," D'aman said, ushering her after Melodie.

Kenzie was still stuck on her former mentor's use of their powers. Why was D'aman disregarding Alliance caseworker rules and regulations left and right? The only reason Kenzie could think of was…

She stopped at the edge of the busy room and stared at D'aman. "You're not working for the Alliance anymore, are you?"

Melodie, who had been leading them toward the bar, looked back, startled. "The Alliance? You worked for those scum?"

Scum? Kenzie had never heard the Alliance called that. But then again, she had never been around many aliens, other than D'aman.

"Not for a long time," D'aman assured Melodie. They

glanced back at Kenzie. "First the rum, then we talk."

They found seats at a booth near a pool table and a jukebox that was spitting out 1980s New Wave hits that seemed to match the optics perfectly. The setting was unremarkable enough, typical American late twentieth century furnishings and decorations, but Kenzie couldn't help staring around at the clientele. Some looked mostly human like her, save for pointed ears or ridged skulls or the occasional extra appendage, but many of the bar's customers were more diverse than she'd ever seen on Earth, with shapes and sizes that varied widely from the typical humanoid model. For a moment, she felt like she was inside *Star Wars*. Had the Alliance approved the settlement of these particular aliens on Earth, or were they here to hide from the reach of the Alliance?

"I didn't know you worked for those bastards," Melodie said once they were seated with glasses of Bandal rum, her voice less cheerful than when she'd greeted them in the alley.

"You did not ask," D'aman said. "But yes, I served as a refugee caseworker for four decades. My loyalty earned me the right to settle on Earth after I retired."

"So that's how you ended up here." Melodie's arm clinked as she raised her glass to drink, the motion disturbing dozens of bracelets of varying metals, some that appeared to be from Earth and others not so much.

"You're retired?" Kenzie asked. "Why didn't you mention that before?"

"We were interrupted," D'aman reminded her. "If you had ever invited me for coffee, I would have."

"It's only been a few days."

"Have you not flown about the city saving people in that time?"

"You're saying I should have let that bus fall off the West Seattle Bridge this morning and gone for coffee with you instead?"

D'aman paused before inclining their head. "Point taken."

"I watched you save that bus on my phone," Melodie put in. "Tell me, what's it like to rescue people?"

No one had ever asked Kenzie that before. She paused for a moment, and then she smiled at Melodie. "It feels good. Really good. Like maybe I finally know why I survived."

D'aman reached over and covered her hand. "I'm pleased you are becoming who you were always meant to be."

Kenzie stared at them. "If you thought that, why didn't you tell me?"

D'aman's gaze was steady. "It was against regulation. Now that I am no longer in the Alliance's employ, I can be more honest, which is why I am telling you that you must be careful. There are forces at work in the universe you don't understand. If you will have me, I would like to stay in Seattle and help where I can."

"Help—like a team?"

"Like a team," they agreed.

"That would be amazing." Having Sloane and Matt assisting her Galaxy Girl work was good, but D'aman was an ancient, powerful being with oodles more experience at all of this. Having them on her side would be a game changer.

Melodie shook her head. "I wish I could remember all of this tomorrow. My friends would be so jealous that I got to meet you!"

D'aman nodded sagely. "All we have is now."

"I thought you didn't remember the song title?"

"It came to me."

Sure it did. But Kenzie only shook her head and

smiled at her former mentor/new superhero partner. "What are you going to wear? I could have Sloane get another suit for you…" She trailed off as she realized that a shapeshifting Kreedilan probably didn't need help in the costume department.

"I have some ideas," D'aman said, stoic face revealing nothing.

Kenzie was sure they did.

This was not how she'd thought her Saturday night would end, she reflected a little while later, warm inside and out from the company, conversation, and alien alcohol. She had assumed she would lay in bed for a while unable to sleep—like usual lately—before giving up to binge-watch something old and familiar on Netflix. Instead, here she was in Portland, having a drink with a Kreedilan and an Elasion at a pop-up bar with aliens of all persuasions around her laughing, playing pool, and singing along with Depeche Mode and New Order. Good thing Zattalians didn't need much sleep—another alien advantage Sloane had always envied.

The flight home was slower. D'aman insisted they take their time since flying with alien alcohol in their system might not be illegal, according to Washington law, but it certainly required more care. Kenzie didn't mind. The breakneck pace of their trip down to Portland had been exhilarating, but she preferred a slower pace, one that allowed her to catch glimpses of the lives of the people whose homes she was flying over. D'aman was quiet beside her, and Kenzie noticed how comfortable she felt in their presence—safe and calm, cared for and seen. The idea of teaming up with D'aman had made her so happy that she'd even forgotten about Ava and her unanswered text. For a little while, anyway.

It was nearly four in the morning when they landed near the schoolyard to retrieve her clothing. She had returned the headband already, so by the time they entered their building, she was back to her usual self. The sense of freedom she'd experienced at the bar had slowly faded as they'd flown home, but the memory of how it had felt to be her genuine self—even outwardly disguised as another—still lingered.

"Thank you," she said as they climbed the stairs.

"Thank *you*," D'aman, back in their human form, replied, and reached for her hand.

At first, Kenzie thought they wanted to hold her hand, but then she realized D'aman had pressed something into her palm. They paused together on the landing to the third floor, and Kenzie peered down at the object. It was a small, beautiful ring with what appeared to be sapphires and diamonds set in a delicate silver band. "This is beautiful, but…"

"Press the button on the side," D'aman instructed her, pointing out the tiny bit of silver she'd missed.

She did and watched as the sapphire in the center flipped to reveal a second, hidden button.

"If you need me, this ring emits a pulse at a frequency only you and I can detect. When I hear it, I will open my mind. Do you remember how to reach out to me?"

"*Yes*," she thought, projecting her inner voice in the way her parents had taught her when she was barely old enough to speak.

"*Well done.*" They smiled at her. "Just like riding a bicycle, as the humans say."

She smiled back and reached for her friend, wrapping her arms around them. "I'm so happy you came back."

"I am, too," D'aman murmured. Then they pulled back and winked at her. "Say hello to Sloane for me."

"What—?" she started, but then she merely shook her head. Of course Sloane was here. "Can I tell her it's really you?"

"You may," D'aman said, and waved as they disappeared into the third-floor corridor.

As she climbed the final set of stairs, Kenzie smoothed her finger over the ring, wondering what D'aman had meant by mysterious forces at work. Did it have anything to do with Melodie's obvious disgust at finding out D'aman had worked for the Alliance? Not everyone in the universe appreciated the Alliance's rule, Kenzie knew. She flashed back to her travels with her parents and the fleet, picturing the mining colonies that provided the materials required to build and power space-faring crafts; the trading posts where citizens of all planets could find what they needed to set up a homestead or manage a migrant fleet; the farm planets that grew food for much of the Alliance's population.

What would her life have been like if she had been placed with a family in one of those places? The Alliance had strict rules about where—and how—Zattalians were allowed to live, D'aman had once informed her. With great power came great responsibility, and her ancestors had not always demonstrated the wisdom to handle that responsibility. It was D'aman's job to help her learn how to use her powers wisely and grow into the type of citizen the Alliance wished her to be.

At the time, Kenzie had thought she understood what D'aman wanted her to learn, but now she wondered. She'd been a child still when she arrived on Earth, reeling from the loss of her family and uncertain what direction her life should take. The Shepherd-Hendersons had offered her love and support, and because of the stability they'd provided, she'd not only healed but had even flourished. When her new family told her that she needed to remain hidden in order to stay safe, she accepted their instructions without question, knowing they cared for her as much as she cared for them.

But had denying her alien identity been the right thing to do? Keeping her cut off from her birthright—and from her fellow off-worlders—had protected her, but she didn't need that protection anymore. She was fully grown and fully powered now, and she had so much to offer, both to humans and to her fellow aliens. For so many years she had been content to fly under the radar—or not fly, as the case might be—but now she was realizing that she didn't want to deny who she was anymore. She was tired of living a fractured existence.

No one was around, so Kenzie blurred down the hall to her unit and let herself in, closing the door quietly. It didn't matter how softly she moved, though. She'd barely stepped out of her shoes when she heard Sloane stirring in the dark loft.

"Kenzie?"

"Shh," Kenzie whispered, floating up to smile at her sister. Sloane was sitting up in bed, rubbing her eyes and yawning. "Go back to sleep."

Sloane made an adorable grouchy noise and lay back, snoring slightly while Kenzie got ready for bed. But as soon as Kenzie lay down beside her, Sloane popped back up, rubbing her face again.

"Where were you?"

"Out," Kenzie said. "I'll tell you in the morning, okay?"

"No," her sister said plaintively. "Tell me now. I've been waiting for you for hours."

"I thought you were with Mika."

"I was, but then the sensor went off and you vanished clear off the—" She blinked and clapped a hand over her mouth, but it was too late.

Kenzie sat up and reached for the bedside lamp. "The

sensor, Sloane?"

"Um, I might have set up a motion detector on your block so I would know if you flew somewhere," Sloane admitted, sounding only a little guilty. "Which was obviously good thinking on my part. Where did you go tonight, and who were you with?"

Kenzie wanted to be irritated with her sister, she really did, but she was too excited to tell Sloane about D'aman and the bar. Besides, given she could eavesdrop on any conversation in her general vicinity if she so chose, being cranky about Sloane's low-accuracy tech seemed a bit uncool.

When Kenzie finished recounting her evening's activities, Sloane sat back with an extra pillow against her belly, shaking her head. "I can't believe that Susan Cheng chick is actually D'aman."

"I know, right? I was about to throw them through the window the other night."

"That would have been classic—a Kreedilan versus a Zattalian."

Kenzie laughed. "Totally. Like something out of the mid-seventeen-thousands."

"I'll have to take your word for that." Sloane paused, her eyes on Kenzie, expression uncharacteristically gentle. "It's good to see you smiling."

"What are you talking about?"

"Hello—your usually sunny disposition was noticeably MIA at the pub tonight."

"No, it wasn't."

"Yes, it was."

Kenzie could feel her forehead furrow and her shoulders hunch, and she tried to distract herself by picking at a thread that had begun to unravel from her green and blue Seahawks blanket.

Sloane reached over and pressed her twitchy fingers. "You don't have to answer if you don't want to, but does your death-glare at Antonio earlier have anything to do with Ava?"

Kenzie shifted, looking into her sister's warm, understanding eyes, and all at once it didn't seem to matter that she'd never told Sloane about her other crushes on girls. This was her sister who she could tell anything. "Maybe?"

"What's going on with you two, anyway?" Sloane asked, her hand still covering Kenzie's.

She sighed, slouching lower. "I don't know. I mean, I think there's something there, but you know I'm not good at reading the signals."

"These signals are pretty hard to miss," Sloane said, laughing a little.

"Really?" Kenzie asked, hope rising.

"Um, yeah. Pretty sure you could see them from space."

Wow. She was being so cool. And yes, obviously, Sloane was queer herself, but she had been so against Kenzie having even a casual friendship with Ava in the beginning that the change felt seismic. "Sometimes I think that, but then at other times I'm like, not only is she human but she's also this literal billionaire who's older and could have anyone she wanted..." She trailed off. Sloane was gripping her fingers so tightly they probably would have broken if Kenzie had been human.

"Are you—you're talking about Ava? Ava *Westbrook*?"

She frowned. "Well, yeah. You asked what was going on with us."

"I meant you and Antonio," Sloane said, staring at her as if she had suddenly morphed into a Troolimpigo. "I thought you were mad at him because he spent so much time talking to Ava last night."

"Why would I be—*oh*." Sloane had thought she was jealous. Of *Ava*. Kenzie tried not to listen to the sudden staccato of her sister's heart. She wasn't being cool, after all. "Forget it," she muttered, pulling her hand away. "It doesn't matter."

"No, it does." Sloane took an audible breath and released it slowly. "So, to be clear, you're telling me you have feelings for Ava? Of the romantic variety?"

Kenzie shrugged, pulling at the thread and watching as the edge of the blanket fell apart.

"I didn't even know that was a possibility for you." When Kenzie stayed silent, Sloane added carefully, "And is this the first time you've, um, been interested in a woman?"

"Not really. But it's never been this, I don't know, *intense* before," she admitted, staring down at her hands.

"Okay." Sloane released another breath. "Then why didn't you say something last year when I was freaking out about being gay?"

"I did!" Kenzie's hands flapped semi-wildly. "I said that it was perfectly normal to have feelings for someone, no matter their gender, and that same-sex pairings were super common among Zattalians!"

"That's anecdotal evidence," Sloane said. "That's not about you personally. I mean, not that you owe me or anything. It's just, it feels like maybe you didn't trust me."

"That's not it," Kenzie said, groaning and slouching even more. "It just didn't seem important when I'm destined to end up a 40-year-old virgin!"

Sloane laughed again and leaned into her side. "Pretty sure that will only happen if you want it to, Kenz."

"I'm not interested in Antonio, okay?"

"I wasn't talking about him."

Kenzie peeked sideways at her sister. "You weren't?"

"Nope."

Kenzie covered her face. "But she's a Westbrook! I can't—I don't even… Seriously, what am I supposed to do?"

Sloane wrapped her arms around Kenzie and rested her chin on her shoulder. "You're supposed to keep on being your fabulous self. Just, you know, maybe a little more fabulous than anyone knew."

Which was cute and all, but Kenzie wasn't in the mood to laugh. She was ready to wallow in angst, not find humor in the ridiculous *Romeo and Juliet* scene she was currently reenacting.

"Think about the costume possibilities!" Sloane continued, nudging her. "You could add glitter to the cowl. Or, I know, you could be the first superhero to wear a rainbow headband! If D'aman really does start heroing with you, maybe they would wear one too, you know, in solidarity?"

After a long pause, Kenzie huffed grumpily, "Bisexual pride is represented by blue and pink overlapping triangles, not your silly gay rainbow."

Sloane laughed softly. "That's my girl."

Kenzie pulled away enough to pummel her arm. "It's not funny."

"It's a little funny."

"I'm serious, Sloane. You're not supposed to just let me off the hook."

"I'm your big sister. It's my job to make sure you're happy. Besides, I *am* gay, you know. That makes me a pretty safe person to come out to."

"That's not what I meant." When Sloane's head tilted slightly, Kenzie added, "You just came out last year, and here I am making everything all about me again. It's like it's all I know how to do."

Sloane had struggled to accept her lesbian identity for

a while, which had led to a variety of unhealthy coping mechanisms. She was happy in who she was now, but that peace had only come with a lot of hard work. Kenzie didn't want to seem like she was showing up Sloane in some way just because she wasn't tortured about her own sexuality. So she liked guys and girls. It wasn't like she had much of an opportunity to date either. Pretending to be human made it difficult to manage a relationship with one.

"You're not making it about you," Sloane said. "You're *being* you. There's a difference. Although, I do have to say that Ava Westbrook might not be the safest person for you to have feelings for. I mean, her family is just a little bit terrifying…"

"Don't you think I know that?" She looked down at her lap again, fingers resuming their restless transit along the blanket's edge. "I haven't heard from her since last night, though, so maybe it won't be a problem."

Sloane snorted. "I seriously doubt that."

Kenzie glanced up, hope stirring again in her foolish, romantic heart. "What do you mean?"

"I've seen the way she looks at you. We all have, Kenz. I just didn't realize there was a chance you might feel the same."

Kenzie scarcely breathed, which wasn't a problem because not only did Zattalians not require as much sleep as humans, they also didn't need as much oxygen. "How does she look at me?"

Sloane rolled her eyes. "Are you really going to make me say it?"

"Yes!"

"Fine. She looks at you like you're the mac to her cheese. The ketchup to her fries. The sprinkles to her freaking sundae."

"Really?" Kenzie felt a small smile steal across her lips, quickly blooming. "She does?"

Sloane nodded and smiled back. "Really. You're incredible, Kenzie, and even if you can't see it, I'm guessing Ava Westbrook does. As does Antonio, obviously."

"Eww." Kenzie made a face. "No, he doesn't."

"Come *on*. That dude has been in love with you for years."

"Well, he shouldn't be. I don't want him to be."

"I don't think that's how emotions generally work. The eggs to your bacon," she added.

"The peanut butter to your jelly," Kenzie replied.

"The ice to your cream."

"The turkey to your stuffing."

At that one, they both cracked up, and Sloane leaned her head on Kenzie's shoulder. "Love you, Kenzie."

"I love you, too, Slo-mo."

Coming out wasn't nearly as scary as Sloane had always made it seem. Even if Ava never spoke to her again—and the thought made Kenzie feel cold and hot at once—at least she'd given Kenzie this.

#

Ava stared out her window. It was a cloudy Sunday morning, and the streets 20 stories below were emptier than usual. She hadn't seen anyone since rising, nor had she spoken to a single soul. Somehow, though, she felt off-kilter.

Except her bad mood wasn't exactly a mystery, was it?

Her phone vibrated on the breakfast bar beside her. Slowly, she turned it over, brow clearing as she saw Bea's name.

"U better not be working thru the weekend!" her best friend had written.

Ava typed, "Nothing else to do around here." Then she added a silly sad emoji and hit send.

"I bet there are plenty of people to do, tho."

Ava laughed out loud at the characteristically cheeky response. Her amusement didn't last long, though. Speaking of hot, unattainable women... Ava squinted at the text thread below Bea's. Kenzie had sent her a message the previous day, inviting her out to dinner and drinks with the crew. Ava, surprised to hear from her after bolting from the pub the night before, couldn't immediately decide how to respond. The text was still sitting unanswered in her inbox, taunting Ava with her own social awkwardness.

She didn't want to ghost Kenzie; she liked her, probably more than she should. That was the problem, actually, because at some point, she was going to have to come out to Kenzie. She didn't think Kenzie was homophobic, not when she obviously adored her gay sister and Sloane's equally gay girlfriend. But even though it didn't seem likely, Ava couldn't stop worrying that Kenzie might respond badly. Having a queer sister was different from having someone you'd been actively friend-dating come out to you, and Ava wasn't ready to lose her. Or, more accurately, she wasn't prepared to be rejected. Because that was what it came down to, wasn't it?

Either way, a confrontation was inevitable. While Ava didn't advertise her sexuality publicly—mostly out of deference to her family's wishes—she also didn't hide it. After a lifetime of familial secrets and lies, the level of dishonesty required to live in a closet didn't suit her. She was going to have to have The Talk with Kenzie, and sooner rather than later if Friday night was any indication.

But not right this second. Right now, she needed to flood her system with endorphins and then, unfortunately, she did have to pop upstairs and get some work done. She and Victoria were scheduled to attend a business luncheon the following day at the Guild House, a former church turned event space that happened to share a lobby with

Hyperion Tower, and she wanted to read up on her fellow attendees ahead of time. The luncheon was supposedly a meet and greet for local business executives, but it was being hosted by Americans for Fairness in Tech (AFT), a national group committed to lobbying Congress to pass legislation that would allow humans to incorporate unpatented alien technology into their own designs with a one-time licensing payment rather than with the permanent royalties dictated by the Alliance. No doubt there would be a presentation that bordered on propaganda, but that was the price of doing business. While AFT's cause may be more the rest of her family's speed, Ava understood that sometimes it was necessary to work with people whose views did not match her own.

Besides, this way she would know which local leaders she needed to keep an eye on moving forward. No doubt there were social conservatives even in Seattle's relatively progressive halls of power. The alien-human question had a way of bringing out the worst in people, in Ava's experience.

She pictured Kenzie again, imagining the disappointment that would darken her beautiful eyes if she found out that Ava—in addition to ignoring her texts—would be schmoozing with a group of rich, white men who literally believed that aliens were sub-human, and for a moment she considered letting Victoria attend the luncheon by herself. But the CEO couldn't be trusted to amplify Hyperion's new branding, and besides, the meeting was invitation-only and hadn't been publicized. It seemed likely that Kenzie would never even find out about the event. And what she didn't know couldn't hurt her, could it?

At least, that was what Ava told herself as she placed her lone plate and mug in the sink and went to change into workout gear.

~

The burst of gunfire was followed, predictably, by screams and general panic. Ava didn't join in, however. As the daughter of a Marine general, she wasn't bothered by gunfire unless it was directed at people, and these particular shots had been of the warning variety. Unfortunately, they'd damaged part of the historic building's terra cotta molding, but at least they'd missed the plethora of stained-glass windows in the domed roof. Guild House was the oldest remaining Beaux-style building in America, which was why Hyperion Tower's builders had preserved most of the original structure in the shadow of the modern skyscraper. Destroying such carefully conserved architectural history now would be tragic.

While people around her stumbled over chairs in their haste to retreat, Ava watched from the second row as the trio of masked gunmen who had leapt onstage shoved the speaker at the podium to the floor.

"Stop, all of you!" the group's apparent leader bellowed into the microphone, military rifle held loosely at his side. "Remain calm and you won't be hurt. But if you try anything, my friend here will be forced to react." He gestured toward one of his companions who had his rifle trained on the crowd of thirty or so executives.

It took a few minutes and several more threats, but eventually the crowd calmed. Everyone took their seats again, some people crying quietly and others gripping the hands of whomever was closest. Ava, meanwhile, held her phone out of sight and hit the panic button her security detail had installed. They would contact the authorities and then, if she didn't respond to their text with a pre-arranged password, they would attempt to extract her themselves.

With the crowd under control, the third assailant

pulled an iPhone out of a hidden pocket and nodded at the leader.

"Right. Here's the deal. All of you should be ashamed of yourselves!" the masked intruder said into the microphone, glaring around the room. "Stealing from immigrants and refugees might be a time-honored American tradition, but that doesn't make it right. We're here to let you know that off-worlders are not commodities you can buy and sell. Aliens are sentient beings who have families and hopes and dreams, and more importantly, a guarantee of protection from the Alli—"

The door to the main room slammed open again, and before Ava could even blink, a blurred form appeared onstage. Within seconds, the three assailants had been disarmed and tied up with—was that a rope from one of the dome's many curtains? Whatever it was, it held the three dazed men securely in a pile behind the podium, their horribly bent guns well out of reach.

Galaxy Girl, Ava realized, feeling a slight chill shiver through her frame. She was here in this very room. First Panopticon and now an AFT meeting—once again, Seattle's new off-world hero had come to the rescue of human beings who didn't necessarily think she belonged on Earth.

Ava's phone buzzed, and she quickly typed in the passphrase to prevent her security team from rushing in, guns blazing: "ALL IS WELL." With Galaxy Girl's arrival, the danger appeared to have significantly lessened.

The hero stepped to the podium, ducking her head almost shyly. "Hi, folks. No need to worry. The authorities are on their way. Is anyone hurt?"

The executives exchanged bewildered glances, Ava noted, but no one seemed any worse for wear. Except, perhaps, the attackers.

"Well, that's great," Galaxy Girl said, and Ava could

hear the smile in her electronically modified voice. "I'm glad to hear it. I'll just keep you company until—" Her head cocked as her gaze locked on Ava. "Av—uh, Miss Westbrook?"

Seattle's alien hero knew her by sight? That couldn't be good. "Yes?" she said, her voice carrying easily across the scant space that separated them. She even managed to keep it steady despite the irrational fear spiking inside as she folded her arms across her chest. "Can I help you?"

"No, um, that is..." She looked away and said, "Does anyone need anything? Anything at all?"

Silence settled over the room until a muttered expletive drew everyone's attention to the assailants, who were currently trying to extract themselves from the hasty restraint job.

"Oh, right," the hero said. "Um, okay, just hold tight. I mean, all of you, not them! It shouldn't be too long now. I'm just going to..." She waved at the trio on stage and blurred to their side, applying pressure to keep them in place. But she wasn't unkind in her ministrations, merely efficient. Ava actually thought she heard the masked hero apologize when one of the assailants complained.

The crowd muttered amongst themselves, and several people began to gather their things as if they planned to beat a hasty retreat. But Ava remained where she was, frowning at the scene before her. Galaxy Girl's awkward blustering and unexpected kindness reminded Ava of someone. She was sure she almost had it when the hero suddenly glanced toward the back of the auditorium and announced, "Oh, good. They're here."

Ava glanced back but didn't see anything. Then, a moment later, the doors flew open and a swarm of black-clad agents streamed in. Somehow, Ava was entirely unsurprised to see Sloane Shepherd in their midst. Panopticon's field office was located only a few blocks away, and the terrorist attack had technically qualified as alien-related even before Galaxy Girl showed up. But still, Ava couldn't figure out how they'd gotten to the scene so quickly—until she watched a spectacled man in his early forties hurry over to Galaxy Girl, Sloane in his wake.

Well, that was certainly new, Ava thought, trying to listen in to the trio's conversation and failing. Panopticon working with an alien vigilante? She could only imagine what her father and brother would have thought of that development. As she pictured her brother punching a wall in his prison cell, she felt a momentary surge of satisfaction. She wasn't the only one who noticed the odd optics, either. More than one of her fellow business leaders caught the scene on their phones as lower-ranking Panopticon agents tried to usher them away. Even Ava managed a quick photo before Seattle's new hero disappeared in a mind-bending blur. One moment Galaxy Girl was standing next to the two agents, and the next she simply wasn't.

Ava blinked at the faint rush of air that enveloped her. What did it mean that the alien hero knew her name? Another question occurred to her: Did Sloane know who Galaxy Girl was in real life? Did *Kenzie*?

Victoria materialized at her elbow. "Why did that creature call you by name?" she demanded, lips pursed in displeasure.

Ava wasn't proud to admit she'd forgotten about her cousin, but that didn't stop her from sniping, "I'm fine, thanks. And you?"

Victoria waved an impatient hand. "You know very well that no one was hurt by those ridiculous intruders. But answer my question. How does that alien know you?"

"Isn't it obvious? I'd be willing to bet she knows you, too," Ava replied, her voice cool.

Her gaze shifted over her cousin's shoulder, drawn to

Kenzie's sister. A moment later, Sloane glanced in her direction and froze, her eyes fixed on Ava, mouth tightening into an even grimmer line. An odd presentiment hovered again at the edge of Ava's consciousness, only to be vanquished by a rush of dismay. So much for Kenzie not knowing about her presence at this cursed meeting.

At least she probably wouldn't find out any time soon. Despite an over-abundance of attorneys threatening political ramifications, Panopticon's agents took their time deposing each attendee one by one in the main event space and in the conference rooms that lined the exterior hall. An Army lieutenant, according to the insignia on his jacket, was just about to interview Ava in one of the smaller rooms when a female agent breezed in. Sloane.

"I've got this," Kenzie's sister said.

"Are you sure—"

She glared. "I said, I've got it."

Ava hid a smile as the younger man fell back quickly. It was hard to believe that Sloane and sweet, nerdy Kenzie hailed from the same family. But then Ava remembered the touch of steel in Kenzie's voice and eyes when she'd confronted Antonio the other night and, yeah, she could see the family resemblance. As an adoptee herself, she knew that biology wasn't everything.

"Ava," Sloane said when they were alone.

"Sloane," she returned, hands folded on top of the table.

"Would you like to share what you remember?"

All business, which was exactly what Ava would have expected. She gave Sloane a quick rundown of events, increasingly aware of the other woman's impatience brimming just beneath the surface.

When she finished, Sloane nodded shortly and said, "That matches what we've heard from other attendees." She glanced down at the unopened file on the table, drumming her fingers against it.

Ava waited, but when Sloane remained silent, she asked, "Am I free to go, then? I need to get back to work."

Sloane looked up, brow furrowed. "Actually, I do have another question. What the hell are you even doing here, Ava?"

And there it was, the accusation Ava had been waiting for. Shoulders straightening, she matched the other woman's scowl with one of her own. "I wasn't aware I was required to run my work engagements past your office."

Sloane ignored her sarcasm. "You have to know how this looks—Hyperion's top two executives attending a meeting sponsored by AFT?"

Ava knew exactly how it looked, but it would have been nice if Sloane, whom she had started to think of as a friend, had given her the benefit of the doubt. Apparently in her mind, Ava was still first and foremost a Westbrook. Good to know.

"I think it looks like we attended a business luncheon with excellent networking opportunities," Ava replied, adding an insolent smirk to needle Sloane even further.

"Are you serious right now? Because I seem to recall you telling my little sister that you cared more about saving the planet than persecuting off-worlders. Or was that just a smoke screen?"

Off-worlders was the politically correct term for aliens living on Earth. Sloane, it appeared, was one of the many Panopticon agents who joined the bureau to protect alien refugees from people like Nick and his minions. Did Sloane know an off-worlder? Ava pictured her talking to Galaxy Girl earlier. Were they friends in real life?

"Well?" Sloane prodded, her frown borderline menacing.

"I'm not sure what my business interests have to do with your investigation, Agent Shepherd," Ava said frostily.

"They have everything to do with my investigation," Sloane said. "But if you're not prepared to discuss business, fine. Let's get personal. What are you playing at with Kenzie?"

Ava paused. "I don't know what you mean," she said, even as her guilt at ignoring Kenzie resurfaced.

"I think you do." Sloane stared at her silently, waiting.

This was an interview tactic Ava had been known to rely on herself. Most people couldn't bear to sit with silence and, inevitably, would start talking to alleviate their own nervousness. But Ava wasn't most people. She lifted an eyebrow at Sloane and sat just as silently, focusing on keeping her breathing even and regular.

After a minute, Sloane sighed and ran a hand through her short hair. "Just, don't toy with her, okay? She's more fragile than she seems." And with that cryptic comment, she stood up and headed for the door.

"So, I'm free to go, then?" Ava called after her.

"If we have additional questions, we'll be in touch," Sloane said over her shoulder, and exited the room.

Muttering to herself about arrogant agents, Ava pulled her things together and left Guild House, taking the steps that led directly from the former church down into the glass-walled lobby of Hyperion Tower, built to encompass one exterior wall of the historic landmark. Hyperion's security chief met her there with a team and, once she'd assured them she was unhurt, escorted her to the express elevator at the far end of the elevator bank, murmuring into the microphones fastened to their lapels as they went.

The sunlight streaming into the high-ceilinged lobby was still bright, the murmur of voices animated, and yet Ava felt as if the world had changed during the past few hours. Not only had she been threatened with potential death—if only because the terrorists hadn't seemed very competent at handling their weapons—but she'd also come face to face with Seattle's local superhero. Even more disturbing was the fact that Kenzie's sister appeared to think that Ava's presence at the meeting meant she might be in cahoots with her brother's followers. Sloane had already viewed Ava as a threat to Kenzie's safety before she'd aligned herself with a regressive group like AFT, separated from Sentinel only by a matter of degrees. But instead of assuring Sloane that she had no love for AFT, Ava had resorted to sarcasm to cover her hurt.

In the elevator, she leaned against the back wall, trying to sort through her emotions. She may not have panicked like some of the other meeting attendees, but the adrenaline that had initially coursed through her system had long since faded, and now she wasn't sure what she felt. As the car glided almost silently to the executive floor, she pulled up the photo she'd snapped of Galaxy Girl. The lighting at the edge of the stage wasn't great, but there was something undeniably attractive about a woman with the power to do what she'd done at Guild House. Attractive, and yet, just a tad frightening, too. Because what was to stop her from doing whatever she wanted? Or, for that matter, renting her powers to the highest bidder? There was the blackmail factor to consider, too. If someone like Ava's brother were to discover the Seattle hero's true identity, it could be catastrophic. Those hungry for power would use any means at their disposal to amass more clout.

Outside her office, Chloe was glued to her screen, eyes avidly skimming something Ava would probably rather not know about. As she swept past, her assistant quickly minimized her web browser—but not before Ava glimpsed the image of a small blue bird in the corner.

"Miss Westbrook! I wasn't expecting you back so soon. Are you—shall I hold your calls?"

Even for Chloe, the wide eyes and slight tremble in her voice seemed extreme. Apparently, the afternoon's events had found their way into the news cycle.

"Yes, thank you," Ava said, and retreated into the refreshing calm of her office.

Soon she was seated at her own desk waiting for her Twitter home screen to load. When it did, she cursed under her breath. No wonder Chloe had looked so titillated. The current top trend in the Seattle area was #AnAlien&AWestbrook. It seemed one of her fellow executives at the Guild House meeting had captured video of the exchange between Ava and Galaxy Girl, and now Twitter was all aflutter with the screen shot of the two of them staring each other down. Only instead of standing a dozen feet apart, some enterprising office worker with too much time on their hands had Photoshopped the picture to make it look like they were only inches apart, thereby providing a very different context for their face-off.

Oh god—had Kenzie seen this? And if she had, was she more horrified by the fact that Ava had been at the meeting or that random Seattleites were shipping her with Galaxy Girl? Meanwhile, Ava's father was definitely rolling over in his grave now, and she imagined her brother would soon be more than angry enough to punch a wall. *An Alien and a Westbrook* sounded like the title of a YA novel, for god's sake. Which, incidentally, was how her life felt at the moment.

When her phone buzzed, she stared at her mother's name in shock. It had been, what—six weeks since the last time they'd spoken? She'd tried to get in touch with her mother numerous times, but Dr. Amelia Thornton was apparently too busy in her alleged "retirement" to bother responding. Ava hit ignore and turned back to the screen, scrolling through stories and threads related to the Guild House attack. Some of the comments about her and Victoria's presence at an AFT event were less than positive, and Ava rubbed her forehead as she absorbed the vitriol. Just when they were finally moving past the upheaval her brother had caused… Hyperion's stock would take a hit if she didn't get out ahead of this. But even worse would be the fallout on her friendship with Kenzie, especially if Sloane got to her first.

Ava opened Kenzie's message from Saturday and typed, "Sorry—I was slammed with work this weekend. Does the invitation still stand? I think I could use that drink tonight!"

Her text notification went off almost immediately, and she eagerly pulled up the new message, shoulders falling when she realized it was from Beatrice: "Oh my god I just saw the news are u ok?????"

"Yes!" she replied quickly. "I promise. No one was ever in danger, except maybe the assailants."

"Really? You sure you're ok?"

To prove her okay-ness, Ava snapped a selfie with an exaggerated thumbs-up and hit send.

"Whew," Bea replied. "So relieved." And she followed with a row of hearts, kisses, and hugs.

Ava sent her back a slightly more sedate row of hearts. "Video chat later?"

"Yes!! I'll text you after the milk monster falls asleep."

Ava sent a smiley emoji and set her phone aside, but it buzzed less than a minute later. She braced herself—but it was only Bea again. She'd sent a copy of the Photoshopped still of Ava and Galaxy Girl facing off that afternoon, along with the words: "Hot!! I approve 1000%. #FindAvaAGirlfriend"

Rolling her eyes at her best friend's antics, she took advantage of the distraction to gaze at the close-up of Galaxy Girl again. But this time as she did, a checklist began to write itself in her mind, almost of its own volition: Ability to fly, check. Invulnerability to fire, check. Untold strength and speed, check. Super hearing—judging by the way she had announced Panopticon's imminent arrival—check. Super vision? Possibly. For now, unconfirmed.

Holy hell. Her eyes narrowed on the photo. Was it possible that Galaxy Girl could be one of the mythical Zattalians, the alien species whose possible existence on Earth had sent her brother over the edge? Could there be an actual Zattalian living here in Seattle, one who knew Ava by sight? But then, why wouldn't Galaxy Girl recognize a Westbrook? Ava's brother's obsession with eliminating powerful aliens was no secret. World-wide coverage of his trial had guaranteed that.

Ava shut off her phone and set it face-down. Even if Galaxy Girl was Zattalian, it didn't affect Ava. Or Hyperion, for that matter. Right now, she should focus on what she could control and let everything else fade away.

For the rest of the day and well into the evening, Ava did what she was good at: She threw herself back into work, skimming emails from colleagues and far-away friends and deleting interview requests from local and national media outlets. There were plentiful project proposals and quarterly financials to review, too, and the avalanche of work kept her so busy she could block out everything else. When at last she took a break, the sky had already grown dark beyond her wall of windows. Time to make a dinner plan, since Kenzie apparently had no intention of responding.

She packed up and headed for the elevator, fighting a growing sense of unease. She could only imagine what Sloane had told Kenzie. For a moment, she considered asking Ramón to take her to Kenzie's building so that she could explain herself, but a quick risk analysis changed her mind. What if Kenzie was really angry about AFT? Or what if she freaked out about the idea of Ava being with another woman, as the hashtag alluded? Frankly, after the day she'd had, Ava didn't have the energy to deal with either eventuality.

In the empty corridor, she punched the elevator button repeatedly, venting her temper. She hoped Bea still wanted to video chat after Rowan was in bed. It wasn't really drinking alone if your best friend could see your wine glass, was it?

CHAPTER SEVEN

Kenzie couldn't sleep. Well, that wasn't exactly true. She'd fallen asleep earlier, and almost immediately the old nightmare had returned, the one where she watched through the porthole on her escape pod as her family's ship exploded, the fireball quickly extinguished in the dark vacuum of space. Now she was lying awake staring at the low ceiling in her loft, afraid to go back to sleep. It wasn't only the recurring nightmare keeping her up. She couldn't stop seeing Ava's expression as she'd stared up at Kenzie on the stage earlier that day: alarm, curiosity, defensiveness. Or, not really at *Kenzie*, because she hadn't known who was behind the mask. Would she have looked at Galaxy Girl differently if she knew? Or would she look at *Kenzie* differently?

Yet another question she probably didn't want to know the answer to.

Then again, why was *she* worrying about what Ava might think of her? If anything, Ava should be concerned about Kenzie's reaction to seeing her splattered all over social media at that shady AFT meeting, looking fierce and unafraid in the face of—no, *no*, that wasn't what Kenzie was supposed to be focusing on. And yet, her mind kept coming back to how fearless Ava had seemed even as actual terrorists had threatened everyone in the room with machine guns. Or was she supposed to call them automatic weapons? Obviously, she was going to need a crash course on weaponry from Sloane.

Reliving the day's events was only making her more sleepless, so after a while, she rose from her comfortable bed and changed back into her hero suit. Instead of checking outside with her augmented vision (her own special version of filing a flight plan) and launching herself from one of her windows at maximum speed, she floated slowly up and over the darkened roof. No need to set off Sloane's flight detector. Frankly, she wasn't in the mood to see her sister right now. She understood why Sloane was worried about Ava, but her sister had amped up her suspicions again way too quickly. Kenzie was more inclined to give Ava the benefit of the doubt—which was precisely why she hadn't texted her back. Sloane had accused her of being willfully blind to Ava's real intentions, and Kenzie couldn't be sure her sister wasn't right.

Once clear of Queen Anne Hill—and, hopefully, Sloane's sensors—she drifted aimlessly over the city. It was lovely to fly through the night air, two-dimensional buildings and neat streets laid out below. From this height, the usually chaotic urban scene appeared peaceful, the sounds of traffic and sirens so much quieter than usual. No doubt if she tuned in she would hear alarms ringing, people shouting, dispatchers directing Seattle PD officers to crime scenes. But she was trying to accept that she couldn't be all things to all people. Sloane had reminded her at the end of her first week of official heroing that she couldn't save everyone, and Kenzie was trying to be okay with that.

Ava, for example. What if those activists had decided to shoot people instead of ceiling tiles? What if Kenzie had arrived to find Ava bleeding out like that Panopticon agent she hadn't been able to save, or worse, already—

Stop, she ordered herself. Hypotheticals would drive her crazy if she let them. To calm her mind, she called up the opening forms of Zalia-Kree, the ancient tradition practiced by followers of the Zattalian deity Alia. Kenzie had never managed to reach Kree-Zal, a spiritual state of enlightenment the ritual's practitioners were said to achieve through measured breathing and guided visualizations, but the traditional exercises helped ground her whenever unanswerable questions threatened to drown out everything else. But tonight, even Zalia-Kree couldn't make her forget how Ava had stiffened, her heart rate ticking upward, when Kenzie had called her name from the Guild House stage. Like most of the humans in the room, Ava had been afraid. Unlike the others, though, she hadn't seemed afraid of the armed assailants, but rather of Galaxy Girl.

Kenzie wasn't surprised when her supposedly aimless trajectory brought her to the corner that housed both Guild House and Hyperion Tower. Built into the hillside above Seattle's waterfront, the tower's elegant steel and glass structure had been constructed on a slight angle beside the old church, with four enormous triangles built into the faceted frame facade. Judging from the photo Ava had sent her the previous weekend, her hotel suite was roughly halfway up the skyscraper on the same side as her executive office.

Ava hadn't been injured in the attack earlier that day, but still, it wouldn't hurt to check on her, would it? Ava had asked her out for a drink that night, so technically Kenzie was merely following up. Sort of. In a very roundabout way.

She slowed and stopped just out of reach of the building's lights. A cursory examination revealed that the rooms in the middle of the skyscraper were mostly dark, so she drifted closer, scanning until she found a corner unit with the lights on. There—Ava was sitting up on a king-sized bed, a tablet propped on her lap. She was alone, a fact that was, like, completely irrelevant. Kenzie focused on the tablet screen, expecting to see Netflix or an Excel spreadsheet. Instead, Ava had a book open in her Kindle app.

Normally, Kenzie didn't use her powers to invade other people's privacy. Not only was it against Alliance regulations, but she had developed her own internal system of checks and balances over the years. In that moment, however, she was so intrigued by the sight of Ava reading in bed that she skipped right over her usual rules. Sneaking a look at someone's reading material wasn't a federal crime; strangers did it every day on public transport. Even D'aman couldn't find fault with her for being curious about what Ava might be reading, could they?

Ethical qualms temporarily appeased, Kenzie zeroed in on the author and title notations at the top of the digital page: Jane Austen, *Lady Susan*. Ava was reading the novella that the recent Austen movie *Love and Friendship* was based on.

"Aww," Kenzie murmured. She adored all things Austen. She loved the books, the movies, the enormous body of retellings out there, some good and some, frankly, atrocious. And now here Ava was, reading Austen on her Kindle. That was just—it was so—

She started at the sound of Ava's phone, sharp in her augmented hearing. Through the glass wall she watched as Ava removed her reading glasses—she looked so smart in glasses, Kenzie thought; she should wear them more often—and reached for the phone on her bedside table.

"Hello, Jack. What can I do for you?"

Jack. Who was this Jack, and what was he doing calling

Ava so late at night?

As a low male voice began to apologize for bothering "Miss Westbrook," Kenzie suddenly saw herself as if from a distance: She was hovering outside Ava's home, watching her without her knowledge, eavesdropping on a private conversation. She was spying on Ava Westbrook for reasons that had nothing to do with an emergency, and what was worse, she was using her powers—her *alien* powers, a voice inside her head whispered—to do so.

She shot away at once, training her eyes on the clouds above and limiting her audible range the way she had learned to do as a teenager still new to Earth. D'aman had warned her that the composition of gases in Earth's atmosphere might effectively supercharge her already superior physical abilities as she matured, but even with that knowledge, it had taken her years to get a handle on her growing powers. And yet, she could count on one hand the number of times she had invaded someone's privacy just because she felt like it.

Stupid, she cursed herself as she flew home. Not to mention unethical, borderline illegal, and plain creepy. At least Ava had no idea. Trying to figure out what to say if—*when*—they eventually came face to face was difficult enough without also having to apologize for stalking her.

Back at her condo, she floated in the dark up to the loft, where she quickly stripped out of her hero suit and crawled into bed. Her mind was racing again, so she closed her eyes and concentrated on the ancient Zattalian spiritual forms. Like before, though, slowing her breath did little to assuage her worry over the afternoon's events. Why did Ava matter so much? Right from the start, Kenzie had found herself drawn to the human woman, despite the fact that Ava was a Westbrook and Kenzie was an alien, and never the twain…

A glimmer of memory sparked, and she grabbed her

phone before tugging the covers back up to her chin even though the Western Washington night wasn't that chilly and, besides, she was impervious to extreme temperatures. But her comforter was soft and cozy, and she needed that extra warmth right now.

It only took a moment to Google Rudyard Kipling's famous verse:

Oh, East is East and West is West, and never the twain shall meet,

Till Earth and Sky stand presently at God's great Judgment Seat;

But there is neither East nor West, Border, nor Breed, nor Birth,

When two strong men stand face to face, though they come from the ends of the earth!

In college, Kenzie's English lit professor had said that most people stopped after the first or second line, and in doing so missed Kipling's actual meaning. The way her prof had interpreted the poem, Kipling was effectively saying that where two equals meet, the accidents of birth—nationality, race, economic status—don't matter. In that case, only character and integrity determine the level of respect each affords the other.

In discussion, the class had expanded the "accidents of birth" bit to include more modern concepts such as gender, sexuality, religion, and disability. When one student proposed "alien status" as an accident of birth, a tense debate had taken place, with a vocal anti-alien minority quick to assert that "ends of the earth" showed Kipling was referring only to human beings. The pro-alien majority pointed out that since the Alliance hadn't officially made contact with the United Nations until 1951, Kipling's sentiments toward those born off-planet could not be legitimately gauged. Meanwhile, Kenzie had sat silently in the middle of the room, trying not to let her discomfort show and wishing she were literally anyplace else. She had been on Earth for years by then, but she'd still worried daily about slipping up and revealing her true nature.

Somehow, she thought she probably knew which side of that debate the Westbrooks would have taken. For a moment, she pictured Nicholas Westbrook on trial, staring at the prosecutor, his mouth twisted in disgust as he declared on international television, "I don't like the idea of aliens walking among us without anyone knowing who they are. Do you?"

To Kenzie, the real question was whether or not Ava agreed with her brother.

When her alarm went off the following morning, Kenzie lay in bed, pressing her fists to her eyes as her memory of the previous night returned. What if someone had seen her hovering outside Hyperion Tower? The hashtag that had sprung up on Twitter—#AnAlien&AWestbrook—along with that doctored photo of the two of them was already bad enough. If she had been caught last night gazing soulfully into Ava's hotel room after midnight... Good thing she wore a mask. The last thing Kenzie needed was for Ava to know that she was secretly mooning over her.

Although, really, was that the secret she should be worried about revealing to Ava Westbrook? She pulled her hands away and lay staring up at the ceiling. *Freaking frack.*

After another few satisfying minutes of wallowing, Kenzie leapt down from her loft and headed for the coffee maker. Today was definitely a bring your own coffee so as to avoid the public eye as much as possible kind of day. In fact, given her ill-advised midnight reconnaissance mission, it would probably be best if she avoided most of humanity for the foreseeable future, especially a certain human who worked in Hyperion Tower.

Having a job, unfortunately, complicated that particular plan. Kenzie had only just reached ECM when Aaron called her into his office.

"Have a seat," he directed, waving at one of the chairs by his desk.

Kenzie dropped into the nearest one, notebook and pen held at ready.

"Can you explain to me why Ava Westbrook is refusing to speak to anyone but you about yesterday's attack at the AFT luncheon?" Aaron asked, his voice studied in its calmness as he pushed away from his desk and eyed her intently.

"Um." Kenzie fiddled with her pen. "Isn't that, like, more of a question for Miss Westbrook?"

He stared harder. "Indeed, but since she won't talk to anyone but you… You see the conundrum, don't you?"

She waited, but when he didn't say anything else, she shifted in her chair. "So, this is a tad awkward, but, well, I don't think I should interview her anymore."

"And why is that?" he demanded.

"Because we're sort of, like, becoming friends?" It wasn't a huge lie. Or, it wouldn't have been a few days earlier. Right now, she had no idea what they were to each other.

"There's no issue with friends interviewing friends, only romantic partners." Aaron paused, blinking owlishly at her. "Unless… Are you saying that you and—"

"No!" she practically shouted. "No, of course not. It's fine. I'll get in touch with her assistant."

"Good. I want a draft by the end of the day. Sound feasible?"

"Very feasible," she said, letting her hair swing across her face as she rose, screening her face from view. A draft was feasible, just probably not going to happen.

As she walked away, she could feel her boss's eyes on her—and not because she had special powers that told her so.

Her powers actually didn't feel special to her because they were part of her, just like her fingers and toes and the hair on her head, all of which looked human. One of the more interesting facts, in her opinion, was the universal nature of life. Some species of humanoids varied greatly, but many were quite similar thanks to the basic building blocks of life. Zattalians and humans shared an astounding amount of DNA, as did other humanoid species from planets light-years apart. That made finding asylum for refugees easier for the Alliance, who liked to assign people to planets where they would blend in. Another universal factor of sentient life was, unfortunately, a tendency to distrust difference.

If previous generations of Zattalians hadn't engaged in genetic manipulation—which most species in the universe had outlawed even before the Alliance banned it outright—Kenzie would have blended in more easily on Earth, too. Instead, the tweaks in her genetic code meant she could never fit in completely. In college, she'd made the mistake of telling Matt about her ancestors' laboratory experiments, and ever since then he'd teased her about not qualifying for the Non-GMO Project. Honestly, the joke was a little funny, not that Kenzie would ever admit as much to him.

Back at her desk, she stared at Ava's text from the previous night. She still hadn't decided how—or if—she wanted to answer. And now, what, Ava was basically ordering her to come see her, as if she hadn't been avoiding Kenzie all weekend? She clearly wanted Kenzie to use her position at ECM to do damage control for Hyperion, but as far as Kenzie was concerned, Hyperion

Tech had more than earned its less than stellar reputation on off-world issues. She certainly had no intention of glossing over their presence at that garbage AFT meeting—not even for Ava.

A half hour somehow passed as Kenzie sat at her desk, stewing over her latest assignment. Finally, no closer to a decision, she did something she'd never done before: She went home sick.

"What? I just saw you a little while ago and you seemed fine," Aaron said when she called him from home, already snuggled up on her couch in her favorite sweats. "I swear to god, Shepherd, if you're doing this to get out of the Westbrook article…"

While he implied in vague Midwestern terms that her job was in danger, Kenzie Googled "communicable diseases" on her iPad. At her boss's first pause for breath, she informed him that her doctor had just diagnosed her with pink eye.

"I'm not supposed to go out in public until twenty-four hours after my first dose of antibiotics, so…"

He released an audibly frustrated breath. "Fine. But you better have a doctor's note when I see you this time tomorrow," he said, and hung up.

Kenzie shook her head as she dialed up Netflix on her television. Skipping out of work was more complicated than she'd expected. Still, Sloane would know how to fake a doctor's note. Panopticon owed her after she'd alerted them to the attack the previous day—and, well, for other obvious reasons. Sloane had been pissed she'd mingled with agents from the bureau again, but Kenzie had jetted before anyone could slap a bug on her. At least, she was pretty sure.

Was it weird that she was now sort of working with Panopticon? Maybe they'd take her on full time if Aaron really did fire her. But lying about a communicable disease wasn't sack-worthy, was it? On a scale of lifetime falsehoods, it didn't compare. Besides, she figured the images of oozing, pus-filled eyelids currently spilling across her iPad screen were punishment enough, really. Never had she been more grateful for her immunity to injury and illness. Being GMO ruled.

Halfway through her third movie of the day, a sound caught her attention, and she poked her head up in time to watch Sloane let herself in with the spare key. This was no longer a surprising event. Who knew that becoming a superhero would mean her already over-protective big sister feared to let her out of her sight for more than a few hours at a time?

Actually, she probably could have seen that one coming.

"You're here," Sloane said, sounding more vexed than happy about this turn of events.

"Why do you sound pissed about that?" She paused the movie and uncurled from her pile of blankets only to discover her studio was a bit gloomier than she'd realized, especially with the blinds drawn and the television volume lower than the average human liked.

"You didn't answer your phone, and Matt said you vanished from work this morning. Why aren't you answering your phone?"

"Sorry, I must have forgotten to turn off night mode," she lied. "Did something happen?"

"No, nothing happened. But you can't just disappear!"

She really did sound pissed, and Kenzie recoiled into her blanket cocoon. "I'm sorry," she repeated. "I didn't mean to make you worry."

Sloane pulled out her phone. "I'm texting Matt. He and Antonio were ready to storm your loft."

"It won't happen again, ma'am." Kenzie saluted, but it must not have been as snappy as she'd intended because right away Sloane sighed and dropped down beside her.

"What am I going to do with you?" she asked, pushing Kenzie's hair away from her face.

She hadn't showered this morning, and she imagined her outsides felt as slimy as her insides. She shrugged, head so low her chin almost touched her chest. "I honestly don't know."

"Rough day?" her big sister asked, voice softening.

"More like a rough week."

"Aww, sweet girl. I'm sorry."

The gentleness in her normally tough-as-nails sister's tone broke something in Kenzie, and she slid down until her head was in Sloane's lap. From this angle, the low light reflecting off the walls reminded her of the perpetual twilight of her family's ship, thanks to the radiation shields. As this thought filtered through, the tears came, hot and painful, accompanied by sobs that actually hurt her throat. Sloane's hands were soothing, one in her hair and the other on her back, and her voice was quiet in the semi-darkness. "That's it, let it out. I've got you, Kenz."

She didn't say it would be okay, and Kenzie appreciated that. They had both seen too much by now to believe in that particular fairy tale. But with Sloane there to shush her softly and smooth back her hair, it was almost like they were home again in Bellingham, and Sloane was comforting her after she'd botched an English assignment or misread a social cue or simply, deeply, missed her parents—which she still did most days even now.

When she was all cried out, she sat up next to her sister, pressing her hands against the splotches she knew must be coloring her cheeks. It was funny. Her body's ability to maintain a constant temperature meant that she rarely flushed from heat or cold. But when she got upset or, say, sobbed uncontrollably, her skin reflected her rare physical discomfort. Maybe that was why she hated crying so much.

"Do you want to talk about it?" Sloane asked.

Kenzie wiped her eyes. "I don't know. It's just, everything is so—I don't even know how—Sloane, what am I even doing?"

"Is this about yesterday?" Sloane hadn't mentioned seeing a certain doctored photo circulating online, but Kenzie knew she must have seen it. The thought made her blush even harder.

"Yes," she said, nodding miserably. But then, as she contemplated admitting to her sister what a huge gay disaster she was—flying by Ava's building and *hovering outside*, for eff's sake—she shook her head. "Actually, you know what? I don't think I want to talk about it right now. Can we just watch the movie?"

Sloane paused, and Kenzie could tell it nearly killed her to nod. "Of course," she said, only a tad grudging. "What's on?"

"*Love and Friendship.*"

"Again?"

"We can watch something else if you want."

"No, it's fine. In fact, upon my word, I find it an uncommonly amiable idea."

Kenzie felt a smile threatening. She'd sent Sloane the link to a Facebook page called "Talk Like Jane Austen" ages ago. "I was starting to think you didn't use your Gmail account anymore."

"I only read messages from people I love."

"So, only Mom and Dad, me, and Mika?"

Sloane's cheeks flushed until Kenzie was pretty sure they looked like twins. "We've been dating for like twenty seconds! Slow down, Speedy."

"I'm guessing you haven't packed your U-Haul yet, then." As Sloane stared askance at her, Kenzie smiled, enjoying her sister's rare speechlessness.

As usual, Sloane recovered quickly. "Start the movie, missy. And turn up—"

"—the volume. I know. I got you, puny Earthling." She reached for the remote, relaxing as the nineteenth century English landscape flickered back across the screen. There was nothing like a well-done period piece to help you forget the turmoil of modern life.

A little while later she said, eyes fixed on the TV, "Thanks, Sloane. For coming to find me, I mean."

"I'll always come find you, Kenzie. You know that."

Sloane scooted closer so that their shoulders were touching, and it was just the right amount of contact to make her feel safe. She was lucky to have Sloane, she knew. She wished the reverse were true, but Sloane's life had revolved around Kenzie ever since she'd arrived on Earth. Their parents had tasked Sloane with looking after her in the early years, and Sloane had admitted that at times she'd resented the role Kenzie's arrival had forced on her. Even so, she claimed she'd never regretted the decision that had made Kenzie part of the family. Their parents had asked Sloane before taking Kenzie in, explaining in detail what harboring an alien might mean to their lives. According to family lore, Sloane had barely hesitated before saying she was all in.

She'd taken protecting Kenzie so seriously that instead of accepting a scholarship to Caltech, she'd gone to U-Dub because it was closer to home. Two years later, Kenzie had followed Sloane the ninety miles south to Seattle. As a freshman, Kenzie had wanted to live on campus, but she required more food than a university meal plan allowed and, oh yeah, occasionally levitated in her sleep. Dorm life was out, so Sloane had rented a two-bedroom apartment near campus and stuck around for graduate school. She'd insisted this was what she'd wanted, but Kenzie knew

Sloane had applied to her PhD program partly so she could continue to keep an eye on her. Knew, too, that she might not have made it through college without Sloane's help.

Not because she hadn't liked college. On the contrary, she'd loved it. As a double major in journalism and history, she had come to understand human beings better, with their endless cycles of war and peace and always, always more war. She became fascinated by the Industrial Revolution and Western Imperialism, by the Holocaust and the decimation of the world's rain forests, by the Atlantic Slave Trade and the American and French Revolutions. She found human history intriguing, planetary history—like, *actual dinosaurs* might have lived in her own back yard—even more so.

Sometimes, though, Kenzie couldn't sleep for wondering if humans were destined to ruin Earth the same way her people had destroyed their home planet. Sloane said that sometimes *she* lay awake worrying the same thing, but Kenzie was pretty sure the thing that kept Sloane up at night most often was worrying about her younger sister. And now Kenzie was demolishing her closet door—correction, *one* of her closet doors—and leaping into the open in the exact way Sloane had always begged her not to. But instead of being angry with her, Sloane was putting her own job at risk to help Kenzie become a hero of the people in as safe a way as possible. Not only her job but her life, because if Sentinel figured out who Kenzie was, her family and friends really would be at risk.

All at once, sitting on her couch with Sloane beside her safe and sound for the moment, Kenzie found herself praying to God, Alia, whomever, that Sloane and their parents and everyone else she cared about wouldn't get hurt because of her. She rarely sent such a plea out into the universal neural network. Like her human family members, her brand of spirituality centered on the breathtaking patterns that could be derived from the universe. But if an action might help and stood very little chance of hurting, why not give it a whirl? Her prayers had certainly been answered when, young and alone after the Zattalian fleet's destruction, she had cast up hope to the universe for a family who would love her. The Alliance had given her the Shepherd-Hendersons, and Kenzie knew how lucky she was to have ended up in a family that had nearly always managed to make her feel loved and accepted even when she had been born so many light-years away.

Of course, being born on Earth didn't guarantee a happy family experience. The Westbrooks proved that much, according to Sloane's case files. They were willing to sacrifice almost anything in the name of their hateful cause, even their closest relationships. Poor Ava. She must feel…

With difficulty, Kenzie stopped herself from going down that particular rabbit hole. It wasn't like she could actually know what was going on inside Ava's head. The only fact she knew for sure about Ava Westbrook was that she didn't trust aliens. Or at least, she didn't trust Galaxy Girl.

Her chin dipped again, and Kenzie let her cheek rest on Sloane's shoulder. She would do better for her sister. She would work hard at protecting her and everyone else she loved. But honestly, she was just as glad she wouldn't have to do any of that today.

On screen, the characters were dining by candlelight. As if in response, Kenzie's stomach growled.

"Pizza?" Sloane proposed.

"Of course," Kenzie said, even though she'd already polished off an entire frozen pizza before Sloane arrived.

Stuffed crust from Zeek's, located helpfully (or *un*helpfully, according to Sloane whose human metabolism wasn't nearly as efficient as Kenzie's) only a few blocks away on Queen Anne Avenue, soon perked Kenzie up. Or maybe it was Jane Austen's droll humor that improved her mood. Or maybe, just maybe, it was the alien alcohol Sloane had nabbed that morning in a raid on a black-market trader and then pilfered before it could disappear into Panopticon's massive warehouse of evidence lockers.

"You're welcome," she said, grinning as she handed over the bottle of Bandal rum, the label blaring its toxicity to humans and certain arthorolopods from the Keteloran system.

Kenzie cradled the bottle carefully. Their parents had presented her with a tiny flask of the stuff the year she'd turned 21 Earth years, but this looked like enough to last her a few months.

"I thought we might toast to your not getting outed as Galaxy Girl," her sister said, heading to the kitchen. "And, of course, to outing yourself as bisexual."

Kenzie was psyched that Sloane wanted to celebrate her sexuality, but, ugh, she was less than pleased about being called Galaxy *Girl*. Freaking sexism. If you counted her time in hypersleep, Kenzie was more than half a human century old. But when she'd griped about the name to Matt, he'd pointed out that Galaxy Girl had awesome alliteration while Galaxy Woman sounded like an Eagles song. Which, accurate.

Sloane soon returned with a pair of glasses and a mostly full bottle of wine. They poured themselves generous servings of alcohol and then pretended to clink glasses—the alien rum really was toxic to humans—while Sloane proclaimed, "To my little sister, vigilante extraordinaire."

"Hey," Kenzie said, smiling, "I resemble that."

"Oh my god, you're such a dork," Sloane said, but she was smiling, too. "Oh, and thanks for saving our butts at the bureau."

"You're welcome," Kenzie said, and sipped her drink,

gasping as the alcohol burned her esophagus.

A little while later, the pizza was gone and they were both tipsy enough that Kenzie managed to convince Sloane to do something they hadn't done in ages: go flying. But only if she wore her Galaxy Girl suit and loaned Sloane a balaclava because getting caught joy-flying with an alien was definitely against Panopticon's rules.

"Remember," Sloane said as they climbed the steps to the rooftop patio, "you can't drop me or Mom and Dad will kill you."

"I mean, even if I dropped you, I wouldn't let you hit the ground," Kenzie said. "What kind of alien sister would I be if I did that?"

"Shh," Sloane whispered loudly, glancing around. "Ix-nay on the ien-alay."

They were about to jump off the roof and Sloane was worried someone would hear them? But Kenzie only nodded and pretended to zip her lips, which made Sloane laugh so hard she almost fell over.

When they had ascertained no one was nearby or had their gazes trained on the rooftop patio, Sloane jumped on Kenzie's back and wrapped her arms around her neck. Kenzie made sure she had a grip on Sloane's knees and then, more slowly than she usually did but still faster than a human being could move, she took off into the night.

Sloane's breath left her in a whoosh, but then she was calling out, "Whoo-hooooooo!"

"Shh," it was Kenzie's turn to say, laughing as she carried them away from Queen Anne Hill. God, she loved this—flying away free with her favorite human, the city laid out all twinkly and sparkly below them. It had been a while since they'd done this, not since the previous summer during a camping trip to the Olympic Peninsula when she and Sloane had gone for a night hike along Hurricane Ridge under a full moon. The sky had been clear and brimming with stars and planets, and the mountains had lain before them, dark, white-tipped masses extending for miles into the interior of Olympic National Park. It hadn't taken much to convince Sloane to go for a flight that night. Earth's beauty had been too enticing to resist.

Tonight's view was significantly different from the perspective they'd enjoyed on the Peninsula. For one, it was cloudy, the mist hanging so low that the top of the Columbia Tower was hidden from view until Kenzie took them above the clouds. The sun hadn't set that long ago, and in the distance beyond Seattle's tallest skyscraper, the peak of Mt. Rainier rose pink and glowing only 60 air miles away. Kenzie slowed to a halt, transfixed, and felt Sloane release her grip and hold her arms out wide, heart racing but body relaxed. Her trust that Kenzie wouldn't let her fall was a gift, and Kenzie made sure to hold on tight despite the off-world rum wending lazily through her system.

After a little while, though, Sloane's human blood felt like ice. Over her sister's protests, Kenzie took her home, dropping down in a dark alley off her tree-lined street and giving her a long hug.

"Thank you," she said, pulling back to smile at her sister.

"Of course," Sloane said, and slugged her, eyes shining from the leftover excitement of flying. Then she shook out her hand. "Ow."

"You have only yourself to blame, puny human," Kenzie said, and lifted off again, laughing as Sloane whisper-shouted something unintelligible after her.

She meant to go home, she really did, but she was feeling so good that she ended up cruising lazily among the buildings of downtown, pulling loop-de-loops and other silly tricks. Somehow—well, it wasn't a mystery, was it?— she ended up near the Columbia Tower again, and before she knew it she was hovering just off the edge of the balcony outside Ava's office, drawn there by the bright light in among the hundreds of other dark windows. Ava was there just as she had been countless other evenings, at her desk with her back to the window, fingers flying over her keyboard. Kenzie didn't try to read her screen this time, only allowed herself the comfort of seeing that Ava was alive and well and working just as hard as ever.

She wasn't usually that impressed by workaholics, but with Ava, she knew it was more about legacy than personal accomplishment. During that very first interview, when Ava had talked about transforming Hyperion Tech for the sake of her family's name, Kenzie had thought she understood what drove Ava to work so hard. But now that she was expanding her own "work" to include moonlighting as a superhero, she had a better understanding of what the term *legacy* entailed. For years, she'd felt like she was floating, uncertain of who she was or what she should do with her life. So much had crystallized since she'd intervened in the hold-up at Cloudtastic. Finally, she was sure of what she was meant to be doing on this planet: helping people to the best of her Zattalian abilities.

Though sometimes even now—like tonight, for instance—she wasn't sure that being a superhero was enough. Shouldn't there be someone to share the ups and downs with, someone to laugh and cry with, someone to be with other than her admittedly awesome friends and relatives? Sloane literally glowed when she so much as thought about Mika. Her happiness made Kenzie hope that maybe she could have that kind of love in her life one day, too.

Inside the office, Ava's phone rang. She picked it up and looked at the screen, and then, before Kenzie realized what was happening, Ava turned and looked straight out into the night, her eyes searching. Kenzie reversed so fast she nearly crashed into a nearby building, and then she shot up into the sky, heart racing.

As she flew home across the city, a single thought played through her mind on repeat: "Please don't let her have seen me."

\#

"Fifteen minutes, Miss Westbrook."

"Thank you, Chloe." Ava nodded at her assistant, expression carefully neutral.

As the door closed again, she allowed her face to resume its earlier, less pleasant expression. She needed a drink. More than one drink, actually. But facing down a hostile Board of Directors required clarity and strength, neither of which she could adequately channel under the influence of two fingers of Scotch.

This had not been an easy week. Not only had the alien activists hijacked the meeting on Monday, but in the days since the attack she'd had to weather dueling Twitter storms: #AnAlien&AWestbrook versus #JustAnotherWestbrook. She hadn't even been allowed to offer up a defense. Victoria had forbidden her to engage, reminding her that the first rule of public relations was that any exposure was good exposure, up to and occasionally including notoriety.

Riding out the wave of public opinion was not in Ava's nature. Her father, a decorated Vietnam veteran, had often said, "The best defense is a good offense," and while he may have been talking mainly about war and athletics, the philosophy had seeped into their family's daily life. Staying silent while her character was debated publicly was one of the more difficult challenges Ava had been tasked with. She had worked too hard to differentiate herself from the rest of her family to feel comfortable being painted with the same brush. Not just in public opinion, either. She had all but promised Kenzie that she wasn't a narrow-minded bigot.

Kenzie, who still hadn't responded to her text from Monday night, or to her interview offer.

As if all of that weren't enough, Galaxy Girl was conducting surveillance on her. Two nights in a row now, Ava had received calls from the head of her security team informing her that Seattle's local alien hero was hovering near her building. Why was she checking up on Ava? Could Panopticon be sending Galaxy Girl to spy on her? They had to know her security team would notice. Were they trying to send her a deliberate message? Sentinel's illegal actions had almost taken down the bureau, a consequence she doubted Nick had considered when he started down the path of avenging their father's murder. Did the agency's new leadership think she was a threat to them, too?

She sat back, rubbing her eyes as the wheels of her subconscious mind turned. Kenzie's sister was a Panopticon agent who appeared to know Galaxy Girl, at least in passing. In turn, Galaxy Girl appeared to know Ava. That was less surprising, and not only because of Ava's last name. Lately, she hadn't been able to shake the feeling that there was something familiar about the hero. But what could it be? Did she know her in real life?

She pulled up the video from Guild House again, watching as Galaxy Girl rambled her way through—wait, *rambled*? Ava peered more closely at the screen. Those broad shoulders and muscled arms, the dark eyes staring out at her with a startled look, as if the hero hadn't expected her to be there... Several connections sped through her mind at once: the Cloudtastic Coffee logo; no discernible fear of heights; an adopted family. Ava remembered how Kenzie had raced away from the Olympic Sculpture Park *toward* the explosion the previous week, how she'd sounded on the phone afterward when she'd mentioned blood seen supposedly through a telephoto lens. She remembered her own momentary flicker of recognition as she'd watched Galaxy Girl in action at the Guild House meeting, quickly extinguished when Panopticon's agents stormed the scene.

Her screen blurred as her subconscious virtually shouted, *Of course!* She couldn't believe it had taken her this long to work out. Sloane Shepherd and Galaxy Girl didn't just know each other. They were… SISTERS?

"Jesus Christ," she murmured, pushing away from her desk. Kenzie was Galaxy Girl. KENZIE was GALAXY FUCKING GIRL. Now that Ava had connected the dots, she couldn't stop picturing Kenzie removing her glasses, unbuttoning her shirt and, transformation complete, launching into the air in her bodysuit and alien mask. Because Kenzie, who was Galaxy Girl, could fly.

Chloe knocked and poked her head in again. "It's time."

Of course it was. Just—*perfect.*

As she headed for the door, she passed her Visiting Executive Entertainment Bar, or VEEB as she liked to call the liquor cabinet hidden in a secret wall panel. When this wretched meeting was over, she promised herself, she was drinking.

Surprisingly, the meeting went—shittily. It went like shit. Fortunately, one of the only women on the board had warned her ahead of time that several of the executives were gunning for her. Not because of any professional misgivings, they were quick to assert, but because of her recent media "notoriety." Outwardly, they claimed that it was the current social media blitz driving their concerns. Sharing a hashtag with a known vigilante, alien or otherwise—even when the corroborating photo of them gazing deeply into each other's eyes was fake—was not good for business, in their opinion. The fact that people were clearly upset over her attendance at Monday's meeting was another contributing factor to the board's serious question: Did having a Westbrook in a position of leadership hurt Hyperion Tech more than it helped?

It had taken more willpower than it should have not to laugh out loud at their transparent scheming. The majority of the board was still old school, which meant they believed that climate change denial was good for business and that aliens were best not spoken of—not that they would publicly admit to either regressive stance. Ava wanted to tell them they weren't fooling anyone, but instead she attempted to downplay their worries because she still wasn't ready to give up the chance to steer her family's company in a different direction.

Probably, she would have fared better if her mind hadn't insisted on fixating on the stunning realization that Kenzie Shepherd, the sweet, slightly bumbling reporter who had only recently entered her life, appeared to be the alien hero the city was currently besotted with. But even as Ava offered up assurances that the PR department was working on multiple major human-interest stories to counteract the Just Another Westbrook narrative, a series of questions kept rattling around inside her head: Was she right? *Was* Kenzie Galaxy Girl? And how could Ava be sure, particularly since Kenzie was the one ghosting her now?

By the time the meeting adjourned, Ava appeared to have convinced the members of the board that she was still the best person for her job—at least for now. Crisis momentarily averted, she smiled through her teeth as everyone else filed out of the executive conference room. As soon as she was alone, she stepped outside. This balcony, located on the opposite side of the building from her office, afforded a less familiar view of the city. Would Seattle ever feel like home? How much longer would she even be here?

Not for the first time, Ava wondered if she could really guide Hyperion out from under the cloud surrounding the Westbrook name. When she was younger, she'd dreamed of earning some small amount of her parents' affection despite the fact they'd reserved most of their love for Nick. When her mother offered her the role as Hyperion's COO, Ava had convinced herself that if she could somehow manage to return the company to the position it had enjoyed before Sentinel turned the Westbrook name toxic, then at least she would know she had done right by her family, even if her parents never acknowledged her efforts.

But maybe the task Ava had set herself was doomed, just like the goal her mother had set: keeping Nick out of prison. Maybe Ava just wasn't smart or ruthless or experienced enough to transform Hyperion into a force for good, especially not when the rest of the firm's leadership team seemed intent on continuing down the very path that was destroying not only the company but the world itself. Freaking capitalism. Wasn't there a better way?

She sighed and lifted her face to the sun, warm but nowhere near as hot as it was in New York City at this time of year. After a lifetime on the East Coast, she was still getting used to the temperate weather of the Pacific Northwest. She didn't miss New York's humidity, she had to admit, or the irritating insects in New England where she'd gone to prep school. Over the years, she had eventually grown to love New England, but when she'd first arrived at Deerfield, Western Massachusetts had felt light-years away from Manhattan. She still remembered crying herself to sleep every night her first week there.

Was that what life on Earth had been like for Kenzie in the beginning? She'd said she was adopted at twelve. Was that when she had come to Earth, or had her family been with her when she arrived? God, she looked so *human*. Another of Nick's fears—that powerful aliens were walking among them, stealing human jobs and resources—come to pass. But reporters were a dying breed, so was Kenzie really taking a job from a human? Assuming she even *was* an alien refugee. It would make sense why Sloane always seemed so protective of her, why Kenzie herself sometimes seemed to watch Ava carefully when she thought she wouldn't be noticed. Another thought occurred to her, and she frowned out at the construction cranes dotting the top of the hill. Was their friendship even real, or was Kenzie only in her life to keep an eye on just another Westbrook?

A siren sounded off in the distance, and she squinted across the city skyline, looking in vain for a small figure blurring past at inhuman speeds. For Kenzie, who was Galaxy-fucking-Girl. Maybe. She *was*, wasn't she?

Right. Time for that drink.

Chloe was on the phone when she reached her office. Ava nodded at her and strode past, her mind elsewhere—Laphroaig or Johnny Walker Blue? Choices, choices…

Behind her, she heard Chloe's voice. "Wait, Miss Westbrook—"

But it was too late. She had already opened the door, only to stop as she noticed a figure sitting near her desk, head bent over her phone, blonde hair glowing in the sunlight spilling through the window.

"—Kenzie Shepherd is here," Chloe finished. "I'm sorry. You said to set up an appointment with her as soon as possible."

Kenzie glanced up and gave Ava a little wave—as if the last time they'd faced each other hadn't been over the prone bodies of gun-toting terrorists; as if Kenzie hadn't hovered outside her windows waiting for her to show her true Westbrook nature. Maybe she really wasn't Galaxy

Girl, but then again, maybe she was.

"It's fine," she told her assistant, hearing the tremor in her own voice. "Hold my calls, please."

"Okay. But you have another meeting in—"

"Hold my calls," she repeated, watching as Kenzie fiddled with a button on her pinstriped shirt.

"Yes, ma'am." Chloe sounded miffed, but what was new?

The door closed and they were alone together, and it was almost too much to grasp. Kenzie was still eyeing her, brow slightly furrowed, and, *Christ*, was mind reading one of her superpowers? But no, it couldn't be or she would know exactly which side Ava was on—hers, namely. Ava took a deep breath and released it slowly, willing herself to remain calm as she crossed to the hidden panel and reached for the nearest whiskey bottle.

"This is a pleasant surprise," she said without turning around. "I was beginning to wonder if you had lost your phone."

"Oh, right. Sorry about that. I've just been swamped the last couple of days. But I'm here now."

"Can I get you a drink?" Ava risked a glance over her shoulder only to find Kenzie watching her with those intriguing blue eyes. Now it made sense why Ava had never seen eyes quite like hers.

"No, thanks. Rough day?"

"You could say that." Ava concentrated on the clink of ice and swish of soda and Scotch. The routine soothed her, and she took a fortifying sip, closing her eyes as the liquid burned through her. Turning, she blinked into the sunlight and offered what she hoped was close to her usual warm smile. "To what do I owe the pleasure?"

And, yep, that was the wrong thing to say. Because while she had enjoyed flirting with Kenzie in the past, had loved the way Kenzie fumbled and flushed at her oh-so-gay attention, that had been before she realized Kenzie was probably, almost definitely Galaxy Girl.

The sun was behind Kenzie, and Ava couldn't make out her features. But then Kenzie rose and, *oh god*, she was walking this way. Kenzie was approaching her, smile hesitant and hands fidgety. Again, it felt like too much, so Ava pivoted toward the couch. There, she sat down, kicked off her shoes, and curled her feet under her, setting her whiskey glass within easy reach.

"May I...?" Kenzie gestured to the opposite end of the couch. When Ava nodded, she sat down and pulled a notepad and pen from her bag, her movements short and choppy.

And, okay, that was disappointing. "Are we getting right to it, then?" she asked, trying to keep her tone casual.

Kenzie followed her gaze to the notebook on her lap. "Oh! No, sorry," she said, quickly setting the pad on the nearby coffee table. She kept hold of the pen, though, twirling it from finger to finger almost faster than Ava could follow. "How are you?"

"I've been better," Ava admitted, her gaze narrowing in on Kenzie's neat button-down. Was she wearing the bodysuit under there even now? Collared shirts were a brilliant superhero disguise. Not only did they convey unheroic averageness, they ensured the hero in question could change quickly without obstructing her sight even for a second. Ava's fingers twitched with the urge to tug Kenzie's top button open. Ava had felt like that around her before, of course, but the impulse had always had an entirely different origin.

"I heard about Monday. I'm glad you're okay," Kenzie said, eyes trained on the cushions between them. "I was... I was worried."

"Were you?" Ava couldn't help the slight bitterness

that crept into her tone. If Kenzie really had been worried, she could have demonstrated her concern by, say, returning Ava's text. An image of Galaxy Girl hovering outside her window two nights in a row flashed into her mind, and Ava blinked. Maybe Kenzie really wasn't lying—about this, anyway.

Kenzie looked up. "Yes, of course. That's why I'm here. I wanted to make sure you were okay."

Right, a voice at the back of Ava's mind whispered. "I thought you were here to interview me."

"Well, yes." Kenzie smoothed the wrinkles in her skirt. "But I'm also here as a friend."

"A friend?" Ava repeated, one eyebrow lifted cynically.

Kenzie blinked. "I thought—but we—" she stammered, gripping her pen so tightly Ava was surprised it didn't snap.

And, *crap*, she was taking her insecurities out on Kenzie, wasn't she? "I'm sorry," she said quickly, barely resisting the urge to reach out and capture Kenzie's hand in her own. "That didn't come out right. I think I'm just having one of those weeks."

After a moment, Kenzie nodded. "Must be catching. I told Sloane the same thing," she admitted. "About me, not you, I mean."

Ava bit her lip. "Is that why I haven't heard from you?"

She nodded and held Ava's gaze at last. "I'm sorry about that. I've actually really missed you."

Ava wanted to tell Kenzie she'd missed her too, wanted to tell her she was sorry for being a terrible friend and even sorrier that she couldn't be the perfect person she longed to be for Kenzie's sake, if not for her own. But then she remembered that every single one of their interactions had been predicated on a lie (probably), and she couldn't help wondering if, even now, Kenzie might be pretending to be something she wasn't.

Her chin lifted slightly. Westbrooks might be many things, but gullible wasn't one of them.

The seconds ticked past, and Kenzie's gaze faltered. After what felt to Ava like entirely too long, Kenzie cleared her throat and reached for her notebook. "Anyway, my editor wanted this story yesterday, so…"

"Why didn't you write it yesterday?" she asked, seizing on the opening to ask an impersonal question rather than the ones trying to tear their way out: *Why didn't you come see me? Did you not even care that I could have been killed?* And yes, she knew the terrorists had been more interested in sternly lecturing the luncheon crowd than in physically harming them, but Kenzie didn't know that—unless she was Galaxy Girl. Her lack of reaction was yet more evidence that she was, more than likely, an unregistered alien who liked to dress up and fly around the city. Ava added another tick to her growing mental list.

Kenzie toyed with her glasses. "I was out sick, actually, which really ticked Aaron off."

"Are you okay now?" Ava asked, frowning.

"I'm fine. It was more of a mental health day. But I had to promise Aaron an interview with you *and* Galaxy Girl to—" She stopped abruptly, blinking as she apparently realized what she had admitted.

Tick. And really, how did she expect to fool the world? No wonder her superhero suit included a mask. "An interview with Galaxy Girl? Do you know her, then?"

"I have a lead," Kenzie said vaguely. "From Sloane. Anyway, back to my questions…"

"Fire away," Ava said, forcing herself to smile even as her own questions swirled and grew: Did Kenzie's mental health day have anything to do with avoiding this interview? Also, was she this terrible at hiding her identity with everyone, or was it only with Ava?

She managed to quiet these questions long enough to go over the basics of Monday's assault, even offering up a couple of coherent quotes. She was still congratulating herself on that accomplishment when Kenzie commented, "It must have been terrifying."

"Yes," Ava said magnanimously, "I imagine it was."

"You *imagine* it was?" Kenzie's head tilted. "Were you not afraid, then?"

"For the stained-glass windows? Absolutely. We didn't go to all that trouble to preserve the dome only to have a cadre of bumbling terrorists destroy it."

Ava was gratified to see Kenzie's tiny smile, but it soon faded.

"Right," Kenzie said, checking her notes. "I understand that Hyperion Tech owns Guild House as well as this tower."

"That's correct."

"In that case, can you tell me a little about the decision to allow an AFT-sponsored event on the premises?" And she looked up straight into Ava's eyes, her own tinged with the steel that made Ava's pulse quicken—and that added yet another tick to her growing list.

She swallowed and touched the tip of her tongue to her lips, aware of Kenzie watching her. "That would be a question for our event coordinator, Andre Stewart. I could put you in touch with him, if you'd like?"

"Not right now, but maybe later." Kenzie jotted something in her notebook. "Can you tell me if Hyperion Tech has an existing company policy that prohibits partnering with anti-alien organizations?"

"Not that I know of." Ava frowned slightly as she wondered why this hadn't occurred to her before. Now that Kenzie made the point, it seemed obvious. But since assuming a position in management, she'd been focused on protecting Hyperion's intellectual property and bolstering the number of renewable energy research teams. She'd never been all that interested in managing personnel, anyway. That was what HR was for.

"I see," Kenzie said, scribbling away, her hand practically a blur.

Tick, tick, tick... "Kenzie," Ava said, and then stopped. She wasn't sure what came next. She only knew she was tired of subterfuge, tired of the game she'd been unwittingly playing since the moment Kenzie had first appeared in her office all those weeks ago.

Kenzie stopped writing and looked up, her brow furrowed even more than it had been on Friday night. "Yes?" she asked, her tone wary.

She really was lovely, Ava noted, her honey-blonde hair in its neat half-bun spilling forward over one shoulder, the black frame of her glasses in sharp contrast to the delicate cream of her skin. Drawn by the question in Kenzie's eyes, Ava shifted closer on the couch until her knee was brushing Kenzie's thigh, trying to find the language to ask what she wanted to—no, what she *needed* to know. Since they'd met, she'd felt drawn to Kenzie's uninhibited smile and apparent kindness, but she had never fully believed in Kenzie's offer of friendship. She was a Westbrook, after all, and had learned not to expect affection from any quarter, not even from someone as open and welcoming as Kenzie Shepherd had seemed.

"Ava," Kenzie said, turning to face her squarely, and even though her voice was soft, it contained a note of warning. Or was it pleading? Either way, Ava had to know. She had to.

"About Galaxy Girl," she said delicately. "I think I know—that is, I have an idea... You're not actually going to interview her, are you? I mean, you can't technically speak with her, can you?" As Kenzie stared at her, eyes widening almost more than seemed humanly possible, Ava reached out a tentative hand, her fingers brushing against the top button of Kenzie's shirt, beneath which lurked (she was almost certain) a dark-colored bodysuit and matching cowl, an image of the Milky Way galaxy splashed across both.

"Ava," Kenzie repeated, only it came out as more of an agonized whisper this time.

Ava looked into her dark blue eyes and said softly, "We don't really need to keep pretending, do we?"

Kenzie's hand came up to trap Ava's, firmly but gently, against her chest. Their eyes held, an electric current passing between them, and Ava felt Kenzie's breath rising steadily beneath her palm, felt the heat rising from her body, sensed the rhythmic beat of her heart. They were so close, and Kenzie was biting her lip again, and… Ava knew that look. Kenzie Shepherd may or may not be an alien, but she was definitely some form of queer.

The confirmation after so many weeks of waiting and wondering should have made Ava giddy. On any other day, it would have. But instead, the recognition of mutual attraction was overshadowed by the other, more urgent question—was Kenzie Galaxy Girl, a hero of almost frightening power? Was she in fact a Zattalian, the unicorn of aliens? Or was she some other alien species entirely?

An image of a Treitan her brother had experimented on—a large, crustacean-like creature with shapeshifting abilities—flickered into Ava's mind. Could Kenzie's humanoid exterior hide a monster, too? She flinched slightly even as she rejected the notion. Shapeshifting was an exceedingly rare ability in the universe, and anyway, Galaxy Girl wouldn't have to wear a mask if she could simply morph into someone else. More than likely, the only external disguise Kenzie wore was her eyeglasses.

Those glasses were slipping down her nose now, and Ava blinked against an onslaught of memories—Kenzie on that first day with Todd Warren, nodding in understanding as Ava spoke of wanting to change Hyperion's mission; Kenzie grinning at her in apparent happiness the night they ran into each other at Shiro Sushi; Kenzie smiling brightly as she led Ava on a tour of the Olympic Sculpture Park; Kenzie looking at her as if it were obvious why she had come today—because they were friends. Then she saw Galaxy Girl striding out of the smoke and flames with a mother and child clutched in her arms; Galaxy Girl stopping the attack on Panopticon; Galaxy Girl blurring onstage to stop the gun-wielding activists from accidentally killing their hostage audience. In whatever form she took, Kenzie had proven how good she was at heart.

The image of the fire rescue triggered another memory—hadn't Kenzie said her parents died in a fire? What had really happened to them to leave her all alone in the universe?

Ava stared at her hand, still clasped to Kenzie's chest. What was she doing, confronting her like this? Kenzie didn't owe her the truth of her identity. She wasn't complex code to be unraveled and parsed. She was a person, and while she may have been born on another planet, she deserved the same respect and autonomy Ava granted her fellow human beings. Despite what the Westbrooks believed, in spite of what they had tried to instill in her, aliens were people just like everyone else, and most of them were only trying to live their lives in peace.

"I'm sorry—" she started, not entirely sure what she planned to apologize for, but Kenzie didn't let her finish.

"I can't, Ava," she interrupted, sounding oddly hollow. "I can't do this." She released Ava's hand and started to stow her pen and notebook in her messenger bag, her movements wooden.

"Wait," Ava said, reaching out again. "It's okay. I'm not going to—"

But before Ava could make contact, Kenzie rose from the couch and bolted away, a mere blur in the light from the floor to ceiling windows. Ava blinked against the dizzying sense of loss. One moment they had been so close, and the next, Kenzie was halfway across the room, mumbling something about a meeting at ECM.

"Wait," Ava repeated, her voice bordering embarrassingly on desperate. She stood up so quickly she bumped her shin on the stupid low coffee table that had been her mother's idea of workplace chic.

Kenzie paused at the door. "I really am glad you're all right, Ava," she said quietly, her sincerity—and her regret—evident in the brief look she cast over her shoulder.

And then, just like that, she was gone.

CHAPTER EIGHT

Kenzie leaned against the back wall of the elevator, barely noticing the car's motion. What the heck had just happened? Except she knew: Ava had all but asked Kenzie if she was Galaxy Girl, and Kenzie had very nearly admitted she was because apparently, what she felt for Ava ran far deeper than any crush had a right to.

She closed her eyes as the elevator stopped halfway down the tower and more people got on, their voices grating in the enclosed space. How was this even happening? Only a couple of months ago, she'd been a happily single photojournalist content with passing as human, and now she was an out alien superhero who was at least partially in love with a human woman whose brother was the most notorious anti-alien terrorist on the planet. Not that the human in question shared her feelings. After the way Ava had just reacted to being close to her—she had been frightened again, Kenzie was sure of it—she couldn't imagine facing her anytime soon.

When the elevator finally reached the ground floor, Kenzie lurched slightly. And okay, very funny, Galaxy Girl being knocked off balance just after being knocked off balance. But really, she thought as she joined the steady stream of humanity crossing Hyperion Tower's beautiful glass-walled lobby, it wasn't funny at all.

The first text arrived that evening while she was at the pub with Matt and Antonio, the latter of whom she was still giving the cold shoulder. In her book, that meant no really big smiles and only short answers to direct questions. Her heart actually skipped when she checked her phone and saw Ava's name. She only hesitated a moment before opening the message.

"I'm sorry about earlier. Can we talk?"

What was she sorry for? Kenzie was the one who had frightened her, not the other way around.

Matt leaned closer. "Is that Sloane? Tell her to get her gay ass down here, pronto."

"Her ass isn't gay," Antonio said. "Besides, who even says *pronto*?"

"Um, Italian speakers? Of whom there are at least 60 million across the world?"

"That might be true if *pronto* wasn't a Spanish word."

And they were off, bickering good-naturedly as usual.

Kenzie stared down at Ava's contact photo, one of the pictures she had taken herself the first time they'd met. It was stunning. Ava was stunning, her green eyes crinkling with her smile. She'd been looking directly at Kenzie when she snapped the shot—a Kenzie she'd presumed to be human, not the alien variant who made her breathing shallow and her skin clammy. Kenzie closed her eyes. She hadn't intended to trap Ava's hand like that. She just hadn't been sure what to do about Ava's interest in seeing what was under her shirt—or about her own startling urge to show her.

She couldn't really reveal her identity to Ava, though,

could she? While Kenzie didn't want to believe someone she cared about was capable of being genuinely villainous, she also wasn't the best judge of character. Humans and Zattalians had such different communication styles. A dozen years in, certain human expressions that should probably mean something to her still went right over her head. Even when she did manage to correctly parse a flick of the eyes or lift of an eyebrow, she wasn't always confident in her interpretation.

Good thing she could fly. That one ability made up for a heck of a lot. And yet, she was only now stretching her wings, so to speak. *Hide who you are*, the Shepherd-Hendersons had taught her since the day she'd arrived on Earth. Somewhere along the way hiding had become second nature, and usually Sloane was the only one who ever saw through her. Now, it appeared, there was someone else who could see what was real and what wasn't. But why did that someone have to be a Westbrook?

Maybe Sloane had the right idea. Maybe denial—or *compartmentalization*, as the kids were calling it these days—was the best option. Kenzie muted her notifications and popped home to take a quick shot of Bandal rum. For the first time in her life, she understood why humans sometimes said they "needed" a drink. Great. Another milestone to not celebrate.

The following morning, the second text was waiting when she turned on her phone: "Please, Kenzie? I only want to talk."

This time, Kenzie had to close her fist to keep from replying. Ava was a gorgeous, brilliant—*no*. Well, yes, but for the purposes of the discussion Kenzie was currently having with herself, Ava was an executive at a firm that specialized in unabashedly pro-human, Earth-first goods. Also, she had been raised by the same family that had produced the evil mastermind of every alien refugee's worst nightmare, as Sloane had reminded Kenzie only a few days earlier.

Kenzie almost turned off her notifications as she walked to work, but an hour later, she was glad she hadn't when Sloane texted during ECM's editorial team meeting to request Galaxy Girl's assistance with a Panopticon mission. Kenzie was thrilled to have something to do other than journalism, which wasn't nearly as distracting as punching bad guys. Not that she usually *punched* the bad guys, per se, but today she might make an exception. An alien detainee—one of a group of Bryllian slavers apparently looking for refugees to kidnap, since they tended to be an easy target rarely missed by anyone—had escaped a Seattle Police Department holding cell and was hiding in a warehouse just south of downtown.

Sloane's text didn't provide these details. Using the code they'd developed, she shared just enough information so that Kenzie would know what to search on. The AP wire provided the rest, including the location of the warehouse where the four-armed brute had taken hostages and was currently refusing to communicate with the Panopticon team arrayed outside.

"Message received!" Kenzie texted back, which in their code meant she was on her way. Admittedly, their communication system was a bit unwieldy, but it was a work in progress.

This would be her first semi-official Panopticon team-up, she realized as she tried to subtly sneak out of the conference room, ignoring Antonio's questioning gaze and Matt's waggling eyebrows. While it might be a bit questionable to partner with the bureau tasked with protecting humans from aliens, she would take the action where she could find it. Besides, Sloane worked for the bureau, and slavers were universally bad (including Kenzie's ancestors), so it was a no-brainer, really. This time, though, she didn't think she would involve D'aman. She wanted to see what she was capable of on her own.

The rest of the day was chaotic, but in a good way. She was so busy with reconnaissance work and the eventual apprehension of the off-world gangster that she barely had time to think about Ava or the unanswered texts stacking up accusingly on their shared thread. Afterward, Sloane and Matt insisted on celebrating the successful Galaxy Girl/Panopticon team-up with a round of drinks at the pub, and Kenzie had to admit that the win did feel pretty freaking good. Compartmentalization accomplished.

Except that it wasn't, really. Sloane had a date with Mika, and Matt had edits to finish up on a story, so everyone headed home earlier than usual. With no one and nothing else to distract her, Kenzie's anxiety came roaring back. Had Ava seen the article about the Guild House attack that had gone to press early this morning? Was she pissed that Kenzie hadn't spun the story in Hyperion's favor? These and other questions refused to let her read herself to sleep, so Kenzie ended up spending the rest of the night trying to soothe herself with Netflix and ice cream. In fact, she ate so much ice cream that she ran out of cookie dough, which was how she ended up in her flannel PJ pants in the freezer aisle of the Ballard Fred Meyer in the middle of the night, questioning all of her life choices.

The following morning, she arrived at work earlier than usual and immediately started tracking down sources for her story about the Bryllian's capture. Given that Sloane's colleagues comprised half her sources and Mika's the other half, minimal legwork was required. Her phone remained quiet throughout the day, and she thought maybe Ava had given up, a notion that caused equal parts relief and sorrow. But then, late that afternoon as she was seated at her desk finishing up her final story edits, texts number three and four arrived: "Saw you on the news yesterday. I'm glad you're all right." And then, "I'm here whenever you're ready."

The second text ended with an emoji that left Kenzie gasping for air, a most unfamiliar sensation. She pushed away from her desk and, chair spinning, stared at the heart emoji Ava had sent her. As in, a red heart that in Earth parlance traditionally meant *love*.

"Dude, what happened?" Matt asked, peering over her cubicle wall. "Is it Sloane? Do you have to—" he lowered his voice—"you know, go?"

Kenzie shook her head dumbly and stood up. Her legs felt weak, but she was sure that was only because she'd used way too much energy beating up on a giant, four-armed fugitive alien the day before. Couldn't be that last text. Except it totally was.

"It's nothing," she told Matt, and sped out of the office.

She ducked into the lobby, nodded at the receptionists, and ran up the stairs to the roof. No one else was around, so she dropped onto one of the patio chairs, tensing as it creaked. She was already on Becky the office manager's bad side; if she broke another chair or phone set, she was going to have to replace it with her own funds. The patio chair held, though, and after a moment she settled on it more gingerly, staring unseeingly at the downtown skyline spread out before her.

Setting aside Ava's potential villainy for the moment, did the heart emoji mean what Kenzie hoped it did, or was it merely a friendly gesture between friends? With guys there seemed to be the assumption that you could always be more than friends, but with girls it was the exact opposite. On the surface, Ava was so far out of Kenzie's league as to be interstellar, which was probably why Kenzie had fallen so hard for her. Not seeing Ava these past few days had been painful. Right now, this very minute, she wanted nothing more than to launch herself into the sky and drop onto Ava's office balcony. Because despite being afraid of her, Ava still wanted to see her, too. Kenzie just wasn't sure if Ava intended to confess feelings of a romantic nature or kidnap her for Sentinel.

She stared at the message thread, mining it for clues. Her gut told her that Ava was nothing like her brother, and that even if she was at the AFT meeting, it didn't mean she wasn't exactly who she'd claimed to be: a business executive trying to move her family's historically regressive company in a more progressive direction. Despite what Sloane might believe, change like that didn't happen overnight. Assuming Ava did return Kenzie's feelings, though, how could it possibly work? Ava was a public figure, and Kenzie had always relied on flying beneath everyone's radar. That is, until she took to flying about the city in her superhero suit. Staying hidden wasn't an option anymore, but to protect her friends and family, she had to at least try.

Clearly, she needed to talk to someone who knew about these things. Sloane? But no, because then she would have to tell her sister why she and Ava hadn't been talking. The same went for D'aman. There was Matt, but his longest-term relationship was with his Xbox console. Antonio obviously wasn't an option because, obviously. Mika, the only other gay person she knew, supposedly didn't know Kenzie was an alien. Besides, anything Kenzie told her would immediately find its way back to Sloane. All Sloane had to do was look at Mika sternly and the usually hard-ass detective cracked faster than Kenzie did when someone waved pot stickers in her direction.

Frustrated, she stood up and shoved her phone in her back pocket, heading back downstairs to wrap up her story. It was going to have to be Sloane, wasn't it? There was literally no one else on Earth she could talk to about Ava. *Freaking frack.*

Her irritation inspired her to turn the tables on Sloane and drop in on her at home to see how she liked being interrupted. Sloane's house—one of the last cute brick bungalows on the top of Queen Anne Hill, as she liked to say—was only three blocks from Kenzie's building. Not long after the bus dropped her off on Queen Anne Ave, Kenzie crept up the sidewalk to her sister's house. But instead of going to the front door like she usually did, she vaulted the eight-foot-tall cedar fence she'd helped Sloane build around the backyard and crept up to the deck. Sloane was inside, and the sliding door to the kitchen/dining area was unlocked as usual.

"Hi!" she said triumphantly as she burst into the house, and then immediately froze. If not for the kissing, she suspected it would have felt great to be the sneaker instead of the sneaked-up-on-er. But there was just so much kissing... and wait, was that a naked shoulder?

"Aargh!" she cried, spinning away and covering her face with both hands. "My eyes! My poor, traumatized eyes!"

"Very funny," Sloane said, over the sound of rustling clothing. "Speaking of eyes, why didn't you use yours?"

Kenzie glanced over her shoulder and noted that the kissing had stopped, and her sister was now safely a foot away from Mika rather than making out with her against the kitchen counter. Relieved, she turned back around to see her sister shoot Mika a nervous look, as if she'd just realized what she'd said.

"Um..." Kenzie said intelligently. If she could have, she would have told Sloane that she *had* used her super vision before sneaking in. But when she'd observed her sister standing at the kitchen counter, it hadn't occurred to her to X-ray Sloane to make sure no one was behind her. Unfortunate, really.

Mika's eyes had narrowed, and she looked between the two of them while Kenzie and Sloane both held their breath. But then Mika only smiled and said, "With as much time as you two spend together, it was bound to happen at some point. I'm actually surprised it took this long."

Kenzie frowned, tempted to argue the point, but Sloane cut in smoothly and said, "Yeah, you're right. Anyway, it could have been so much worse!" She turned a look on Kenzie that clearly said, *If you ruin this for me I will cut a bitch.*

"Whatever," Kenzie grumbled. "It's not like you don't barge into my studio whenever you feel like it."

"She's got a point," Mika said, and Kenzie beamed at her because solidarity with Sloane's girlfriend was not to be taken lightly.

"That's different," Sloane said. "I'm in a relationship, whereas you…" She stopped and stared as Kenzie kicked the rug under the table in the dining alcove, refusing to meet her gaze. "Wait, what's that look?"

"No way," Mika practically shouted. "Did you and Ava hook up?"

"Dude," Sloane hissed. "That's my little sister you're talking about."

And, *great*, Kenzie thought. Everyone knew she had a crush on Ava. Just fantastic. "No, we didn't hook up. More like the opposite," she said, and gave Sloane what she hoped was a subtle look.

"The opposite?" Sloane asked. "What does that mean?"

"It means I had a very interesting conversation with her." She waggled her eyebrows at her sister.

Mika held up a hand. "I sense a sister chat coming on.

How about I run out and grab some wine and cheese? Trader Joe's has that Stilton you like, babe, and I'd love to try it with that new Port."

Usually Mika seemed so much like the quintessential rough and tumble city cop that Kenzie forgot she came from a wealthy family. But then she would say something like that and it all came flooding back.

"That sounds really gouda," Kenzie said, cracking herself up.

Sloane rolled her eyes and leaned in to kiss Mika. "That would be great. Thanks."

Kenzie looked away, fearing a repeat of earlier, but instead she heard the sound of keys jangling and a quiet laugh as Mika exited the kitchen.

"She's laughing at me, isn't she?"

"I mean, who isn't?" Sloane folded her arms across her chest. "Now, out with it. What's going on?"

"I just want you to know, this isn't my fault. Do you promise to remember that?"

"Kenzie…" her big sister said in her best exasperated secret agent tone.

Sloane might want to have this conversation standing up, but Kenzie most definitely did not. She pulled out a chair from the Ikea dining set she'd helped build without breaking a single part—an accomplishment considering she literally forgot her own strength at times—and settled carefully on the fake wood seat. Ikea furniture was the worst, but it was also easily replaced.

"Okay," she began. "So, you know how I interviewed Ava the other day about the Guild House thing?"

"Yes."

"Well, it seems that… The thing is, I think maybe, and again, this really isn't my fault—"

"Spit it out, Kenzie."

She looked down at the dark red placemat set with Sloane's nice dishes, the orange ones with the Southwest design. There were two place settings, actually, and a pair of unlit taper candles beside a small vase of flowers, and— "Crap. I totally interrupted date night, didn't I?"

Sloane shrugged. "It's fine. You obviously needed to talk, or you wouldn't be here, right? So talk. She's not going to be gone all that long, and I have an agenda item to discuss, too."

"You do? You can totally go first if you want," she offered generously.

"I swear by the light of Alia, Kenzie…"

"Sloane! That is not okay!" As her sister just stared at her, Kenzie huffed. "Fine. Anyway, as I was saying, I met with Ava the other day and, well, I'm not sure but I think, maybe, possibly, she might have—" she paused and then said in a rush, "figured out I'm Galaxy Girl."

"She—" Sloane bit off whatever she was about to say, closed her eyes, and took a deep breath, waiting to speak again only after she had released her breath slowly and steadily. It took a while. For a human, she had decent lung capacity.

Kenzie tapped her fingers against the tabletop, waiting for the inevitable explosion. But it never came.

Instead, Sloane opened her eyes and said succinctly, "Tell me everything."

She did, although she *may* have left out certain details like the biting of lips and the way Ava had toyed with her shirt button, almost as if she were going to take matters into her own hands. Sloane, she had a feeling, would not be okay with the non-consensual nature of that particular interaction. Kenzie hadn't minded, though, not really. She knew Ava was a scientist, an engineer accustomed to taking gadgets apart to see how they worked. Not that Kenzie was a gadget whose internal parts could be disassembled and tinkered with. Fortunately, Ava had seemed to be aware of that fact, too.

When she finished, she sat back, waiting again for the outburst of anger from Sloane that typically accompanied any threat to Kenzie's identity, but once again her sister surprised her. Sloane only nodded slowly, brow slightly furrowed, and tapped her chin as she said, "That's not entirely unexpected."

Kenzie stared at her. "It's not?"

"No. Like I said before, you and Ava have been spending a lot of time together, and you've been all over social media in your costume—sorry, your awesome suit. Plus, she's a literal genius. How did you leave it?"

"Um, I left?"

"You left?"

"I didn't know what to do!"

Sloane shook her head. "You need to find out for sure what she knows. You need to talk to her, Kenz."

"Isn't that the kettle calling the pot black?"

"It's the pot calling the—*whatever*. What are you even talking about?"

"I'm talking about Mika. You should at least tell her I'm unregistered."

Her sister snorted. "Telling her would only put you and her at risk. She works for Seattle PD, remember?"

"She's also not an idiot," Kenzie pointed out. "She's going to figure it out sooner or later, just like Ava did."

Sloane's mouth flattened into an obstinate line that Kenzie was more than familiar with. "That may be, but until she does, she's not hearing it from me."

Even Kenzie, who was famously bad at human emotions, understood that this was a bad plan. But Sloane would do whatever she thought was right, and Kenzie had learned long ago that swaying her from her chosen path was nigh impossible.

"There's something else," she said, and pulled up her text thread with Ava before tossing Sloane her phone.

Sloane made an exasperated sound as she caught it. "Kenzie! No wonder you go through so many phones."

"What? You caught it, didn't you?"

Sloane ignored her and scrolled through the messages. Then her thumb paused on the screen. "Holy shit! She sent you a heart?"

"I know. That's why I'm here," Kenzie moaned, hiding her face in her hands again.

"Huh. Maybe I got her wrong, after all. Or maybe this is just the next move in her diabolical plan…"

"Sloane!" If she had been standing, Kenzie would have stomped her foot. But fortunately for Sloane's wood floor, she was seated. "You have to stop saying things like that. Ava is not like the rest of her family, okay?"

"And you know this because…?"

"Because I just do. I have superpowers, remember?"

"If D'aman says she's cool, I'll believe them. But until then, I reserve the right to be suspicious."

"Only if you keep your suspicions to yourself," Kenzie retorted. "I'm serious, Sloane. I really like her. I think she really likes me too, despite the whole unregistered alien walking among us thing."

Sloane nodded slowly. "Okay. I hear you. I'll try to be more open-minded, okay?"

Mollified, Kenzie nodded back at her. "Thank you. Now, what the heck should I do?"

"Honestly? This is a bit outside my purview. Are you okay if I share this with Mika? She's more experienced in the whole lady love department."

Kenzie expelled her own decently long breath. "Yes, but only if you promise never to say *lady love* again."

"Totally. My bad." She brightened. "As long as we're waiting for her, can I pick your brain about something?"

Kenzie didn't point out that the phrase *pick your brain* wasn't the best thing to say to an alien on post-Sentinel Earth. She simply nodded and listened as Sloane explained the idea she'd come up with for how to contact Kenzie for future Panopticon team-ups.

"Seriously?" Kenzie said when she'd finished. "And you call Matt the comic book geek. Your idea is to shine a giant bat signal into the air?"

"It wouldn't be a *bat* signal, it would be—"

"What then, a glowing green mask?"

"Hilarious," Sloane said, clearly unamused. "Apparently you missed the part where I said it would be an *audio* beacon. Basically, we would station a speaker on Panopticon's roof and anytime we needed you, we could send out a message at a frequency only you and D'aman can hear. I got the idea from the ring they gave you."

Kenzie fingered the ring on her right hand. Her left wrist was occupied by her Galaxy Girl tool belt bracelet, and honestly, she was relieved that Sloane didn't want to give her additional paraphernalia. Her body was getting a little crowded as it was.

"It has to be something Panopticon can't use to trace your whereabouts," Sloane added. "I want all communications to originate with us, not with you."

"It sounds like you don't completely trust your employer."

"That's because I don't," Sloane said. "And you shouldn't either."

"Fair enough. Actually, an audio beacon is perfect because then D'aman would also be able to hear it."

"I'm not going to say I was thinking that too, but I was totally thinking that, too."

Sloane's smile was more of the charming variety than the smug one, and Kenzie found herself smiling back at her impossible older sister. "You've certainly changed your tune, haven't you? Whatever happened to me keeping a low profile?"

Sloane shrugged. "I guess I finally realized how important this is to you. I don't want to stand in the way of you achieving the life you've always wanted, Kenzie. Safety isn't everything, especially if it means living a shadow life. Plus, this way D'aman and I both get to do the superheroing with you. Because, let's face it, I'm totally the Q in this scenario."

Kenzie laughed, shaking her head. There was the control freak she knew and loved. Still, she couldn't argue with facts. "I'll check with D'aman, but I'm pretty sure they're in, too."

"Awesome. Pretty soon we're going to have our very own Hall of Justice."

"Again with the comic book reference." A sound outside caught her attention, and she added, "Mika's on her way in. But yes, let's proceed with the beacon idea."

"I already had one of my agents set it up."

So typical. Ava wasn't the only genius in the crew. Although, was she technically in the crew at this point? *Aargh.*

"I come bearing smoked gouda," Mika said as she padded into the kitchen, a bottle of red wine and several chunks of cheese held before her like a sacred offering.

Which, Kenzie could totally get behind. Food was the closest thing to a religious experience she had found on Earth. An image of Ava leaning close, eyes dark and lips slightly parted as her fingers toyed with the edge of Kenzie's shirt collar, flashed into her mind, and Kenzie felt herself blush. Well, the closest thing so far, anyway.

While Sloane finished making dinner, Kenzie shared

Ava's text thread with Mika. "What do you think? Is the heart, like, a friends thing? Or does it mean more?"

"It can totally be a friends thing," Mika said, and Kenzie's heart started to sink. "But in this case," the diminutive detective added, glancing up at Kenzie with an impish grin, "I'm going to have to go with more than friends."

Kenzie pushed up her glasses. "Really?"

"Really. You forget, I've seen the two of you together. Ava is definitely into you. I just didn't realize it was mutual before." And she held up her hand for a high five.

Kenzie dutifully—and carefully—slapped her palm. "I thought you hated the Westbrooks."

Mika, like Sloane, had joined the Seattle PD Alien Affairs Bureau because she wanted to protect aliens from humans, not the other way around. In previous conversations, Mika had expressed her fury with Sentinel's actions against the alien refugee community, decrying in particular Nicholas Westbrook and his false claims of pro-humanism.

"I hate the anti-alien Westbrooks," Mika clarified. "Your girl seems different from the rest of her family, which I can appreciate."

Kenzie nodded. She knew from Sloane that Mika wasn't close with her parents, apparently because of the gay thing. Mormons weren't huge fans of the rainbow crowd, according to Mika, who had been raised in the religion that Kenzie still had a hard time believing was as popular as it seemed to be. She didn't have a problem with polygamy in theory; there were plenty of alien cultures where multiple marriage partners were embraced or even encouraged. But when only men were allowed to have more than one spouse, that was clearly just patriarchy at work. Plus, the whole magic underwear thing Mika had described was kind of hard to grasp.

"Can I ask what's stopping you from texting her back?" Mika asked.

So many things, Kenzie thought, catching Sloane's warning look. "Nerves, I guess?" Which was true enough.

"I hear you. Sloane said you just came out as bisexual. Congratulations, by the way."

"Oh. Well, thanks," Kenzie said awkwardly, and it was her turn to flash a glare in her sister's direction.

"We totally have to go out to celebrate," Mika continued. "Right, Sloane?"

"Definitely. *Tomorrow* night," Sloane said, her tone firm.

Kenzie could tell when she wasn't wanted. The memory of all the kissing from before made an unfortunate return, and she jumped up from the table so quickly she almost knocked her chair over. "All right! Well, you two enjoy your date. I have pizza to order and video games to play with Matt and Antonio."

She didn't actually have a pizza/video game plan already in place with the boys, but that didn't mean she wouldn't be eating pizza and playing video games with them tonight. After all, it was a Friday. Matt, at least, probably wouldn't have a date.

"Have fun," Mika said, giving her a quick hug.

Sloane stopped tossing the salad long enough to give her a hug and murmur in her ear, "Don't overthink it, okay? If it's right, it's right."

"Even if she's a Westbrook?"

"You heard my brilliant girlfriend. She's not like the rest of her family. Probably."

Probably. Kenzie pulled away and smacked Sloane's shoulder, ignoring her sister's muffled grunt of pain. "By-ee!"

As she left the way she had come, she resisted the urge

to pull out her phone and read through the text thread with Ava yet again. She would have to respond at some point, but that heart emoji made it clear she better figure out what she wanted before getting in touch. Because this thing with Ava was serious, and not only because Ava had guessed that Kenzie had multiple layers to her identity.

Pizza and video games it was, she decided, pulling up her ongoing thread with Matt. Everything else could wait for now.

#

When Ava heard the knock on her hotel suite door, she almost dropped the plate she was washing. Could it be Kenzie? She hadn't texted, but maybe she'd decided to drop by again, only inside the building this time. Or, no, what if her mother was back? Amelia had visited unexpectedly two nights earlier to demand Ava accompany her to dinner to answer her questions about the masked alien who could pick Ava out of a crowd. Ava had agreed to go mostly because she knew her mother would behave in public, and sure enough, what had followed was a stilted conversation mainly about business and politics. Amelia had left all mention of anything personal until the end, when she insisted on dropping Ava back at her suite.

"Have you spoken with your brother?" she'd asked as she stood just inside the hotel room door, eyes averted as if this question wasn't the true reason she had come to see Ava.

"No," Ava had replied, tossing her key card on the nearby breakfast bar.

"Have you written to him?"

"Why would I?"

Her mother tossed her head in irritation. "I thought perhaps you would have found it in your heart to apologize to him by now."

"*Apologize*? What do I possibly have to apologize for?"

Ava had asked, deliberately trying to provoke her mother's temper.

Amelia regarded her coldly. "Do not pretend to be naive. Your testimony single-handedly placed your brother behind bars."

"He was kidnapping and torturing people! That's what landed him behind bars, not my testimony."

Her mother waved a dismissive hand. "They can hardly be called people, now, can they?"

Ava had pictured Kenzie, with her kind smile and awkward gestures, her genuine concern for others and her willingness to risk her own life for the sake of strangers. Kenzie, an alien, demonstrated the best of humanity on a daily basis, far better than Ava's own purportedly human family members.

Ah, family. Couldn't live with them, couldn't avoid them every single day for the rest of time.

There was really only one way to find out who was at her door on a quiet Saturday afternoon, so Ava dried her hands on a towel and started forward. If the rumors about Zattalians were true, *some* people might be able to see through inanimate objects, so she made sure to keep her pace slow and measured as she approached the door and peered through the peephole. On the other side, a familiar face greeted her, but it didn't belong to the person she'd been simultaneously hoping and dreading to see. Straightening her shoulders, she pinned a smile to her face and opened the door.

"Beatrice!" she said. "What are you doing here?"

Her best friend's smile faded slightly. "You're acting weird. Why are you acting weird? Is this not a good time?"

Ava held the door wide for her. "No, it's fine. I'm so glad to see you, really! But, um, how exactly did you get up here?"

"Blaine at the front desk remembered me from last

time."

"Really? Apparently, he and I need to have a talk."

"Don't scare him. He's like ten years old. Now give me some of that sweetness, sweetness." Without waiting for a response, she dropped her bag and enveloped Ava in a spine-crunching, rib-shattering hug.

Ava squeezed back, inhaling the scent of jasmine in her friend's unruly cloud of hair. Ava always claimed not to be much of a hugger, but being in her best friend's grasp felt good. For a moment, she remembered the heft of Kenzie's arms around her the night they'd had their picnic at the sculpture park, how warm and strong and *perfect* Kenzie's taller frame had felt against her... Nope, not going there.

"How are you?" Beatrice asked as she pulled away.

"Peachy." She picked up the bag and ushered her friend inside the suite. "Where's Rowan?"

"Home with James and both grandmothers. You know what that means, don't you?" She wiggled her perfectly tweezed eyebrows.

Ava's smile was genuine this time. "White or red?"

"Are you kidding? Break out the good stuff. For once I don't have to worry about my milk jugs."

Hand on the freezer door, Ava paused. "Does this mean you're staying for the weekend?"

"Damn straight. Assuming you'll have me."

"Oh, I'm always up for having you," Ava drawled, winking over her shoulder as she unscrewed the top to the vodka. "But definitely not in a straight way."

"If only." Beatrice sighed and collapsed dramatically on the couch. "Unfortunately, I am an old married woman. But that doesn't mean you can't have fun."

Ava scoffed. "Like that's going to happen."

"It could."

"An asteroid could strike the planet tomorrow and end all sentient life on Earth, too."

"Ah, I see we're channeling Dark Ava today."

"Today? More like this year." Ava handed Beatrice her drink and sat down beside her. "To the Dangs," she added, holding up her glass for their traditional toast.

Beatrice clinked it and offered her customary rejoinder: "To the Westbrooks."

"To the Dang Westbrooks," they said in unison, and took a drink.

More like the goddamn Westbrooks these days, really, but Ava kept that thought to herself. She could feel her friend watching her as they sipped their vodka tonics, so she studiously trained her gaze elsewhere. She loved Beatrice, she did. It was just that today she felt closer to the edge than usual. A sympathetic look and a kind word from her oldest friend on the planet would probably make her bawl.

Of course, that wouldn't be anything new. In the nearly thirty years they'd been friends, they had seen each other at their worst innumerable times. Beatrice's mother had worked at Hyperion Tech's New York office, and the two girls had met at a birthday party for another executive's child. By the end of the party, they'd bonded over their shared love of all things horse-related, thus beginning a friendship that lasted through prep school, college, and beyond. Ava still maintained that Beatrice was the only reason she'd had any friends at Deerfield, and honestly, Ava had spent more weekends at Smith College with Bea than at MIT. If not for Smith's liberal, lesbian-friendly culture, she may not have come out as early—or as easily—as she had.

Ava was pretty sure Beatrice's friendship had saved her from potential suicidal ideation on more than one occasion. Beatrice, meanwhile, claimed that the Westbrook clan's flair for dramatics had saved her from dying of boredom, so they were even.

"I see what you're doing over there," Beatrice said.

"What am I doing?"

"That stoic WASP bullshit. Come on, A, talk to me."

Ava let her head fall onto her friend's shoulder. "I don't know what to say, Bea. Everything is absolute shite right now."

"If you had only come to LA for Easter like I wanted you to…"

"I told you, I had to work."

"I don't know," Beatrice said, reaching for her free hand and tangling their fingers together. "Are you sure Hyperion is worth it? You could always come home with me and run my label, you know. The offer still stands."

Beatrice ran a small recording studio out of her home in Laurel Canyon, while her husband worked as an entertainment lawyer at Warner Brothers. She'd won a Grammy a decade earlier as a solo artist, but she'd always preferred production work to performing. Now her Grammy nominations were for helping other musicians realize their dreams. When Ava had shown up on Bea's doorstep the week Amelia had arm-wrestled her into coming to work at the Seattle office, Bea had tried to convince her to move to LA instead.

"Be careful," Ava said now, only half-joking. "I just might take you up on it."

"I wish you would."

Ava closed her eyes. "I have to at least try to save the company. Not that that's going particularly well. The board is threatening a vote of no confidence if our shares keep falling."

"It's kind of hard to shore up the company's stock when your family is determined to blow up the world."

"Not the world, Bea. Just the aliens."

"Do you want to talk about what your terrible, horrible, no good, very bad mother was doing here?"

"No, I think we covered most of it the other night," Ava said, waving a hand in a gesture that immediately reminded her of her mother. "Let's do something fun. Want to go out for sushi and a movie?"

"We could. But I have a better idea." And she smiled devilishly.

Uh-oh. Beatrice's "better" ideas had landed Ava in more trouble over the years than her own family's plots. As long as she didn't end up on Instagram making a drunken idiot out of herself like the last time Beatrice had dragged her out… She had a feeling the board's vote of no confidence would come sooner rather than later if she did. Worse, Kenzie might get wind of their shenanigans, and Ava didn't want the other woman to think any worse of her than she already did.

Her memory helpfully provided an image of Kenzie leaning into her side at the pub on Queen Anne Ave, their faces close together, Kenzie's warmth stealing into her, their hands nearly touching on the smooth wooden tabletop. Resolutely, she pushed the thought away. Kenzie hadn't spoken to her since the incident at her office, and there was no reason to think she would anytime soon. Or, possibly, ever.

Thank god for best friends who somehow magically knew when you needed them most.

Unsurprisingly, Beatrice's ideas were pretty awesome. Declaring that Ava was in desperate need of retail therapy, Beatrice took her shopping at a handful of boutiques that made Ava swear she was in Beverly Hills, not uber-casual Seattle. It had been a while since she had shopped for anything other than professional clothes, and she found herself enjoying the swanky shops where they were served wine in crystal goblets while they browsed.

After dinner at a rooftop restaurant with an amazing view of the city—though Ava couldn't help checking the skyline for a certain blurry figure each time a siren sounded—Ramón drove them to a Capitol Hill speakeasy that Ava had read about in ECM's weekly magazine. The speakeasy was located above a busy restaurant. To reach it, they had to wind through crowded tables, stop near a locked door, and give their names over an old-fashioned telephone. A dark, narrow stairway lined with vintage photos of naked dancers (thankfully all female) led them to a small room with a polished brass bar and antique furniture. There was no drink list. Instead, the bartender dressed in period clothing interviewed each of them about their favorite cocktail flavors, and then brought them a custom drink based on their answers.

As they tried each other's cocktails and reminisced about past adventures, Ava treasured the rare opportunity to catch up with Beatrice without James or Rowan to distract them. Ava loved her godson, and James was a good guy. But going out like this with Beatrice reminded her that she'd had a life before her father died, before her brother had tried to destroy the world (or at least the aliens), before her mother had walked away and left her at the helm of the family company. Bea's visit signaled that if everything fell apart in Seattle, Ava would be okay. She would always be okay—assuming her family's enemies didn't kill her, of course.

Focusing on the details of someone else's life was another welcome change. Beatrice's days were hectic in a completely different way from hers. On top of a job she loved, Bea had to juggle a baby, a spouse, and clients who were mostly young and often not very responsible. Fortunately, she had family support. Her mother had recently retired from Hyperion and moved to LA to spend more time with the baby, her first grandchild.

"She sees him more than she ever saw me," Beatrice groused, swirling the lime green liquid in her martini glass.

"Maybe she realizes what she missed with you and doesn't want to make the same mistake again."

Beatrice shrugged, but Ava could see how much her mother's belated shift in priorities grated on her. "Maybe. But what about you? Is there a wife and kids in your future? Or are you still determined to pour all of your passion into your mother's company only to realize later how many regrets you have?"

"You know I can't afford to get involved with anyone right now," she said, evading the question *and* her friend's sharp gaze.

"That's just something you tell yourself so you don't have to risk getting hurt. Not everyone is a cheating ass like Mallory."

Ava winced at the mention of her ex. Mal had gotten a job in Chicago a year before Ava had relocated to Seattle. They'd tried the distance thing for a couple of months, but they'd failed. Spectacularly and semi-publicly, in fact. Ah, for the pre-social-media era of the past, when your friends typically found out about your partner's affair *after* you had.

"I know my instincts lean more toward flight than fight," she said, "but think about it, Bea. How could I in good conscience bring some innocent, unsuspecting person into my life, knowing she could become collateral damage?"

Even maintaining a friendship with Beatrice put her friend's family in danger—from pro-alien activists as well as from anti-alien terrorists. But even as Ava reminded herself of these facts, an image of Galaxy Girl flashed into her mind. Galaxy Girl, who was practically indestructible and routinely triumphed over armed attackers. Galaxy Girl, who was actually Kenzie, her crush who sometimes seemed like maybe, just maybe, she might want to kiss Ava, too.

Beatrice nodded, brow furrowing. "Valid. Still, that doesn't mean you can't get laid, you know. You don't have to get engaged to every girl you sleep with."

"I'm not like you," Ava said. "I don't do casual."

Unless she was really, really drunk and Beatrice started throwing her at randos. *Note to self*: time to slow down on the cocktails.

"Maybe you should learn because it cannot be good for your lady parts to go this long without sex. Besides, it doesn't have to be a complete stranger. What about that cute reporter, Kenzie? I thought you two were getting closer?"

"Yes, well, she's not exactly speaking to me right now."

Beatrice lifted an eyebrow. "What did you do?"

"More like what did my family do," Ava hedged, which wasn't *entirely* untrue.

"Ah." Beatrice nodded. "The Westbrook curse. In that case, what about Galaxy Girl? She's hot and, as a bonus, can obviously hold her own."

Ava almost snorted her drink, which would have been really bad given that it contained peppercorn. "Galaxy Girl?"

"You know, the superhero from the hashtag? I doubt she has room in her life for anything serious, and besides, I thought you had a thing for her?"

"I didn't say that," Ava denied quickly. "I don't even know what she looks like under that mask. I mean, she could be hideous. Or, like, a thousand percent straight. Am I right?"

Beatrice's eyes narrowed. "Why are you rambling?

Wait, have you actually met her in real life?"

Ava gulped her drink and then coughed as the heat burned her throat. Goddamn custom cocktail.

"You have, haven't you?" Suddenly, Bea's eyes widened. "Holy shit. Is *that* why the reporter isn't speaking to you?"

"Kenzie is *not* Galaxy Girl," Ava hissed, and then glanced around to make sure no one was close enough to hear their exchange.

Bea frowned. "No, I meant was she jealous of you and…" She trailed off, looking at Ava, and then covered her mouth to stifle a laugh. "Oh my god, I can't believe you just outed Galaxy Girl! You are so bad at keeping secrets, Ava. I swear."

"I am not," Ava groused, picking at imaginary lint on her tailored pants. But denying a thing didn't make it untrue. No wonder Kenzie and her sister didn't trust her. She hadn't even known for a week yet and she was already giving away Galaxy Girl's identity. In her defense, she'd been drinking way too much tonight, and Beatrice knew her better than anyone else on Earth. Or any other planet, for that matter.

"You cannot tell a living soul," she added as Bea continued to laugh silently at her. "Not even James."

Bea recovered enough to assure her, "Don't worry. You don't succeed in LA if you can't keep secrets. Interesting, though. I'll have to ponder this one."

"You really don't."

"Well, someone needs to think about how to fix your disastrous love life."

Love. Ava sipped her drink more slowly this time, picturing the sad look Kenzie had cast her as she'd left Ava's office. God, she really was romance-challenged, wasn't she?

"Speaking of disasters," she said in an unsubtle attempt to shift the focus, "whatever happened with that young artist you found last month?"

The distraction worked, and Beatrice was off and running on a tale that involved a dog walker and a missing contract.

Ava only half-listened, her mind replaying Bea's earlier words, which had echoed her own idea: *Galaxy Girl can obviously hold her own.* Was it possible that Kenzie was the only person in the world Ava could safely date? Then again, "safe" was a relative term given Ava's brother's obsession with kidnapping and torturing a Zattalian. If he found out his sister was dating one... But Kenzie would have to be speaking to her in order for the whole dating thing to occur, so there was that.

They were just finishing their cocktails when Beatrice held up her phone in triumph. "Found it!"

Ava, who had assumed she was texting James, frowned. "Found what?"

"A gay bar hosting ladies' night. Have you been to the Balcony Club?"

"No, and we are not going there tonight, Beatrice. I told you, I'm not interested in meeting anyone right now."

That argument rarely swayed Beatrice when she was in find-Ava-a-hook-up mode, probably because she had a fierce aversion to being alone herself. Fortunately, she had never needed to be for long. Since adolescence had gifted her with long legs and large breasts (for an Asian, Beatrice always qualified), men and women alike had fallen at her feet. Back in college, when Beatrice flitted from boy to girl and back occasionally with more than a slight overlap, Ava used to tease her about giving bisexuals a bad name. Beatrice would only shrug helplessly and say, *I can't help it that I'm just that good.*

Predictably, Beatrice ignored her protests and downed

the rest of her drink. "All right, then. Let's go get you laid."

An hour later, Ava placed her hands on the hips of the woman twerking against her and moved in time to the music pulsating through the club. With the lights flashing and the crowd of mostly women dancing around her, she almost felt like she was back in college, when she and her friends had a standing date at a Boston all-ages club where they would drink and dance for a handful of hours every Thursday night. Or was it Tuesday? Ten years later, college was beginning to recede from her memory.

Beatrice glanced over her shoulder and gave her a huge smile as she worked her hips in mesmerizing fashion. At least Bea was still in her life—her one constant through all the moves and changes. Ava smiled back and realized that she actually felt happy in that moment. Despite everything, she could still find shining moments of pure joy in among the detritus. Her former pop star best friend was brilliant. But then, Ava had always known that.

They danced for an indeterminate amount of time, bouncing off other bodies and each other, and any self-consciousness Ava had felt in the beginning over what she was wearing soon faded. She didn't mind showing skin, but the sequined halter top Beatrice had picked out for her revealed significantly more side boob than she was accustomed to. Front boob too, for that matter.

At last Beatrice made the sign for a drink, and they headed to the bar, where they surveyed the seating area. Most of the tables were occupied, with a few male couples sprinkled in among the groups of women. Ava eyed the laughing couples enviously. She hadn't realized how much she missed being in a relationship until Kenzie came along. Work was useful for deadening any otherwise unmanageable human impulses.

"You know what time it is, don't you?" Beatrice asked

once she'd paid for their bottles of water. It was quieter here than the dance floor, so she didn't have to lean as close to be heard.

"No," Ava warned. "Don't you dare."

Beatrice smiled evilly. "Don't worry, I'll do the heavy lifting. Ooh, she looks cute." And with that she skipped away, headed for a brunette seated alone at a table not far from them.

Bea's target was attractive, but her profile also seemed familiar. She almost looked like—*oh, shit!* Ava leapt from her bar stool and rushed over, but Beatrice was already saying flirtily, "Have you met my friend Ava?"

"Actually," the brunette said, rising to her feet, "I have. Hello, Ava."

"Hi, Sloane," Ava said, forcing a smile. Because this wasn't awkward or anything.

Just then another woman appeared and slipped her arm around Sloane's waist. "Hey, Ava! Imagine seeing you here."

"Mika," Ava said, her smile more genuine. Mika had always been the friendliest of Kenzie's crew—which, honestly, wasn't saying much. Sloane and Antonio behaved toward Ava like Kenzie's personal security detail, while Matt's admiration was a little too awe-imbued to feel friendly. Still, she would take awe over the unimpressed stare Sloane was shooting her now. Of all the lesbians for Beatrice to hit on…

Her friend looked from the couple to Ava, eyebrows raised.

"Beatrice," Ava said, "this is Sloane Shepherd, my frien—um, Kenzie's sister, and her girlfriend, Mika Hansen."

"Kenzie," Beatrice repeated. "As in, reporter Kenzie?"

Ava nodded, praying Beatrice wouldn't give anything

away—like, for example, that a Westbrook knew Galaxy Girl's secret identity.

"Hey," Mika said, waving.

"Nice to meet you," Sloane said, but only after her girlfriend nudged her. "So what are you up to, Westbrook? Other than hitting on random women."

Ava tried not to clench her teeth too hard. Her dentist already wanted her to wear a mouth guard at night to prevent further damage. "I wasn't hitting on—"

Beatrice cut in. "Sorry," she said, adopting a semi-chagrined tone, "that was totally my fault. Ava was feeling a little low, so I dragged her out to have some fun."

"Oh," Sloane said grudgingly. "Don't worry about it. How do you guys know each other?"

"We went to school together," Ava said.

"Yeah—elementary school, middle school, prep school…" Bea supplied, smiling sideways at Ava. "We go way back."

Sloane's look thawed a little more. Bea had always been good at charming people she needed to be on her side. Or, as in this case, on her friend's side.

"Where are you from?" Mika asked.

"New York originally, but now I live in LA. I needed a break this weekend, so I flew in this morning to surprise Ava. It's harder than I expected to be away from my son, though."

She looked so pensive that even Ava felt a rush of empathy, despite the fact Bea had assured her earlier that she was loving her time away.

"Oh? How old?" Mika asked.

"Eleven months." Bea pulled her phone from her clutch and showed Mika her lock screen, which was a picture of Rowan curled up on James, thumb in his mouth, curls falling in perfect ringlets around his beautiful face.

"He's adorable," Mika cooed. Then she elbowed Sloane and jerked her chin at Ava. Sloane shook her head slightly, frowning as Mika repeated the gesture.

Ava watched the interaction closely. The amount of alcohol swimming through her bloodstream was making it hard to be sure, but they appeared to be communicating about her.

Mika rolled her eyes at Sloane and turned to face Ava. "Look, I'm apparently not supposed to tell you this, but in the interests of reducing unnecessary lesbodrama, I think you should know that you just missed Kenzie."

It took Ava's mind a second to catch up. Then her gaze flew to Sloane before snapping back to Mika. "Wait. Are you saying that Kenzie was *here*? As in, at this bar?"

"Yeah," Mika said easily. "Until about fifteen minutes ago."

Fifteen minutes earlier, Ava and Beatrice had been grinding semi-obscenely on the dance floor. Ava closed her eyes for a second, and then she asked Mika, "She didn't happen to mention seeing me before she left, did she?"

Mika's gaze was sympathetic. "She did, actually."

Ava expelled a frustrated breath. Just when she thought things between her and Kenzie couldn't get any worse… She grabbed her phone from her tiny sequined purse and started a new text.

"Kenzie," she typed, and then stopped. What the hell was she going to say? She needed to clear her head, a feat that was impossible in a crowded gay bar with Kenzie's sister watching her.

"I'll be right back," she told Beatrice, not even waiting for an answer. Then she maneuvered through the crowd and ducked outside into the cool night. Leaning against the bar's brick exterior, she stared down at her phone. Kenzie hadn't answered any of her previous messages. Why would she now, especially if she had seen Ava grinding on the dance floor with a seemingly random woman?

Still: "Hi," she typed. "I just talked to Sloane. I wish I'd known you were here."

She hit send and waited, her eyes on the steady flow of foot traffic along the sidewalk. The club was near Pioneer Square, where bars, night clubs, and comedy clubs drew patrons from city neighborhoods and suburban districts alike. That couple, with hipster haircuts and skinny jeans, probably lived in the city. The three men behind them, though? She would bet they were Bellevue soccer dads trying to relive their youth.

Her phone's chime startled her and she glanced down. Kenzie had responded. Ava hadn't allowed herself to hope, and yet there it was in black and white: *Kenzie Shepherd*. Quickly she clicked on the new message.

"You seemed pretty happy where you were."

Maybe it was Ava's imagination, but the words seemed to carry a very un-Kenzie-like bite. Had she left the club because she didn't want to see Ava, or because she didn't want to see her with anyone else?

The day's alcohol—and despite her best intentions, there had been a lot of it—flowed through her bloodstream and into her fingers: "I would have been happier with you."

The message app whirred, and then the "Sent" icon popped up, followed almost immediately by "Delivered." There wasn't really any way to misinterpret what she'd written, was there? She read it over again. Nope. The heart emoji from the day before could have been interpreted in a variety of ways, but with this message, she'd basically just confessed—*something*—to Kenzie. Now the ball was unquestionably in her court. Again… Ava chewed her bottom lip as she waited for a response, so focused on her phone that she didn't even register the man approaching.

"Hey, baby," he said, veering into her personal space.

"What are you doing out here all by your lonesome?" He loomed over her, a drunk, aging frat boy in a button-down shirt and pleated (pleated!) khakis, his thinning blonde hair slicked back from his red face.

Hyperion security was only ever a phone call away, but Ava could handle this sexist fuck. In fact, her restlessness could use a little venting. "I'm definitely not waiting for you," she said coolly. "Move along, jackass."

His expression slowly morphed into outrage, and he leaned closer, his mouth opening to release what would no doubt be a torrent of abuse. Before she could intercept his arm and flip him over her shoulder—she hadn't practiced in a while, but she was fairly sure judo was like riding a bicycle, except for the obvious differences—a blur of blonde hair, pale skin, and black rayon suddenly appeared between them. And then the frat boy was on his ass on the sidewalk several feet away, gaping up at the new arrival.

"She said she wasn't waiting for you," Kenzie said, fists clenched at her sides and gaze harder than Ava had ever seen.

And, *wow*. Kenzie was here in a short strappy dress that made her legs look fabulous, *and* she'd jumped in to protect Ava. Apparently, she took her hero identity seriously.

"I thought you left," Ava blurted, her tongue nearly tripping over the words.

Kenzie turned back to her, eyebrows lowering even further. "I did."

"But…?"

She shrugged, her usually expressive eyes unreadable. "I came back."

"I'm glad."

Ava moved a little closer, relieved when Kenzie didn't step back. She was so pretty in her short dress with spaghetti straps, her collarbone sharp and delicate at the same time. Usually her outfits kept so much of her body hidden that now Ava felt a little light-headed with all that creamy skin on display.

"Are you okay? He didn't touch you, did he?" Kenzie asked, eyes trailing over Ava in a similar appraisal. As her gaze seemed to get stuck on Ava's cleavage, she cleared her throat and pushed up her glasses. And it was such a familiar, sweet gesture that Ava wanted to—

"You bitch!"

Oh, right. The frat boy had regained his footing. As he advanced unsteadily upon them, Ava stepped neatly around Kenzie and delivered a swift knee to the man's groin. He crumpled back to the ground, both hands cupping his genitals while Ava stood over him. That was what he got for interrupting their almost-moment.

"Go back to the suburbs, asshole," she spat.

A crowd had started to gather now, and just as someone pulled out their phone—to record the scene? to call the police?—Ava felt a hand grip hers. She let Kenzie pull her away from the now purple-faced man and back inside the nearby club, her feet barely touching the ground as they zoomed past the bouncer.

"Kenzie." She squeezed the other woman's hand. "Slow down."

Halfway across the bar already, Kenzie stopped and let go of her hand. "You shouldn't have done that," she said, running her fingers over her neat bun as her eyes flitted around the dark room.

Ava stepped closer again. "Why not? Why should you have all the fun beating up the bad guys?"

Kenzie stared at her, a question rising in her gaze, and Ava remembered a beat too late that they hadn't actually discussed the fact that she knew about Kenzie's crime-fighting alter ego.

"Ava," she started, her voice low. But then her eyes

focused in the distance, and she stepped back.

Ava knew before she looked what she would find: Sloane, Mika, and Bea were headed their way.

"You came back," Sloane said when she reached them, her voice and eyes full of sisterly concern.

As Kenzie muttered something unintelligible to her sister, Beatrice leaned into Ava's side. "God, I love lesbodrama. P.S., your girl is a hottie. I definitely see the attraction."

Kenzie's gaze flew over to them, and Ava inwardly groaned. Super hearing, check.

She cleared her throat. "Kenzie, I'd like you to meet my friend Beatrice."

Kenzie's eyebrows shot up. "Beatrice? As in, Bea from LA?"

Ava nodded. "She's visiting for the weekend."

Bea shook the hand that Kenzie held out. "You're the reporter, right? It's nice to meet you. Ava has told me all about you."

"Oh. Um, thanks," Kenzie said, stumbling over her words in her usual manner. "I've heard a lot about you, too."

Beside her, Ava felt Bea's confusion. This adorable nerd was Galaxy Girl, possibly the most powerful woman on the planet? *See*, Ava wanted to say. There was a reason people didn't just automatically figure it out.

Mika grinned mischievously into the awkward pause. "Bea isn't just your friend, though, is she?"

Ava frowned, trying to work out what she could possibly mean. Other than that one ill-advised kiss senior year at Deerfield—

"Mika thought I looked familiar," Bea explained. "So I had to admit—"

"Wait, are you B Dang?" Kenzie interrupted. The

tightness around her mouth eased suddenly, and she smiled as she practically squealed, "Oh my god, Ava, you didn't tell me your friend Bea was B Dang!" And she momentarily gripped Ava's arm more than a little bit too tightly for comfort.

Ava glanced at Bea. Normally her friend didn't appreciate such extreme fangirling, but it appeared that seeing Galaxy Girl this excited about meeting her was something altogether different.

"I am," she said, smiling back. "I take it you're a fan?"

Even Sloane was smiling now. "She had a poster of you hanging on her ceiling back in the day. Now that I think about it," she added, eyes on Kenzie, "maybe that was a sign we should have picked up on sooner."

"Like your affinity for motorcycles and guns?" Kenzie returned.

If they hadn't been standing in a gay club, Ava might not have believed that the Shepherd sisters were teasing each other about being queer. Kenzie glanced at her shyly, and Ava smiled, trying to tell her with her eyes, *It's okay. So am I.* In case that wasn't already blatantly obvious.

A sense of lightness began to rise inside her, a steady unfurling of an emotion she didn't usually allow herself: hope. With Kenzie standing before her smiling her sweet smile, Ava could almost see a way forward from this moment. They would drink and laugh together with their friends and Kenzie's sister, and then, eventually, Ava would ask her to dance. On the dance floor they would move together in the darkness, the lights illuminating one half of their faces at a time as they drifted closer and closer. Ava would slip her arms around Kenzie's neck, Kenzie would place her hands at her waist, and when the moment was right, Ava would kiss her. They would simply be two women who liked each other, no more, no less.

But even as this fantasy played out in her head, a series

of notifications distracted her. Mika and Sloane were already reaching for their phones, and Kenzie—well, Kenzie was frowning, her head cocked to one side as if she saw or heard something off in the distance. Once again, super hearing for the win. Except that in this case, it felt more like a loss to Ava.

Bea was gazing around the little group. "I feel like I'm missing something."

"They have to go," Ava supplied, her eyes on Kenzie. "You have a story to cover, don't you?"

Kenzie nodded, her gaze flicking briefly to Mika, who Ava noted was looking between Kenzie and Sloane as if working out a puzzle. And, interesting, the detective didn't appear to know that her girlfriend's sister was Seattle's new superhero. Although how much longer that would be the case seemed debatable.

Mika stepped forward and pulled Ava into a quick hug. "I'm so glad you guys are getting your shit together. Finally!"

Startled by both the contact and the comment, Ava hesitated before hugging her back. "Thanks. I think."

Mika released her and turned to Bea, and soon the two were embracing and chattering about seeing each other again as if they were the old friends in the bunch.

Sloane caught Ava's eye. "Westbrook," she said, with a sharp nod.

Somehow Ava managed not to flinch at the use of her surname. Sloane's tone held a note of warning, and as she nodded back, it occurred to Ava that she and Kenzie could never be simple.

"Sloane," she said, just as serious. She knew why Sloane didn't trust her with Kenzie. Ironically, it was the same reason she didn't trust herself.

"We'll wait for you outside, Little Shepherd," Mika said, grabbing Sloane and pulling her along even though it was clear her girlfriend did not agree with this plan in the least.

Little Shepherd? What an adorable nickname—and further proof the cop had no idea Kenzie was one of the most powerful beings on Earth.

Beatrice reached out to hug Kenzie. "It was lovely to meet you, but I have to pee. I'll be right back, A, okay?"

Ava nodded at her friend, hoping Beatrice could see how grateful she was for the moment on their own. Well, sort of on their own—if you didn't count the dozens of other people dancing and talking around them.

"A and Bea, huh?" Kenzie fiddled with her glasses. "That's so cute."

"Not as cute as Little Shepherd," Ava returned, drifting closer again. She reached for Kenzie's hands and held them lightly in her own. Her pulse raced at the contact, and she knew Kenzie could tell from the way her eyes narrowed as she looked at Ava, her gaze slightly awed, slightly scared, slightly—something Ava couldn't read.

"You're the cute one," Kenzie said. "Actually, no, you're beautiful. I've always thought so."

Ava breathed in. She hadn't been wrong—Kenzie did have feelings for her, too. *Oh, thank god.* "I know you have to go, but will you call me later?"

Kenzie blinked, her glow fading slightly. "I don't know if I'll be able to. At least, not tonight. Will tomorrow be okay?"

"Of course." She hesitated. "I'm glad you came back."

Kenzie watched her for a moment, and then she nodded. "So am I." And swiftly, so incredibly swiftly and yet, at the same time, so gently, she pulled Ava into a hug. "Super glad."

Ava smiled into Kenzie's hair, which smelled of mint shampoo and something she didn't recognize, and let herself relax against the alien body pressing into her. She wasn't as hard as Ava had expected. Her arms and shoulders were firm but her skin was soft and silky beneath Ava's touch, warm and smooth and just a touch inhuman. But that realization didn't scare her this time. Instead she wanted more—more contact, more time, more everything.

"I really do have to go," Kenzie said.

"I know."

But Ava didn't move. She had told herself for a while now that she didn't need this sense of connection in her life; that she could be happy on her own. And she could. She genuinely believed that she didn't need a romantic partner to feel complete. But then Kenzie Shepherd had stumbled into her life with her nerdy glasses and her sunny smile and her unshakable sense of justice, and now Ava could feel how desperately some part of her had always been waiting for her.

Kenzie started as if she had been shocked. "Crap. My sister's waiting for me." She sighed, and then tightened her grip infinitesimally before pulling back.

"Be careful," Ava said, finally relinquishing her hold.

"I will. You, too—don't go fighting any drunk jerks without me, okay?"

"I'll try, but no promises."

Kenzie shook her head, but she was smiling. And then, slowly, she leaned in until their noses were almost touching, closed her eyes, and lifted her chin. That was all the invitation Ava needed to close the distance between them and press a warm, lingering kiss against Kenzie's mouth.

Kenzie made a slight, surprised sound in the back of her throat, and it took every bit of Ava's considerable willpower to pull away.

"Be safe," she said again, and then she pushed Kenzie's slipping glasses back up her nose.

"I will." For the first time in a week, Kenzie smiled at her in the way Ava had grown accustomed to: widely, happily, truly.

"Kenzie!" Sloane's voice sounded faintly from the doorway where she was now standing, arms folded, but Kenzie reacted like she'd been shot. Or, rather, like something that had the power to affect her negatively, since bullets apparently didn't. Ava would have to ask her about that later because while she fully believed Kenzie wasn't a machine to be poked and prodded, she also understood now in a non-abstract way how fundamentally different they were.

"Thanks," Kenzie said inanely, still smiling as she backed away. "I'll call you!"

Ava waved, biting back a smile as Kenzie nearly ran over a pair of women at the edge of the dance floor. At the last second she changed courses before turning and racing over to Sloane. And then they were gone, and Ava was left looking at the spot where they had just been, knowing it could be the last time she ever saw either—*both?*—of them alive.

And here was the part of the relationship plan she hadn't thought out: Kenzie being Galaxy Girl meant she could safely date Ava, yes. But Kenzie being Galaxy Girl also meant that she was only ever a step away from a missile to the chest or a potentially fatal blow from a vicious four-armed Bryllian. Kenzie being Galaxy Girl meant that if they dated, Ava would always have to worry about losing her, and not just in the "what if things don't work out" way that was endemic to any romantic entanglement. No, she would have to worry about murderous aliens and rogue government agents trying to pick Kenzie apart in an underground lab much like the one Ava used to call home in New York City.

She jumped a little as she felt arms wrap around her

from behind, but relaxed as the scent of jasmine drifted over her.

"Wow," Bea said, resting her chin on Ava's shoulder. "An alien and a Westbrook for real, huh?"

Ava sighed. "Fuck."

"I'll say. Come on. Let's get you home."

As she followed Bea from the bar, Ava heard sirens in the distance and sent a prayer up into the universe: *Please keep her safe. Please, please, please bring her back safely.*

CHAPTER NINE

"Oh my God, Sloane, she kissed me! I kissed her! We kissed!" Kenzie paused, waiting for a response.

Unfortunately, she couldn't really get a good look at her sister's face seeing as Sloane had her motorcycle helmet on. Also, they were in midair, Sloane tucked under one of Kenzie's arms and her motorcycle under the other. Normally Sloane would never allow Kenzie to fly her to a crime scene. But tonight there were extenuating circumstances—mainly that, in a fit of giddiness, Kenzie had grabbed her and launched into the air without asking permission, only just taking time to change into her Galaxy Girl suit first.

"Slow," Sloane gasped. "Can't... breathe..."

Whoops. She always forgot about G forces since they didn't affect her. Kenzie reined herself in. "Sorry. Are you okay? I was just so—"

"I know." Sloane panted a little. "And I'm happy for you, Kenzie."

"You are?"

"I want you to be happy, and if Ava... Wait, Mika can't see us arriving together."

237

"Oh, right." Kenzie landed a couple of blocks short of the Capitol Hill address the audio beacon had specified.

"But, um, are you sure she doesn't already know?"

"Pretty sure." Sloane slung a leg over her motorcycle. "Now go. We're late enough as it is."

"Okay. See you!" Kenzie shot into the air perhaps a bit overzealously, correcting her path as she went. She was just... Ava was just... Wait. What the heck was that guy doing?

She landed again and quickly assessed the scene. On a side street on lower Capitol Hill that was filled with condos and parked cars, a humanoid with pale blue skin was holding a car over their head and shouting in a language that sounded familiar to Kenzie, who had learned dozens of alien languages in the way all Zattalians did: through an AI implant. The steady rant was too fast for Kenzie to completely understand, but she was pretty sure she heard the phrase "everyone I ever loved." Her elation faded a little. She knew exactly how they felt.

A gentle touch to her mind had her glancing down the street, which had been closed to traffic by a pair of Seattle PD cruisers with lights flashing but sirens, thankfully, silent. Mika was there with her colleagues, staring in the same direction. Kenzie blinked as she saw what looked like a carbon copy of herself approaching, only taller and definitely male.

"*I couldn't exactly appear as Susan Cheng, could I?*" an amused voice sounded inside her mind.

"*D'aman?*" she thought back.

"*In the flesh. So to speak.*"

As soon as they reached her, thoughts flooded her unguarded mind. The Pendran man before them was distraught because it was the anniversary of the deaths of his mate and children. He had worked for a mining company on his home world, but while he was away on business, a reactor blew, taking out half of the company town. For a moment, Kenzie felt the man's pain settle over her, a dark cloud pressing down, down... But then it evaporated, and she glanced up at D'aman.

"We need to help him," she said aloud.

D'aman—*Galaxy Man*; crap, she could already imagine the Twitter response—nodded. "Indeed, before the Alliance gets wind of the disturbance."

The telltale sound of a motorcycle grew louder, and Kenzie watched as Sloane stopped near her girlfriend. Mika was looking at Sloane in a way Kenzie couldn't quite interpret, so she kept one eye on the Pendran and the other on their conversation. If it had been anyone else, she would have respected their privacy. But Mika hadn't been super psyched at first to be dating a *baby gay*, as she'd referred to Sloane in the beginning, and had seemed a bit flighty in the early days of their relationship. Apparently, lesbians broke up and got back together a lot, according to Kenzie's research, but predictability didn't make angst any less painful.

"*This* is our rogue alien?" Sloane sounded irritated as she pulled her bulletproof vest and other gear from a nearby Land Rover bearing the Panopticon crest.

"We've got the street sealed," Mika replied, "so unless Pendrans have suddenly gained the ability to fly, he isn't going anywhere."

"Any idea what set him off?"

"Nope."

Even from a distance, Kenzie could see the tight set of the detective's shoulders. Apparently, Sloane could too because she reached out a hesitant hand and touched Mika's sleeve. "Hey. Is there a reason you won't look at me?"

"Gee, I don't know, Sloane." Her gaze flicked over Sloane's shoulder and settled on Kenzie for a brief, heated moment. "What could I possibly have to be upset about?"

"Jesus fucking Christ." Sloane made a frustrated noise and unholstered her gun.

Kenzie recognized that tone. It usually precluded a rash and impatient act. Sure enough, she watched disbelievingly as Sloane aimed her weapon at the agitated Pendran.

"Sloane!" Mika and Kenzie shouted at the same time.

She lowered her arm slightly. "What? I was only going to wound him. I am an expert mark, you know."

"I've got it!" Kenzie positioned herself between Sloane and the anguished man, shielding him from her trigger-happy sister. Not that she really believed Sloane would shoot him. At least, she didn't think she would.

Mika seemed less convinced. As Kenzie advanced toward the distraught alien, one hand held out reassuringly, she heard the detective comment, "For someone whose sister is an alien, you sure don't seem to like them very much."

Sister—so, okay, she'd figured it out. It was only a matter of time, as she'd tried to warn her sister.

This wasn't the time for that conversation, though. Kenzie pushed everything out of her mind except the Pendran—*Laquine*, D'aman helpfully supplied—who was weaving on his feet now, car barely held above his head. It was a nice car, too, a Jaguar. Which, good taste, but where would a refugee get the money to pay for a replacement? The Alliance stipend was generous, but not that generous.

"Laquine," she called, searching through her mind for a Pendran phrase. She took a breath and tried, "Laquine of Pendra, you are not alone. We are with you. We are your friends." Or at least, she was pretty sure that's what she'd said.

The car teetered precariously as Laquine spun to face her. "Wha—Galaxy Girl?" he asked, gazing at her woozily.

"He has taken something," D'aman thought to her. *"I see an image of a bottle of pills. An opiate, perhaps, reconfigured for non-human systems."*

What the hell? Who would take advantage of downtrodden aliens…? A face flashed before her. Nicholas Westbrook. He had collected biometric readings and blood samples from hundreds of his victims during his search for the elusive super alien he was convinced must be living, hidden, among the ordinary citizens of Earth. The media had called him a crackpot, but he hadn't been wrong, had he? In a way, it was her fault that Sentinel had experimented on so many innocent refugees. While Nicholas Westbrook and his minions hated people like the man before her, they both hated *and* feared her. And everyone knew how male humans dealt with fear.

She held out her hand to the Pendran, whose eyes seemed desperate to close. "Give me the car, Laquine. It'll be okay. Let me help you."

"You can't," he said, his voice raw. "No one can because they're all gone. I left them there and they all died. I let everyone I love just… *die.*"

Tears pricked her eyes, and she blinked them back. It wasn't the same for him as it was for her, obviously, but survivor's guilt was awful whether you survived as a teenager or as a full-grown adult. Whether your parents put you in the escape pod or you drove it yourself.

"You didn't know," she said, hand up placatingly as she advanced again. "There was nothing you could have done."

His face contorted as he stared at her. "You're right. It was the Alliance's fault. If not for them, my mate and children would be alive, my nieces and nephews… They died for the Alliance!"

In situations like this, Kenzie automatically engaged whatever super-sense she needed. As the Pendran's shoulders tensed, she could hear tendons tightening, the creak of his shoulder joint, the slight displacement of the air around the car. By the time he hurled it at the closest building, she was already hovering off the ground at the ready, D'aman at her side. Together they caught the car, allowing it to drive them back just enough to absorb its force the way a softball player would field a pop fly. Or, maybe not exactly like a pop fly, but similar.

Kenzie and D'aman set the car gently on the pavement and, before the Pendran could recover his equilibrium, she flew to him and pinned his arms to his sides. He thrashed against her, eyes red and damp, but she kept her hold, careful not to hurt him. He wasn't angry at her, not really. If anyone understood the pull of anger in the face of great loss it was her.

"You are not alone," she repeated in his native language, wishing she could convince him it was true. And then, "Please let us help you, Laquine. Please?"

As her voice cracked on the last word, he deflated like a football she'd once squeezed too hard, the anger and venom fizzling out of him in a long, painful sob. He buried his face in her shoulder, and she blinked back more tears as she felt him shuddering against her, this stranger with whom she shared so much.

"It's okay," she murmured. "I've got you. I'm here."

She held him as he cried, wishing she could do more. She hated to see other people hurting. Sloane said she possessed super sensitivity, but Kenzie only knew that she had an innate need to try to help anyone she could. Most people weren't born evil. They became that way after something traumatic, something that tore them down, something that wounded them so deeply they could no longer see the good in themselves or others.

An image flickered in her memory—Nicholas Westbrook in a leaked video looming over one of his subjects in Sentinel's secret laboratory, an almost bored expression on his face as he purposely operated on a screaming alien without anything more than a local anesthetic. What had happened to Nicholas Westbrook to make him so craven, so cruel? And how had Ava managed to escape the same fate?

Mika and Sloane appeared at her side, and Kenzie glanced at D'aman, sending a quick question: *"Can you talk to them?"*

"Of course," they responded, and turned to the other pair. "Can you make sure he gets somewhere safe? We think he might be on some sort of opiate."

Mika nodded, her eyes still on Kenzie. "We can take him to my precinct. He can sober up in one of our holding cells."

"I'd rather take him," Kenzie said, ignoring Sloane's shushing look. She had the voice modulator, and besides, the cat was well out of the bag. Although, where that particular human idiom came from was… probably best not analyzed too closely.

She lifted the distressed man, who half-heartedly protested. "It's okay," she repeated as they shot into the air, D'aman close behind. "I've got you."

Below, she heard Mika say, "Since when are they a matched pair?"

"I don't know."

"Sure you don't. And how do they know what precinct to take him to? Want to explain that one, Sloane?"

"I don't know," Sloane repeated stubbornly. "Maybe they're telepathic."

Now who was skirting awfully close to revealing secret identities?

"Sorry about my sister," she told D'aman as they flew

toward SPD's Alien Affairs Bureau, headquartered in an old brick building just south of downtown.

"It's fine," they said. "I thought it went quite well."

"So did I," she said, and even though her friend and new partner in crime-fighting couldn't see her face, she was smiling. "Nice costume, by the way."

"I've been told it's called a suit." Their voice contained a definite smile, too. "Now, if it's all the same to you, I was in the middle of a tasty Blenvilliette cake, so if you think you have this covered…"

"Fly away, my winged friend," Kenzie said, laughing. "I've definitely got this. Thanks again for your help."

"You're welcome," D'aman called as they peeled off and zoomed away.

As she flew, Kenzie pictured the angry set of Mika's mouth again, so different from her easy smile at the club earlier when she'd teased Kenzie about her crush on Ava. She hoped Mika wasn't too angry that Sloane had kept Kenzie's identity a secret. The last thing she wanted to do was cause issues in Sloane's relationship, but they needed to figure out how to manage her presence in their lives on their own, without her interference. At least Sloane had finally picked someone who was her equal, in more ways than one. The men she had dated in the past had let her walk all over them, but Kenzie had a feeling Mika Hansen had never let anyone walk over her in her life.

That description matched Ava, too, she thought, flashing back to the moment outside the club when the khaki-clad creep had nearly accosted her. Kenzie had been pacing the block trying to decide if she should go back to the club when she'd received Ava's text, and the drunk's intrusion had made her decision fairly quickly. Which, now that she thought about it, maybe she should be grateful that jackass had shown up when he did. He'd forced her to act, and Ava… had kissed her. Ava actually had feelings for her, real, solid feelings that made her do things like hold her hands and smile at her as if no one else existed. Kenzie hadn't sensed any fear in her this time. That didn't mean she wouldn't ever be afraid again, of course, but at least for now her feelings seemed to lean more toward adoration than fright.

Or maybe Kenzie was thinking of her own feelings.

At AAB headquarters, she handed the semi-conscious Pendran off to a male agent who was already expecting them, and then, assured that Laquine was in good hands, she skedaddled. She meant to pick up her gear from the nearest safe roof and head home following Sloane's protocol, she really did. But somehow she found herself on a beeline across the city to Hyperion Tower, gear bag tucked under her arm. Ava had said to call her later, hadn't she? A house call counted, surely.

As she neared Ava's building, she slowed. Inside, she could see the two women sitting on the couch facing each other, feet touching as they talked. The realization that Ava, too, had a sister of sorts made Kenzie happy, and she hovered off the corner of the skyscraper listening to the low hum of their voices for a moment. Maybe she should leave them in peace. What would she say to Ava, anyway? *Just thought I'd drop in on you because yes, I am that whipped after one kiss.* Sloane had counseled her to play it cool with previous crushes, but playing anything cool wasn't really in her playbook.

All at once, she realized that the suite was quiet, and she refocused in time to watch Ava set her phone down and move toward the windows. She was coming this way, as if she knew Kenzie were there.

Kenzie backed away. She hadn't intended to interrupt Ava's time with her friend. Or, like, actually get caught stalking them. How would Ava explain her presence? Beatrice had seen them together as Kenzie and Ava. What would she think of Galaxy Girl conducting a late-night fly-by?

Ava stopped beside the window, squinting into the darkness. "Hello?" she said, not bothering to raise her voice.

Kenzie hovered just out of sight. This was bad. This was so bad. What had she been thinking? Worse, what was Ava thinking?

"I know you're there," Ava added, her voice soft. "You're hard to miss. Usually the largest objects the security cameras pick up are seagulls."

Security…? Kenzie closed her eyes tightly. Of course there were cameras. Did that mean Ava knew of the other instances when she'd been fundamentally unable to stay away? Had she seen her almost crash into the neighboring building the night D'aman had taken her out drinking? *Fricking frack!* She turned away, intending to go home, bury herself in a pile of blankets, and never ever show her face again.

But then she heard Ava say through the window, "Please? You have to land sometime."

And, come on, how was she supposed to resist that? Obviously, she couldn't. No mortal creature could, she was fairly certain. Except maybe some species from the Vegan and Andromedan systems. They weren't big fans of humans. Neither were Vorings, for that matter… and, great. She was rambling inside her own head.

She reached into her gear bag and pulled out her phone. "I'll be there in a minute," she texted. "Just have to change."

Ava gave the window a thumbs-up, and Kenzie flew away as fast as she could to a nearby roof on Sloane's safe list. Then she made her way back to Hyperion Tower, skipping most of the steps Sloane had specified. It wasn't every day she got kissed, okay? Besides, she could tell no one was following her. Hello, superpowers.

Checking in with The Westbrook receptionist and waiting for the elevator was excruciating, but soon enough she was standing before Ava's hotel room door, heart racing as she lifted her hand to knock. Was this a bad idea? This was totally a bad idea. She knocked anyway.

"I wasn't listening in on your conversation," she said as soon as Ava opened the door. "I promise."

"Okay." Ava smiled easily at her. "I trust you."

The phrase should have curled inside her like a reassuring wisp of smoke, but instead she wanted to blurt, *Why?* Because frankly, she hadn't done much to deserve that trust. In fact, she was pretty sure Ava ought to kick her to the curb for being dishonest since the day they'd met but was just too nice to do so. Or too accustomed to being treated poorly by the people in her life, maybe? What did it mean that Kenzie had slipped into that role herself, lying to her and suspecting her of evil-doing just because of who her family was? All Kenzie really wanted was to immerse herself in the beautiful dream they'd conjured earlier in the dim light of the bar, far from their everyday lives. But there were things they needed to talk about if they were going to move forward.

And, by Alia, did she ever hope they moved forward, assuming she hadn't ruined everything by being the worst super-stalker ever. Sloane always said she didn't have a subtle bone in her body. While Kenzie usually replied that that was because her bones had been formed in space, she couldn't disagree.

"Maybe I should go," she said, still wavering on the doorsill. "I just wanted to check on you. I don't actually need to interrupt."

"You're not interrupting." When Kenzie stared at her disbelievingly, she added, "Well, you are a little. But it's fine. Bea and I have spent the entire day together. She doesn't mind sharing me, do you, Bea?"

Through the open door, Ava's friend gave them an exaggerated thumbs-up, and Kenzie smiled shyly, still slightly thrown that Ava's best friend Bea from LA was her one-time pop idol—and, possibly, her first girl crush. "If you're sure...?"

Ava held out a hand, palm up. "I'm sure."

Kenzie hesitated one last time, and then she reached out, grasping Ava's hand as she stepped inside. "In that case, hello again."

"Hi." Ava tugged, and Kenzie let herself be pulled closer, allowed Ava to kiss her cheek, allowed herself to sink into the warmth of a hug that she was already beginning to crave. "I'm glad you're safe. It's not every day you get a car thrown at you." When Kenzie drew back quickly, Ava added, "It was on Twitter."

"Okay, but what are you doing?" Kenzie whispered, brow furrowed as she glanced over Ava's shoulder at Beatrice, whose smile appeared conspicuously unruffled. "What about...?"

"Oh." Ava bit her lip in that way she had that immediately made Kenzie forget about every other thing. "Bea already knows. Who you are, I mean."

"What?" Kenzie stepped back, her foot bumping up against the closed door.

"I didn't tell her," Ava said quickly. "She figured it out on her own. But it's okay, she's great at keeping secrets. It's a huge part of what she does in LA."

"Ava!" Kenzie gaped at her. "You can't—I can't—*Sloane is going to kill me.*"

"I know, and I am truly sorry, Kenzie. But Sloane doesn't have to know, does she?"

"In theory, no, but it turns out I'm not very good at not telling Sloane things..."

Ava squinted at her. "That's not really surprising. But there's nothing to be done about it right now. Come sit down? You don't have to stay long if you don't want to."

As if that could actually be a thing.

"Okay," Kenzie said, and squared her shoulders. She could do this. She could hang out with Ava Westbrook, who had kissed her, and B Dang, who wasn't even bothering to pretend not to avidly watch them. Kenzie couldn't blame her, though, because an alien and a Westbrook? It was crazy. Dangerous. Outright foolish. And yet, here they were.

Forget Sloane. Her parents were definitely going to kill her.

They had been leaving her messages and sending her texts for a few weeks now, asking if there was anything she wanted to tell them. But they had no real evidence that she was the masked hero. Galaxy Girl could just as easily have been one of the many other unregistered aliens who called Seattle home. Sloane had insisted that Kenzie be the one to tell their parents about her new career path, and so far, she had managed to evade their delicate questioning. But that wouldn't last much longer. It was the end of spring quarter at the university and they were crazy busy right now—too busy to drop in unexpectedly—but as soon as graduation was over, she had no doubt that Jane and Benjamin would drive down to Seattle and stake out her condo if she continued to dodge them.

As she followed Ava to the couch, she tried not to wonder which news would shock them more: that she was Galaxy Girl, or that she was bisexual and currently dating—they *were* dating, weren't they?—Ava Westbrook.

Probably, it was best not to overthink.

A little while later, Kenzie shifted on the couch as Beatrice told a story about college-aged Ava that Kenzie had a hard time envisioning.

"So wait," she interrupted, "girls at your college—sorry, I mean, *women*—actually streak across the quad? Like, completely naked?"

"Well, yeah," Beatrice said, shrugging. "It's a great stress reliever. Not to mention empowering."

"The primal scream during reading period was my favorite," Ava said, voice tinged with nostalgia.

"You didn't even go there!" Kenzie said. "Why would you participate?"

"Alcohol probably had something to do with it," Ava admitted, smiling sideways at her.

They were sitting close together on one end of the couch while Beatrice occupied the other, and Kenzie felt herself flushing as Ava's eyes lingered on her. Their thighs were touching and so were their shoulders, and Kenzie had to keep resisting the urge to slip her hand into Ava's and… or maybe she didn't. Why couldn't they hold hands?

Tentatively, she slid her palm beneath Ava's, holding her breath until Ava intertwined their fingers and squeezed. Relieved, Kenzie glanced up at her, immediately caught by the darker gray-green ring around her paler irises.

"You have beautiful eyes," she breathed, noting the way they widened momentarily at her words.

"Thank you," Ava said softly. "So do you."

"And on that note," Bea announced, rising, "I'm going to go text my husband."

"Oh, sorry," Kenzie said, looking up at her. "I didn't mean…"

"It's fine. I'm actually really looking forward to a quiet night of sleep without the demon child to awaken me every three hours looking for a boob. Seriously, sometimes I feel like a walking breast."

Kenzie tried very hard not to gaze at the body parts in

question, but while she might not have been human, she was more than a little bit gay. And Bea, it should be noted, had very nice lady parts.

Beside her Ava snickered, and Kenzie quickly tore her eyes away. This was bad. She should not be holding one woman's hand and checking out the rack on another. *The rack?* Great, now she was using sexist language. But only in her own mind, right? She hadn't said any of that out loud? No, she hadn't. She was almost certain.

Ava released her hand and stood up to walk Bea to the den—which, a hotel room with a den, seriously? Kenzie made sure to aim her senses elsewhere to give them a semblance of privacy. It wasn't all that difficult. In the hotel room below, a guest was watching *The Force Awakens*, one of Kenzie's favorite movies ever. She got so caught up in the dialogue—Kylo Ren was just about to confront Han Solo!—that she didn't notice Ava returning until just before she dropped down beside her.

"Hi," Ava said, and reached for her hand.

"Hi." Kenzie wove their fingers together and leaned closer. "Sorry I chased your friend away."

"I'm not. I'm really glad you're here. It's a bit surreal, but good."

"It is surreal, isn't it?" Kenzie stared down at their linked hands, noting how pale Ava's skin was compared to her own. She was cooler, too, and softer, of course—human. Whereas Kenzie was unarguably alien.

"You look cute in my clothes," Ava said, resting her chin on Kenzie's shoulder.

Ava and Bea had just changed out of their club clothes when Kenzie arrived, so Kenzie had accepted a T-shirt and leggings from her host. Much more comfortable than sitting around Ava's living room in the short dress she'd worn out tonight, and, as a plus, the T-shirt smelled like Ava's perfume.

"Not as cute as you," she said. "In your clothes, I mean. Or, really, any clothes. Probably in no clothes, too..." She trailed off. Smooth, as usual.

Ava only smiled more and hummed under her breath as she toyed with Kenzie's fingers. "So."

"So."

It really was nice, despite the surrealism, to be sitting here in Ava's brightly lit hotel suite, their bodies flush on the overstuffed couch. Ava's office furniture might be modern bordering on severe, but the suite was done in warm Pacific Northwest colors and rustic surfaces. Ava matched the decorating style currently, her hair loose about her shoulders, her usually stark make-up washed away to reveal pale pink lips, a few freckles, and laugh lines at the corners of her mouth and eyes. In this space, she was softer, more relaxed, her polished Westbrook veneer noticeably absent. She was just Ava, and Kenzie was powerless to keep from falling even further for her.

"How are you doing?" Ava asked, her eyes growing slightly serious.

"I'm good. How are you doing?"

"Also good." She hesitated. "Should we, I don't know, talk about everything? Because I haven't actually seen you much recently."

Of course it would be Ava who would bring up what was between them because while Kenzie might be a superhero, her courage mostly extended to action, not to the discussion or processing of emotions, which frankly frightened her more than all of Sentinel's agents combined. Ava, on the other hand, apparently understood that sometimes it was necessary to talk about elephants in the room, particularly when the elephant in question had refused to speak to you for days on end.

"I'm sorry," Kenzie said, folding her legs beneath her. "I should have come to see you after the Guild House attack, or at least answered your texts."

"You did come to see me," Ava said, her eyes again on their hands in her lap. "Maybe not in person, exactly, but you were around."

Kenzie shook her head. "I'm sorry about that, too. It's so embarrassing. I can't believe I did that."

Ava smiled a little, gaze still cast downward. "I thought you were watching me under official orders. You know, like maybe your sister and her colleagues might not trust me?"

"They don't distrust you."

Ava squeezed her hand. "You're a terrible liar."

Kenzie tried again. "No, I mean they distrust your brother, but they don't actually know you."

"Which means they don't trust me, either."

She relented, shoulders dipping. "Okay, fine. They don't trust you. But, you know, Monday didn't exactly help in that regard."

To her surprise, Ava nodded. "You're right. I'd convinced myself it was only business, but then you asked me if we had that policy about partnering with bigoted firms, and I realized that maybe I'm more of a Westbrook than I'd like to believe."

Kenzie wanted to defend Ava against any and all critiques, but she contented herself with, "I don't know about that, but the fly-bys were entirely my idea. Sloane doesn't even know."

"Look at that. You *can* keep something from your sister."

"I couldn't keep how I felt about you from her," Kenzie admitted, trailing her free hand across Ava's arm and feeling the goosebumps her touch elicited. She could hear Ava's breath hitch, and she tried not to smile at the sensation of power flowing through her. She was used to being powerful. But the way Ava responded to a simple touch? This was so much better. It made Kenzie wonder what would happen if she replaced her fingers with her lips—which was something she had never actually thought about doing before, not even with the boys she'd dated. Not that there had been many—one in college and one her first year at ECM. Neither boy had made her feel like this.

"And how *do* you feel about me, Miss Shepherd?" Ava asked, her voice low and sultry, her breath feathery against Kenzie's collar bone.

And, oh, right, the power was mutual, Kenzie realized belatedly, feeling her own system stutter and restart at the question. "Um," she said, swallowing audibly, "I, uh, like you. A lot." Which, fantastic, sounded exactly like something a thirteen-year-old boy would say.

"Well, good," Ava said, and leaned in until her breath ghosted over Kenzie's lips. "Because I like you, too. Also a lot."

Kenzie wasn't sure which one of them closed the gap. All she knew was that one moment they weren't kissing and the next they were, all soft lips and warm breath and tentative tongues. Then one of them moaned—was it her? She honestly didn't know—and the kiss changed from hesitant to urgent, from gentle to hot. Operating on instinct, Kenzie pushed Ava down against the couch cushions and moved over her. They fit together perfectly, Kenzie's hips pressing against Ava's, their legs instantly tangling as Ava wrapped her arms around Kenzie and pulled her even closer. Kenzie gasped as she felt Ava's knee slip between her thighs, and then it was like her brain had lost control of her body as she felt her own hips shift and grind into Ava's softness. Ava pressed up against her, and the movement put pressure on a part of Kenzie's body that no one else had ever touched. Her eyes were closed, and she was having trouble focusing on all the different sensations erupting inside of her, and then suddenly there was cool air between them and she opened her eyes to see Ava staring at her, mouth open, as Kenzie floated up and bobbed against the ceiling.

"Well, shoot," she said, and fell back to the couch, careful not to land on Ava.

Meanwhile, Ava covered her mouth with a hand and sat up, eyes crinkling and shoulders shaking with the nearly silent laughter that Kenzie could hear just as clearly as the sounds of an off-world battle rising from the room below.

"That totally just happened, didn't it," Kenzie said, letting her head fall back against the couch.

Ava leaned into her side and slipped an arm around her shoulders. "At least I already knew you could fly. Otherwise, that might have been a bit more shocking than it was."

"You think?" Kenzie looked over at Ava, curiosity overcoming her embarrassment. "How did you figure it out, anyway?"

"I don't know—maybe it was all the time I spent admiring you in *and* out of your Galaxy Girl suit," Ava said.

Could individual human beings have more potent fields of gravity than others? Because Kenzie would have sworn at that moment that she could feel herself being drawn steadily closer to Ava, unable to resist her pull.

"Wait," Ava murmured, placing her hand on Kenzie's chest. "Talking, remember?"

"Whoops. That's right." She scooted over so that the temptation to touch Ava wasn't quite so strong. "What did I ask you? Oh, yeah. How you knew about Galaxy Girl."

"You don't really talk about yourself in the third person, do you?"

"What's wrong with that? Galaxy Girl is a hero, and Kenzie is pretty awesome as well…" She giggled at the look on Ava's face, unable to keep a straight face any longer.

"Thank god you're joking. Otherwise this would end up being the shortest relationship in history."

Kenzie licked her lips. "Um, relationship?"

"You know what I mean." Ava glanced down and smoothed her palm over her black leggings.

Actually, Kenzie didn't, having never been in a real relationship in her life. "Uh-huh," she said vaguely. "So. Did you know before or after you texted me on Monday?"

"After. I put it together right before you came to my office the other day."

"I thought you were in a board meeting?"

Kenzie was pretty sure that was what Chloe had said because she remembered thinking that it wasn't very accurate to use the word "board," a homonym for "bored," for a meeting that gathered together all the most powerful people within an organization.

"I figured it out immediately before the meeting," Ava admitted. "I'm not even really sure why, except that once I pictured you turning into Galaxy Girl, I couldn't unsee it."

Kenzie sighed. "I'm starting to think more people know than don't."

"Like who?"

"Like you and Bea and Mika, for starters."

"Mika knows?"

She nodded. "As of tonight, it would seem."

"What about the boys?"

Kenzie squinted. "Yeah, they know. Or, I mean, Matt does. Antonio knows I'm an off-worlder, but that's about it."

"So, I'm guessing that Antonio isn't your new doppelganger, then?"

Kenzie perked up. "You mean Galaxy Guy?"

"You wish they called him that."

"It's totally Galaxy Man, isn't it?" When Ava nodded, Kenzie blew out a breath in frustration. "So freaking sexist!"

"Always." She hesitated, and Kenzie saw the uncertainty flicker across her face. "It's really not Antonio, though, right?"

"No, I promise. Galaxy Guy—what, I'm totally calling them that—is an old friend. Literally," she added, laughing to herself at the joke. When Ava looked at her expectantly, she explained, "D'aman is more than three centuries old. And, also, non-binary. They go by they/them, which is why they should totally be called Galaxy Guy."

"Huh." Ava nodded. "You know some very interesting people."

"And some total douchebags, too," Kenzie said, squeezing Ava's hand. "What happened the other night with you and Antonio, anyway? What did he say to scare you off like that?"

"He was being territorial," she said, eyes narrowing.

"But without cause, I presume?"

"Completely without cause," Kenzie confirmed, and huffed in irritation. Stupid boy. As if she would ever pick him over Ava. "Do you want me to punch him into space?"

Ava's head tilted to one side. "I'm going to assume you're being euphemistic."

After a moment, Kenzie nodded, because that seemed like the smarter option.

"So, you and your sister are both queer," Ava said, changing the subject with a lack of subtlety that rivaled Kenzie's.

"I know. I was surprised, too." She paused. Mika had worried with Sloane that she might be a straight girl's experiment. What if Ava shared that concern? Or what if she didn't want to date someone who was—what did Matt always call it—AC/DC? Biphobia was fairly prevalent, if the Internet could be believed. "You should probably know I'm bi, not gay. And, well, you're the first woman I've ever kissed."

Ava nodded slowly, her expression inscrutable. "Okay. Then you should probably know I *am* gay, and you're not the first woman I've ever kissed."

"Okay." They regarded each other, and then Kenzie asked, "Do you know where I'm from?"

"I have an idea," Ava admitted.

"And?"

Ava frowned slightly. "And what?"

Kenzie swallowed against a sudden flutter of nerves. "Your brother would have killed to find someone like me."

Ava looked down, smoothing her hand over the cushion between them. "I think we both know he did kill trying to find someone like you. That's why I testified against him."

Kenzie tried to imagine what it would take for her to testify against Sloane and failed to come up with a single thing. Not because she would let her sister get away with murder, but because she couldn't imagine Sloane ever doing anything so utterly horrible. "I'm sorry your brother made you do that," she said, inching closer again.

Ava glanced up, her smile mixed with an emotion Kenzie couldn't quite read. "You're incredible, do you know that?"

Kenzie stared at Ava, her heart stuttering inside her chest. "You're incredible, too."

Ava shook her head. "If that were true, I would have stopped Nick before anyone got hurt."

"Your brother's actions aren't your responsibility,"

Kenzie said. "You didn't have any idea what he was up to, did you?"

"No, but I should have. His feelings on the subject weren't exactly a secret."

"You helped stop him before he could hurt more people, Ava. That was you. That *is* you." Kenzie slid a finger under her chin and tipped her face up, wanting to see her eyes. "You know what?"

"What?"

Kenzie took a breath and recited, "You is kind, you is good, you is—"

"Kenzie!" Ava exclaimed, laughing.

"Sorry," she said, smiling. "I totally felt like I was channeling *The Help* there, for a minute."

"Which is problematic on so many levels."

"Just, so many levels," she agreed.

Ava paused. "Would you have told me if I hadn't figured it out? Or would you have gone on ignoring me?"

"I couldn't have kept ignoring you," Kenzie told her. "But in full disclosure, I didn't have any plans to tell you, either."

"Did you not…?" Ava cleared her throat. "Did you think I was like the rest of my family?"

"When?" Kenzie asked, stalling.

The furrow returned to Ava's brow. "You did, didn't you?"

"No, I really didn't," she said, willing Ava to believe her. "Ask Sloane if you don't believe me."

"I'm not going to ask your sister, Kenzie." The furrow deepened slightly. "What about at Guild House? When you spoke to me from the stage."

"Okay," Kenzie admitted. "There might have been a moment when I wasn't sure whose side you were on. But at some level I knew or else I wouldn't have come to see you after that, no matter what my boss threatened."

"Why did it take a threat from your boss for you to come see me?"

"You didn't exactly seem like you wanted to talk to me last weekend," Kenzie pointed out. "Besides, I was scared."

"Of what?"

"Of you." She realized how that sounded and added quickly, "Or I guess, more how I felt about you. I thought I knew you, and then it seemed like I didn't, and that feeling was so—painful."

"I know." Ava scooted closer, narrowing the gap between them again. "When I realized you were Galaxy Girl, I felt the same way. Like I hadn't really known you at all."

Kenzie turned to face her more fully. "And now?"

"Now I'm glad there aren't any more secrets between us." Ava leaned back momentarily and fixed Kenzie with her chief operations officer gaze, penetrating and sharp. "There aren't, are there?"

"No," Kenzie said. "Not unless you count my working with Panopticon..."

Ava's eyebrows lifted. "That's right. I think I'm going to want to hear about that."

"Another time," Kenzie said, smiling at her. "Right now I'm going to kiss you again, 'kay?"

"'Kay," Ava said, and smiled back at her.

They were both still smiling as Kenzie leaned in, which made it hard to kiss, honestly. Then Ava slipped her arms around Kenzie's neck, locking her hands at her nape, and tugged her closer. With their lips still pressed together, Kenzie maneuvered them so that this time, Ava was stretched out on top of her. *I'm kissing Ava Westbrook*, Kenzie thought, her eyes closed, and the realization brought on such a delicious shiver that they both left the couch this time.

Ava gasped into her mouth, and Kenzie slowly floated them upright in midair, easily supporting the additional weight.

"You're amazing," Ava murmured against her lips.

"No, you're amazing."

"Agree to disagree," Ava said, and then she resumed kissing a very willing Kenzie.

Meanwhile, in the room below, the battle for the Star Killer base continued. But Kenzie didn't care what came next in the movie. For now she only had space in her mind—and heart—for the very real woman in her arms.

CHAPTER TEN

Ava blinked sleepily, smiling as she felt the weight of the arm around her waist. Then she focused on the hand with its long, slender fingers and professionally manicured fingernails and—*wait*. Her smile faded. When had she arrived, and how had Ava not noticed?

Rolling over to face the interloper, she reached out a finger. "Wakey wakey," she murmured, biting back a laugh as the other woman's nose wiggled *Bewitched*-style. She brushed the tip of the twitchy nose again. "Come on, bed hog. Wake up."

Bea frowned, eyes still closed. "Shhhh. Sleeping."

"Not anymore, you're not. Wake up, Dang!"

Yawning, Bea stretched her arms above her head. "You do realize this is my only day to sleep in for like the next calendar year, right?"

"You do realize I am constitutionally incapable of sleeping in, which you knew when you decided you were afraid to sleep alone in the den, right?"

"Bitch, I'm not afraid!" As Ava just stared at her, one eyebrow raised in challenge, she added, "Whatever. I can't help it if this suite is freakishly silent. I mean, seriously, we're in the heart of the city here."

"The hotel floors were sound-proofed when the building was constructed. Now come on, let's get going. We have to meet Kenzie for brunch in less than an hour."

Kenzie. Ava barely suppressed a dreamy sigh as she pushed a button on the bedside table to open the floor-to-ceiling blinds. It had been all she could do to let Kenzie leave the night before, but after walking her to the door and pressing her up against it for a while, she'd finally managed to keep her hands to herself long enough for Kenzie to leave in her borrowed clothes, her other gear folded neatly inside her black, nondescript backpack.

"Nine AM brunch on a Sunday?" Bea groaned. "Are you trying to kill me?"

Ava pushed back the covers, stretching in the morning sunlight. "We wanted to beat the rush."

"Right." Bea's voice was smug as she sat up and leaned against the upholstered headboard. "More like you're so whipped you couldn't wait to see each other. I was a little surprised to find you alone in here last night."

Ava slipped out of bed so that Bea wouldn't see her face when she said, "We decided to take it slow."

But Bea, who had known her longer and better than anyone else, caught on immediately. "Oh my god, she's never been with a woman before, has she? She's a virgian!"

"A what?"

"A virgian. You know, a lesbian virgin?"

"No comment. And that's not actually a word."

Ava headed for her walk-in closet. Not only had Kenzie never been with a woman, but she had never slept with a man, either. While Bea may be one hundred percent trustworthy, Kenzie had seemed so embarrassed the night before when she admitted her lack of experience that Ava had no intention of betraying that particular confidence.

Like, ever.

"Ingrate," Bea grumbled.

"Excuse me? What exactly am I supposed to be grateful to you for?" Ava asked as she rifled through the casual side of her wardrobe. Jeans, scoop neck tee, and the cashmere mock turtleneck from Ireland that brought out the green in her eyes. Perfect.

And then, suddenly, it hit her: She was going on a date with Kenzie. And Galaxy Girl. And, well, Bea.

"If not for me dragging you out last night," her best friend reminded her, "your girl still might not be talking to you."

Which, she had to admit, was true. She poked her head out of the closet. "Thank you, Bea." And then she threw a soft, pink slipper at the bed. "Now get up! I know how long it takes you to get ready."

Bea lifted her hands defensively. "I'm up!"

As she showered, Ava replayed the events of the previous night in her mind. Kenzie had been so sweet—and a natural when it came to kissing girls. The news that she'd never slept with anyone wasn't exactly a surprise, though, especially after she'd explained how she had spent most of her dozen years on Earth hiding who she was from everyone and everything. It wasn't until her favorite coffee shop was held up that she finally decided it was time to start using her powers to help people.

"I remember that," Ava had said, picturing the image that had been shared millions of times online of a blurry figure in a raincoat. "And then you saved those people in that fire, right?"

"Yep. And a cat," Kenzie had added. They were lying on the couch by then, Ava pressed into Kenzie's side, each toying with the other's fingers. "Sloane was actually really angry with me for revealing myself, if you can believe it."

"But you saved those people."

"And the cat," Kenzie repeated, nudging her. "She was just worried about me. It's something of a perpetual state for her, to be honest."

"I had noticed. That night she showed up at your studio, I thought she was going to pull me aside and tell me to stay the hell away from you."

"I'm pretty sure she wanted to. But don't take it personally. She's like a grumpy 1950s dad sometimes. Anyway, she couldn't threaten you there, what with the whole super hearing thing."

"Well, yes," Ava had said, and leaned up to kiss one of Kenzie's ears. "I realize that now."

The ear in question had been tinged with red, and Ava had settled back against Kenzie's side, amazed that she could have such an effect on Galaxy Girl, of all people. How had she gotten this lucky—and when would the other shoe drop? Because in her experience, there was always a shoe somewhere waiting to drop.

Now she closed her eyes and lifted her face to the hot spray. Decades of training in glass-half-emptiness would be difficult to unlearn. But for Kenzie's sake—and her own—she was damn well going to try.

"I'm so sorry—they just showed up and invited themselves along!" Kenzie whispered in Ava's ear as she hugged her on the sidewalk outside the restaurant near Pike's Place Market.

While Ava may have been a bit shocked to receive Kenzie's text informing her that Sloane and Mika were crashing their brunch date, she was still floating high enough that she couldn't find it in her heart to care all that much.

Okay, so not literally floating at this point, but only because they were in public.

"It's fine," she murmured in Kenzie's ear, delighting in

the way the other woman shivered against her. "I'm just happy we're doing this."

Kenzie smiled down at her, a mildly perplexed furrow pulling her eyebrows together. "Me, too. But, um, this as in Sunday brunch? Or this…?" She gestured between them.

"Both." Ava tried not to laugh as Kenzie grew flustered and practically shoved her glasses into her own head. Which couldn't really happen, could it? She was impervious—but only physically. In nearly every other way, Kenzie was so, so pervious.

"Westbrook. Beatrice." Sloane's voice was neutral. But when Ava glanced at her, she could see the coolness in Kenzie's sister's gaze. "Good to see you again."

Kenzie stepped back quickly, almost guiltily, and Ava heard Bea snicker under her breath beside her. She knew exactly what her best friend was thinking: *Yay, lesbodrama!* On the walk over, Bea had reminded Ava that as a married mother, she had to take her drama the way she took her women—vicariously. And frankly, she'd added, Ava had been doing a crap job recently of keeping her entertained on both fronts.

Mika stepped forward to pull Ava into a hug. They were about the same size, and Ava found herself returning the gesture with genuine warmth. It was impossible not to like the smart-ass detective.

"Don't mind Sloane," Mika said, further endearing herself to Ava. "She sometimes forgets that her baby sister is an actual adult."

"Hey!" Sloane transferred her glare to her girlfriend. But it softened, and a smile lurked at the corners of her generous mouth. "I heard that."

"That was the idea, babe." Mika winked over her shoulder as she moved on to hug Bea.

"An adult with superpowers, even," Kenzie added, frowning at her sister.

Sloane gaped at her. "What the actual hell, Kenzie?"

Kenzie waved her hand dismissively. "It's not a big deal. Everyone here already knows."

"Oh. My. God."

Mika slipped her arm through Sloane's. "Breathe. It's her secret to share, remember? Your words, Shepherd."

"But—so many—they have to—our parents…" Sloane's eyes were wide as she looked around the small group, and all at once Ava felt sorry for her. They were all treating Kenzie's secret like something of an inside joke, but if her identity were to be known widely, the real danger would be to all of them, the unarguably vulnerable human beings who loved—er, *cared about* Galaxy Girl.

"I hope you know that Bea and I don't take the knowledge lightly," Ava said, trying to reassure her.

Sloane's eyes narrowed, almost as if she thought she would be able to see inside Ava's head if only she squinted hard enough. Then she nodded abruptly. "Thank you, Ava. I appreciate that."

Ava nodded back, hoping that the move away from her surname signaled that Sloane was willing to at least try to accept her presence in Kenzie's life.

"So, how long have you been up?" she asked Kenzie, wishing she could touch her in some way. But not only did she not want to make Bea feel like a third/fifth wheel, she also wasn't sure where Kenzie stood on PDA. If Ava was the first woman she'd ever kissed, she might not be ready to come out publicly for a while. Besides, Westbrooks didn't exactly fly below the radar. If Ava were to be seen out and about with a reporter who had interviewed her, questions of a potential conflict of interest were bound to arise. Definitely a conversation they should have sooner rather than later—she didn't want to cost Kenzie the job she so obviously loved.

"I got up around seven," Kenzie told her. She started

to reach out—for Ava's arm? hand?—but stopped, twisting her own hands together instead.

"Seven?" Bea repeated. "What is wrong with you people? None of you have children. How do you not grasp the enormous privilege you have to sleep in?"

"Hazards of the job," Mika said. "Besides, working out first thing is not only fun but also a healthy lifestyle choice. Right, Sloane?"

Beside her, Sloane turned a delicate shade of pink that instantly clued everyone else into what sort of workout Mika meant.

Or, maybe not *everyone*.

"Did you guys go to the gym this morning?" Kenzie asked.

"Totally," Mika replied with an impressively straight face as Sloane looked anywhere but at her sister.

"Does your girl really not get—" Bea started quietly, and then oofed as Ava's elbow caught her in the gut.

They clearly needed to have a chat about Kenzie's super hearing. Fortunately, before Bea could do more than scowl at her, a college kid in an apron paused in the doorway. "Shepherd, party of five?"

"That's us," Kenzie said, smiling brightly at him as they headed inside the old brick building.

Ava glanced around the interior with interest. Mirrors and abstract art from local artists lined the exposed brick walls all the way up to the high ceiling, where wooden beams and copper pipes gleamed prettily. The interior was long and narrow and opened out onto a wisteria-lined patio at the back, she discovered as the waiter led them to a table in the center of the patio. It was quieter in the courtyard, away from street traffic. She liked it, she decided, taking a seat between Bea and Kenzie. She liked everything about this experience. For a little while, she could just be herself, instead of Ava Westbrook, Hyperion Tech second-incommand and heir to the Westbrook fortune.

It was blood money, all of it. But with her mother withdrawing more and more from public life and involving herself in god knew what—Ava's security sweep had found no fewer than three bugs after Amelia's visit to her hotel room earlier in the week—control of the Westbrook financial strings would soon fall to Ava. She couldn't wait to throw her parents' cash at deserving groups like the Alien Anti-Defamation Committee and Equal Rights for Off-Worlders, among others. She could only imagine the look on Amelia's face when she found out. Then again, maybe Amelia had already cut her out of the will, given Ava obviously didn't subscribe to the Westbrook clan's anti-alien fanaticism.

She almost wished she hadn't destroyed the bugs in her hotel room, just so she could see Amelia mottled in apoplectic rage. After all, dating an alien was about as far as you could get from Sentinel's master plan.

"I like your sneakers," Kenzie whispered when they were seated.

Ava had chosen an ancient pair of green Converse tennis shoes that matched her sweater. "Thanks," she whispered back. "I like your cardigan."

Kenzie was wearing a blue zip-up sweater that somehow managed to appear both conservative and sporty. "Thanks. It's easy to remove…" She seemed to realize what she'd said and added hastily, "I mean, for Galaxy Girl stuff, not—"

"Hey, no whispering over there," Sloane interrupted from across the table.

Ava remembered what Kenzie had said about Sloane being a grumpy 1950s dad. Yep, she could definitely see the resemblance. She knew a thing or two about how to handle blustering old men, though, seeing as she dealt with them in droves at Hyperion.

"I'm glad you and Mika could make it on such short notice, Sloane," she said.

"Oh." Sloane gripped the laminated menu in both hands. "Well, thank you. I'm hoping we can get to know you a little better. This one here—" she nodded at Kenzie, who appeared to be holding her breath— "thinks very highly of you, as I'm sure you know."

"The feeling is mutual." Ava glanced at Kenzie with a soft smile, unafraid of letting her adoration show. Kenzie, the prettiest, dorkiest, most badass woman she'd ever met, smiled back at her with a look that Ava suspected perfectly matched her own smitten expression.

"I hate to interrupt the moment," Bea put in, "but I need coffee. Like, two hours ago."

"You weren't awake two hours ago." Ava reached for Kenzie's hand under the table, happy when Kenzie immediately laced their fingers together.

"Details," Bea dismissed. "Now, who's been here before and can tell me what to order?"

As Mika chimed in with a recommendation for the eggs benedict, Ava pretended to study the menu. In fact, she was watching Sloane look at her girlfriend, analyzing the way her face and shoulders relaxed, the small smile that eased her previous tension. Apparently, Ava wasn't the only one who was whipped.

The restaurant wasn't crowded yet, so their orders didn't take long to arrive. Everyone was happier with some food and caffeine inside them, and Ava was pleased to see a little while later that brunch was going beautifully. Conversation centered mostly on popular culture— television shows, movies, web series, and, of course, the music industry, thanks to their out-of-town guest. Kenzie appeared to still be getting used to the idea of Ava's best friend being a musician she'd idolized, but then again, Bea was almost as enamored with her superhero status.

Ava wasn't sure why she'd worried Bea might feel like a third wheel. Throughout the meal, Bea chatted easily with Mika and Kenzie in particular, not always bothering to include Ava. She didn't mind, not when Kenzie refused to let go of her hand even to eat. Good thing she was apparently ambidextrous. If not, Ava suspected the situation would have gone a bit differently, given the amount of food Kenzie seemed intent on consuming.

"This isn't even her first meal of the day," Sloane said after Kenzie ordered a second entrée and Ava made a laughing comment about her hollow leg.

"Donuts don't count." Kenzie swallowed a large bite of hash browns. "They're like appetizers for breakfast."

"One donut might qualify as an appetizer," Mika said. "But half a dozen?"

"Half a *dozen?*" Bea echoed. "Seriously?"

"Seriously," Sloane confirmed, looking nearly as proud as she sounded.

And Sloane Shepherd, Ava thought as brunch wore on, was pretty okay, not least for her steadfast affection for her sister. Kenzie had lucked out with her adoptive family. Briefly, Ava wondered what it might have been like to grow up with a family like the Shepherds, but then she let the thought go. She had spent years in therapy working on issues involving her family of origin. They still came up, but it helped to remind herself that the Westbrooks had given her every material thing she had ever wanted or needed. The General and Amelia had both encouraged her to follow her passion for science and technology, and her father had even paid for a laboratory to be built in one of their garages for her to tinker around in whenever she came back to New York from prep school or college. She didn't come home that often. Mostly she spent her breaks with school friends and their families—her parents were both on the road so much with their respective jobs, and

Nick was long gone by then, so it was usually easier to go home with Bea or one of their other friends.

The Westbrooks may not have been perfect, it was true; but they had taken care of her when she needed a family. Some kids who lost their birth parents ended up in the foster system or in truly abusive families where they sustained wounds that never fully healed. Emotional neglect was shitty, but Ava had been able to find love and comfort from other people in her life. She was incredibly lucky, and she hoped she never stopped reminding herself of that fact.

They lingered over coffee (and an extra side of toast for Kenzie), talking about children. Mika had nieces and nephews she adored back in Utah, and Bea needed little persuading to share photos of Rowan. She even let Kenzie swipe through the images on her phone, an action that had Ava staring at her with a single brow raised. Bea, an infamous phone miser, only smiled as Kenzie oohed and ahhed over pictures of her son.

On the other side of the table, Sloane had her arm around Mika, her chin on her girlfriend's shoulder as Mika scrolled through Facebook looking for a particular picture of her namesake niece. They were sweet together, Ava thought, watching the way Sloane's nose scrunched up as Mika laughed at something on the screen. They seemed to match each other in ways Ava and Kenzie didn't—they worked in similar fields at jobs they loved, they were both equal parts bravado and poorly disguised fluffiness, and they were really into each other, if appearances could be believed. Kenzie had told her they had been friends for a while before finally getting together only recently, but the way they acted, Ava would have guessed they had been dating much longer.

"Oh my god, look at you!" Kenzie's squeal captured Ava's attention, and she realized Kenzie had paused on a photo of her dozing on Bea's couch, Rowan asleep on her chest. "When was this taken?"

"A few months ago."

"Oh, right. Duh, the time stamp." Kenzie looked closer at the photo and then glanced up at her. "Wasn't this right after you were promoted?"

"Yeah. I needed to clear my head, and what better way to do that than by spending the weekend with my godson?"

She stared down at the photo, remembering how calm and loved—and loving—she'd felt with Rowan asleep on her chest, Bea and James napping a couple of rooms away on a lazy Sunday afternoon. That was real life. Hyperion Tech, on the other hand, was work and family obligation. If it all came crumbling down, she would move on and forge a different path for herself, even if she couldn't imagine what direction that path would take. The thought was surprisingly exhilarating.

"I tried to convince her to stay in LA that weekend," Bea said. "I even offered her a gig managing my label so I would have more time to work with new clients, but alas, she turned me down."

Kenzie glanced up from the phone, her eyes on Ava. "You wouldn't leave Hyperion, would you?"

"Not by choice." Ava noticed all eyes were on her now. "But there is a board of directors, and even though I own a substantial share in the company, I am beholden to their expectations."

"But you're doing an amazing job," Kenzie said, straightening her shoulders. "They'd have to be blind not to see that."

"What they aren't blind to is falling share prices. It's fine, though. I always knew it wouldn't be easy to shift the direction of the company. Most people don't like change, especially not those accustomed to a certain level of return on investment."

"That's a nice euphemism for greedy as hell," Bea said, and the table broke out in laughter.

Their server was going off shift, she informed them a few minutes later, so unless there was anything else they wanted—and here she paused, eyes on Kenzie, who shook her head quickly—she was leaving their bill.

The time had come to leave, the group agreed reluctantly. The restaurant had filled up since their arrival, and no doubt there were people who'd gotten a later start to their Sunday waiting for a table. Ava and Bea argued briefly over whose treat it was over the protests of the others, but Bea was closer to the server, so she won that battle.

"Thanks for being so cool about my sister crashing our date," Kenzie said softly as they waited for the receipt.

"Thanks for being so cool about me bringing a friend on our date," Ava replied.

"I mean, she *is* B Dang ..."

Which was a very good point.

A few minutes later, on their way back through the restaurant, Ava caught two women at a table along their route do a double-take as the group passed, and she was almost certain she heard a voice whisper both her name and Bea's. Or maybe she was just being paranoid. But what if she wasn't? Maybe going out in a group like this hadn't been the best idea. All they needed was to be tagged together on Instagram, and then Nick's minions would go after Beatrice *and* Kenzie...

She took a breath as they exited the building. Worrying accomplished nothing. Besides, Nick already knew what Bea and her family meant to her. If anything happened to the Coleman-Dangs, being punched into space would be the least of her brother's worries. Speaking of which, even if (when) he did find out about her and Kenzie, she and her Panopticon agent sister could take care of themselves. To keep everyone safe, Ava's only real option was to isolate herself completely, but that wasn't any way to live, was it?

And yet, everyone she cared about would be safe, so there was that.

Outside, Mika and Sloane said their farewells and left together. Kenzie's gaze trailed after them; Ava guessed she wasn't used to seeing her sister leave with someone else. Sloane looked back a few times, her forehead similarly furrowed. Yep, Kenzie had definitely won the adoption lottery. Nick had either been disinterested in Ava or jealous of her relationship with their parents, especially their father. Convinced the General cared more about her than about him, he had followed in their father's footsteps, determined to earn his love and approval. But Alexander Westbrook, an old-school Marine, had believed that discipline was more important than affection when it came to rearing children.

Poor Nick. He'd never understood that his delusions weren't based on reality. Ava, meanwhile, had responded to his toxic jealousy the way most siblings of people with personality disorder react, according to her therapist: by keeping her distance from the rest of the family. That strategy had allowed her to remain insulated from Nick's fits of jealous rage for years upon years. So why, exactly, had she allowed her mother to lure her back to the fractured family fold now?

At least moving to Seattle had given her Kenzie, she reminded herself, trying to banish thoughts of her family of origin.

Bea slipped her arm through Ava's and said cheerily to Kenzie, "You're coming back to Ava's with us, aren't you?"

Ava shot her friend a look, though she couldn't decide

if she was more grateful to or irritated with Bea for extending the invitation she had been psyching herself up to offer. Maybe Kenzie had other plans. Maybe she was sick of them. Maybe she was still hungry and wanted to go home and put on her fat pants and eat a pizza or two. Not that Kenzie Shepherd had fat pants.

Kenzie glanced between them. "Oh. Um, I don't know. I hadn't really..." She trailed off, letting her gaze rest on Ava.

"Come with us," Ava said, smiling warmly. "Please? I bet Bea could be convinced to sing, right, Bea? I'll even play the piano...or, the keyboard, anyway."

"You play the piano?" Kenzie's eyes lit up like someone had just waved a plate of french fries in front of her.

"Does she play the piano?" Bea repeated. "She's only the best keyboardist I've ever known!"

Ava elbowed her. "Liar."

"Yes, that is a lie," Bea confirmed. "But you do have a keyboard in your hotel room, and you know a ton of songs, some of which aren't even mine. We used to play for hours," she told Kenzie, "plotting our future in the industry."

"What happened?" Kenzie asked.

"Some of us had to grow up," Ava said.

"Excuse you? Which of us is married with child and which is married to her job?"

Speaking of... Kenzie's phone went off at that moment, and Ava watched her close her eyes and take a breath. Then she checked her screen. "It's Sloane," she said, her tone apologetic. "I'll just be..." And she stepped away, voice low as she answered the phone.

Was this how their plans would always end? With Kenzie called away and Ava watching her go, wondering if she might not see her again? Dating a superhero was—not easy. But then again, neither was dating a workaholic Westbrook. This weekend was the most time Ava had taken off from Hyperion since February, when she'd run away to LA and almost hadn't come back.

"Superhero time?" Bea asked.

"I hope not," Ava said. "But probably."

Except Kenzie was smiling as she turned back, her phone at her side. "It's okay. Sloane just wanted me to tell you thanks again for brunch. She hopes we can do it again soon."

"She does?" That was pretty much the last thing Ava had expected from Kenzie's big sister.

"She does," Kenzie confirmed, wide smile warming her beautiful eyes.

Ava couldn't hide her matching smile. "Does this mean I passed the sister test?" Because while she had met Sloane on numerous occasions, it had only ever been as Kenzie's friend.

"You passed the sister test," Kenzie agreed. "Also, she wanted us to see this." And she held her phone up for the other two to see.

Ava squinted, trying to parse the image on the screen. It was clearly a photo of a mural painted onto the side of a building, but one Ava hadn't seen before. Wait, was that the Milky Way stretching over a city skyline? And the Space Needle? Hovering above the indistinct buildings was a familiar figure, her strong, feminine form as clear as the cowl that covered everything except her eyes. At the top of the mural was painted a message in giant letters: "THANK YOU, GALAXY GIRL! ♥" At the bottom corner, the artist had signed, "Off-Worlders of Seattle" in flourishing letters.

"Sloane said they walked past it a minute ago," Kenzie explained, her eyes bright. "Isn't it incredible?"

"Yes, and so are you," Ava said.

Kenzie started to lean in and then caught herself, glancing around nervously. Ava would have bridged the distance and simply kissed her there on the sidewalk, but she didn't want to make Kenzie uncomfortable. Besides, there was no need to rush things. They had—well, maybe not *all* the time in the world, but enough time. She hoped.

Bea laughed. "It's official, you're both too adorable for words. Now let's go make music together, ladies," she added, waggling her eyebrows suggestively.

Kenzie looked at Ava, faintly alarmed. "Doesn't that mean…?"

"Ignore her." Ava slipped her arm through Kenzie's, pulling her away down the sidewalk. "She's an old married lady trying to live vicariously through us."

Bea fell into step beside them. "I only wish I could say that wasn't true. So, Kenzie, does your squad call themselves the Super Friends, by any chance?"

Kenzie snorted a laugh. "No, I can't say we do."

"You totally should! I do have one suggestion, though."

Ava braced herself, hoping her body language clued Kenzie into the crassness that was undoubtedly coming.

"You'd probably be better off calling yourselves the Super Gay Friends," Bea said. "Because, let's face it, y'all seem to have a certain vibe going."

Kenzie nodded regally, her face frozen into a smile that Ava recognized as one of her less comfortable looks. She smiled so much that one needed to study each variation closely to figure out what she was feeling. Fortunately, Ava was more than willing to accept the challenge.

"You okay?" she asked quietly, pressing into Kenzie's side.

Kenzie glanced over at her, smile morphing into something far more comfortable as they gazed at each other. "Never better," she said, and then—because while she might be a superhero, she was still Kenzie Shepherd—she tripped over a crack in the sidewalk. Ava, walking close to her, lost her balance and started to fall forward, too, but before she could hit the pavement, Kenzie had somehow righted them both.

"Shoot! I'm so sorry, Ava. Are you all right?"

Bea was sighing exasperatedly beside them, and Ava got it. Kenzie couldn't just levitate on a downtown sidewalk and hope to preserve her identity for long. But she'd caught Ava before she could fall, and honestly, Ava couldn't remember the last time someone had looked at her the way Kenzie was looking at her now: as if she were the most precious thing in the world.

"I'm good," she said, and continued down the sidewalk, flanked by her best friend on one side and on the other, the woman who was fast becoming more important to her than anyone else in the universe.

They had almost reached Hyperion Tower when Ava's phone dinged. She knew that alert, and her heart immediately sped up, thumping inside her chest. Trying to be subtle as Kenzie and Bea chatted on about favorite musicals—the brilliance of Lin-Manuel Miranda *may* have come up once or twice—Ava glanced at her screen, only to stop in her tracks as she read the words: "I've found something. Call me when you can."

Ava bit her lip, hair rising on the back of her neck. *Something*—what did that mean? Was her theory correct? Had the spreadsheet she'd recovered from Chloe's hard drive borne fruit?

"Ava?" Kenzie asked. She'd stopped a few paces ahead and was turning back now, her eyes concerned. "You okay?"

"Yeah, A, are you okay?" Bea echoed, her tone serious for once.

Ava slipped her phone into the back pocket of her jeans and painted a smile on her face. "Of course, my lovelies," she said, slipping her elbows through each of theirs and tugging them forward. "How could I not be with the two of you at my side?"

Reassured, they continued their walk—and their conversation—while Ava paced between them, eyes focused on the street ahead. Her mind was on the mural. It was only one image, but it signaled a change. Normally, the city's alien community remained hidden, she knew, living in the shadows even in a city where they were generally accepted. In other parts of the country and world, even the shadows didn't feel safe. Sentinel had brought the hatred and mistreatment of off-worlders into the mainstream, and the American government's involvement, knowing or not—and Ava had her theories about that—had given Nick and his minions a degree of credibility they didn't deserve.

But now things were changing. First, Kenzie had stood up for her favorite barista, and then she had saved complete strangers. From there, her heroics had grown to encompass more and more people—even the people who approved whole-heartedly of Sentinel's mission and actions. Now it wasn't just her but others standing tall beside her: Galaxy Guy, Sloane, Mika, and all the others within Panopticon and the local authorities who believed as they did, not to mention a community of aliens with someone at last to inspire them. Kenzie really was her brother's worst nightmare, Ava realized, but not because of the power her body held. Her power lay in her ability to unite the world's alien refugee community, to give them the hope and confidence to step out of the shadows and claim their space. Or, at least, to move through the world feeling a little more secure.

Sentinel had better watch out, Ava thought, leaning into Kenzie's side. An alien and a Westbrook—the world didn't know the half of it.

Yet.

ABOUT THE AUTHOR

Kate Christie, author of fourteen novels including the Girls of Summer series, *Beautiful Game*, *Leaving LA*, and *Gay Pride & Prejudice*, was born and raised in Kalamazoo, Michigan. A graduate of Smith College and Western Washington University, she lives near Seattle with her wife, three young daughters, and the family dogs.

To read excerpts from Kate's other titles from Second Growth Books and Bella Books, please visit her author website, www.katejchristie.com. There, you can also check out her blog, *Homodramatica*, where she occasionally finds time to wax unpoetically about lesbian life, fiction, and motherhood.

To receive updates on her work, including future installments in the Girls of Summer series, sign up for her mailing list at www.katejchristie.com/mailing-list.

PATREON SUPPORTERS

Last year, one of the faithful readers of the Girls of Summer series suggested I start a Patreon account so that those with the means and desire could help support my work in ways other than purchasing titles. So I did, and the experience has been eye-opening. Not only do I worry less about the business side of writing, but I've also formed online friendships with patrons of my work. So much of writing is a solitary slog away from family, friends, and co-workers, but with Patreon I can interact with readers who I know care deeply about my work. That is a really powerful gift, even more than the financial support.

One of the benefits listed on my Patreon page—in addition to behind the scenes glimpses and free e-books, audiobooks, and paperbacks—is the publication of my patron list in the back of my books. Thank you to each and every one of you for letting me know that my books have found their way to generous readers who just might care about my characters as much as I do.

Amy T., AZ, Barb B., Bernie C., Charley K., Chris Z., Cristina K., Ed M., Erica G., GZ, Hugh R., Jan B., Jeff J., Jessie W., Jordan W., Katherine J., Kim M., Kristina G., MW, Pat G., Richard S., Shannon R., Spencer K., Stephanie A., and Suzi S.

Thank you, and happy reading!

CPSIA information can be obtained
at www.ICGtesting.com
Printed in the USA
LVHW050831261121
704455LV00007B/851

9 798695 387438